# GOSSIP AND GORGONS

MANNERS AND MONSTERS BOOK 3

TILLY WALLACE

Print ISBN: 978-0-473-51015-2



To be the first to hear about new releases, sign up at:

www.tillywallace.com/newsletter

# 1

*Westbourne Green, May 1816*

Hannah woke to a scream. The high-pitched wail turned into a warble, and then tapered off into more of an outraged shout.

"Not again," she muttered as she opened her eyes. There was sufficient dawn light peeking through the open curtains that Hannah could see without the need of a glow lamp.

Sheba lay curled up in her dog bed. The spaniel raised her head and thumped her tail at the movement from the human bed. Hannah threw back the blankets and lowered her feet to the floor. She patted the puppy's head. "Come along, girl. We shall use the opportunity to take you outside."

Hannah padded to the chair where she had left her robe. She shrugged on the purple dressing gown and tied the belt as she headed down the stairs, the spaniel at her heels. This was the third such wakeup call in less than a week and the time had come to take matters in hand.

She was joined on the stairs by her husband, also with a robe knotted around his middle...though the blue and gold paisley seemed at odds with his stormy personality. Sheba wagged her tail and sidled along the stairs to his side.

"Again?" Wycliff asked as they descended.

"I presume so," Hannah replied.

She couldn't help staring at her husband's naked feet. They had been married for two weeks now and the sight of his toes was the most she had seen of him.

Not that she intended to see her husband naked. Theirs was a marriage of convenience and they kept to their separate rooms. But Hannah was curious enough that when an early morning scream warbled through the house, she wondered what it would be like to open her eyes and find another person next to her in bed.

Thumping noises and muttered curses came from the front parlour. Lord Wycliff pushed open the door to reveal Mary, fire poker held high over her head, preparing to do battle with the light fitting.

"Barnes, get down," Hannah called as she stepped into the room.

"He did it again, ma'am!" Mary swiped with the poker, but his lordship's quick hand caught it in its descent before the glass shade protecting the candles was smashed.

"So we heard," Lord Wycliff said.

Mary relinquished the weapon and stepped back to the fireplace. "I cannot get my work done with him lying in wait to jump out at me, Lady Wycliff."

"Yes, I agree with you entirely, Mary." An object dropped from the light fitting to the carpet with a solid thump, and Hannah scooped it up before it could scuttle away.

She held Barnes between her own hands and raised him to eye level. "This has gone on quite long enough, Barnes, and will not be tolerated any longer. You have two options before you. If you frighten Mary again, you will find yourself confined to the cage in the laboratory. If instead you value your freedom, you will leave Mary to do her work unharassed. Do you understand?"

The hand slumped in her palms, then he raised the index finger and waved it up and down.

A steady thump rumbled from the floor and up through Hannah's feet, the accompanying noise like the distant approach of thunder. A shape completely filled the doorway and blocked the exit.

Mary gave a sob and rushed to the newcomer. Frank, formerly the Chelsea Monster, sheltered the maid and turned his body to hide her from view. He raised a hand and pointed at Barnes with a growl.

"Perhaps we should leave the two monsters to fight it out," Wycliff suggested. "Do you think you can take Frank one-handed, Barnes?"

Barnes arched and stood on his fingertips in what appeared to be a vain attempt to look taller.

"There will not be any fighting under this roof." Hannah knelt and released Barnes on the carpet. "Go find Timmy. The lad will be awake soon."

Frank lifted Mary off her feet as the disembodied hand scuttled across the carpet and shot between his two tree-trunk legs. The larger creature growled again before setting Mary down.

Lord Wycliff returned the poker to the fireside set. "How is it, Mary, that you have no problem with all seven feet of stitched-together Frank, but scream when confronted with Barnes?"

Mary curled her hand into the front of Frank's shirt and spoke to him when she answered Wycliff. "Because Frank here has a gentle soul—plus arms, legs, and all the bits in between, my lord. That Hungarian hamster...*thing* ain't right."

Hannah held in a sigh. She doubted this was the sort of domestic dispute other married women had to mediate; but then, theirs wasn't like any other household. "Right or not, Barnes is a part of this household. If he drops on you again, he will be confined to his cage. I believe he has had sufficient warning that he will not bother you again. Now, Mary, kindly be so good as to ask Cook to make some hot chocolate. Since I am awake, I will do some reading in the library. Frank, could you please take Sheba outside?"

"Yes, ma'am." Mary unwound her hand from Frank's shirt and wiped her face.

The former monster bent down to pick up the

puppy, who squirmed and licked his face as the odd trio left the room.

Lord Wycliff inclined his head in Hannah's direction. "Let us hope that is the end of the matter."

"Yes, I too hope that is the end of it," Hannah said as her husband left the room.

She rubbed the gold band on her left hand. There had been many adjustments to life in the Miles household over the last few weeks.

Frank, the stitched-together man reanimated by the late Lord Dunkeith's potions, had moved into the stables. His gentle nature was ideally suited to working with the horses and Old Jim appreciated the help. For all they knew, the monster's hands and arms might have come from a groom, as he seemed to know instinctively what to do.

Hannah's father studied the man while they tried to make sense of Lord Dunkeith's notes and what he had done. Somewhere in the animation of Frank and Barnes was the knowledge they needed to help the Afflicted, if only they could determine the nature of the liquid in which both had been immersed.

Another change affected Hannah. Mary and the other staff referred to her as either *ma'am* or *Lady Wycliff*, but on the inside, she still felt like Miss Hannah Miles. What did it take to truly become a married woman, if a piece of jewellery, the marriage articles, and the parish register were insufficient?

Their marriage was little more than a business arrangement. The viscount had extended the protection of his name and body should anything happen to Hannah's father. Many such aristocratic marriages were made every year. Their participants lived separate lives, even if they happened to share a roof.

Yet Hannah's heart yearned for something more. How was she to fill the void within her? If she found common ground with her husband, could friendship blossom between them?

Hannah considered the idea in the library, as she laboured over Egyptian hieroglyphs in the book she studied. Her husband was like an inscription carved on a stone obelisk—inscrutable and unmoving.

Mary delivered a cup of hot chocolate and the puppy, then left with a quick smile. The sunlight coming in through the window grew in warmth and reminded Hannah she still wore her dressing robe. Sheba was nestled inside a blanket, asleep, and Hannah left her to her dreams as she hurried upstairs to dress for the day.

Once properly attired, she found the family gathered in the dining room. All except Timmy—the youth preferred to eat in the kitchen with Frank and Cook, but Hannah suspected he was really afraid of the viscount. She would have to find a solution to the lad's hesitancy. If he were to become a surgeon like her father, he would need to face a variety of patients in order to carry out his work.

She glanced at her husband's stern countenance from under lowered lashes. Truth be told, Timmy wasn't the only one a little afraid of the viscount.

Hannah said her good mornings, drew a deep breath, and stood a little taller. She was married to Lord Wycliff and her mother was a powerful mage. There was nothing for her to fear. In that moment on the threshold, she decided to consider their marriage a type of experiment. She would try different approaches to grow an amicable relationship with her husband, and would record and measure any improvements or setbacks.

She kissed her mother's cheek and then took her chair opposite Lord Wycliff.

"Another early start, courtesy of Barnes," her mother said with a chuckle.

"Yes, his behaviour is intolerable. If he jumps out at Mary again, he will be put back into his cage." Hannah poured another hot chocolate and nursed the cup between her two hands.

"It would appear *Hungarian hamsters* have a puckish sense of humour." Her mother slid the toast rack along the table toward Hannah.

"This particular Hungarian hamster is in danger of being flattened by Frank. The constructed man has taken quite a shine to Mary and is rather protective of her," Lord Wycliff said from across the table.

"Barnes might simply be enjoying every day of life available to him. We do not know the exact mechanism that keeps him healthy and animated. He may at any time begin to rot or simply collapse, lifeless." Hannah had her own such dilemma. If her mother's spell failed, the French curse would snatch away her life. Perhaps she should be more like Barnes and enjoy each moment.

"From my investigations, Barnes was known to be an argumentative man before he was murdered. If he carries on like this, he will be killed twice over. Or thrice, if what Dunkeith did to him counts." Wycliff pulled the newspaper closer to scan the headlines as he ate his breakfast.

Sir Hugh entered with the mail in one hand. "One for you, Lady Wycliff," he said as he placed a heavy envelope by her plate.

"This will be from Lizzie." Her friend was much amused, and curious, about Hannah's newlywed state. Although with nothing gossipworthy to impart to her friend, Hannah was afraid Lizzie would have to wait until her own wedding to find out what marriage was really like.

Hannah picked up the envelope and read the direction. The handwriting was unfamiliar. She broke the seal with her knife and pulled out a sheet of paper, curious as to who was writing to the new Lady Wycliff.

She read the enclosed letter twice, then picked up the envelope and stared again at the name on the front. It was addressed to Lady Wycliff, but perhaps it was meant for another such lady or someone with a similar name? "This must be a mistake."

"Why is it a mistake, dear?" her mother asked.

"This is an invitation for Lord and Lady Wycliff to attend a house party in a week's time." Hannah stared at the letter as though it were a summons to Hell by

Beelzebub himself. A house party? How absurd. "I have no intention of being paraded about like some curiosity to be ridiculed. Let them find some other sport to fill their days in the country."

Lord Wycliff glanced up from his newspaper. "Who wants us to perform like baited bears?"

Hannah read the signature at the bottom of the sheet. "Lady Frances Pennicott."

"The Earl of Pennicott's daughter?" The viscount folded up the newspaper and placed it on the table.

"Yes. Do you know her?" Did he have some previous association with the young woman that had prompted the invitation? An odd sensation rippled through Hannah at the thought.

"No. But I am aware of the earl by reputation. He owns a thriving banking establishment and I have been trying to secure a meeting with him for some time. The earl rarely comes to London and mostly conducts his business from his country estate." He rapped his short nails on the tabletop.

Hannah stared at her husband. "Are you saying you wish to attend?"

"Ordinarily I would agree that you ought to refuse the invitation. I have neither time nor inclination for silly house parties. But this would be a rare opportunity for me to talk to the earl. His managers in London will not see me and Lord Pennicott is the only avenue I have to acquire new breeding stock for my estate."

"Hugh and I would be willing to invest in your farm," Seraphina said.

Dark brows knitted together. "No, thank you, Lady Miles. I will not have it said I married your daughter to access your finances. I will recover my family home through my own endeavours."

"We are to attend, then." Hannah tried to smile but she was chilled on the inside. She enjoyed her time spent with her friend Lizzie, but it was one thing to stay with a dear friend and another entirely to be surrounded by strangers. Her every movement would be scrutinised for faults, as would her clothing.

"I think a trip to London is required, Hannah, to acquire a few new outfits for the week? I'm sure Lizzie would be delighted to assist in the matter." Her mother clapped her hands, reading her daughter's thoughts.

Her father waved his knife in the air as though he performed invisible surgery. "Pennicott has an estate out Swindon way. My old friend Doctor Colchester lives there, he's an aftermage with a gift for healing similar to that of our Timmy. It would be an excellent chance for the lad to spend a week with someone with magic similar to his."

"It is agreed, then. Lady Wycliff will reply and accept the invitation." Lord Wycliff went back to his newspaper.

"I will offer you one snippet of information about your host, because I am sure that as soon as you meet the earl, a question will spring to your mind," her mother said.

"Whatever do you mean?" Hannah asked, curious as to why her mother raised the issue.

"Lord Pennicott is a goblin. He hails from a long line of goblins who are exceptionally good with finances. But they are rather unusual to look upon."

"Goblins are real? What other fairy-tale creatures are living quietly in the countryside? What of fairies? Do they fly over the fields with gossamer wings?" It wasn't even ten o'clock in the morning and already Hannah's head felt crammed full with nonsense. House parties and goblins. Whatever next?

Seraphina laughed. "Who would know, with the Fae? They think us ugly and uncivilised and keep their own company."

Hannah stared at her mother, not sure whether she should believe her, or if she spoke in jest. A veil hid so much and she couldn't tell if her mother's eyes crinkled with humour or not. "I think you tweak my nose, Mother. Fairies could not fly around England and remain a secret."

This time a gentle laugh did puff out the thin veil. "Oh, it's true. Ask your father. Hugh longs to have one of the Fae on his autopsy table to see how they fly."

Her father waggled his eyebrows. "Entirely true. I nearly got my hands on one during the war, you know. A French Fae collided with a cannonball, but no one could find where the body fell. We searched for it all day, until we lost the light." He sighed like a young lass after a lost opportunity.

"I shall write a note to Lady Frances accepting the invitation. Then I shall call upon Lizzie and seek her assistance with what to pack for a goblin's house party."

Hannah traced a finger along a gilded spiral on the paper. Her life was most certainly not like the married life of other women. Then a warm trickle of curiosity curled through her. A goblin? What else would she discover in her time away?

# 2

Hannah called on her friend that afternoon. The butler showed her through to the front parlour, with its wallpaper of ferns and shrubbery where all sorts of birds hid. Lizzie reclined on a chaise, fanning herself with a blank wedding invitation.

"Hello, Lizzie. No more wedding arrangements to make?" Hannah glanced around the parlour. The stacks of cards, envelopes, and large sheets of paper with instructions and arrangements were conspicuous by their absence.

"I have banished all wedding matter to Mother's study." Lizzie pointed with the card.

"Whatever is the matter? There is nothing amiss with the duke, is there?" Hannah sat on the chaise next to her friend as Lizzie swung her feet to the floor.

Lizzie took Hannah's hand. "Goodness, no. Everything is done or arranged and there is nothing left to do save the act itself. I wish I could marry him tomorrow instead of enduring this horrid waiting."

"The day will be here soon—only a few more weeks to wait. There is the Royal Wedding next week—are you not looking forward to that?" Many Londoners would line the street, hoping to catch a glimpse of the bride and groom. Lizzie and her parents had a coveted invitation to the celebration ball.

Lizzie dropped her head back to the arm of the chaise. "I don't know if I can stand watching another woman marry the man she loves when I cannot have Harden. I believe I shall expire from waiting. How I wish I had married him already—then you and I could share the delicious details only married women know."

Hannah would have to disappoint her friend on that particular subject. Despite having been married two weeks, the only detail she had to share was the state of her husband's bare toes.

Lady Loburn entered and Hannah rose to greet her mother's friend.

"Hannah, to what do we owe this pleasure?" Lady Loburn took a seat upon the sofa opposite her reclining daughter.

Hannah sat back down. "I am in need of Lizzie's assistance, Lady Loburn. Lord Wycliff and I have been invited to a house party and Mother instructed me to acquire some new gowns for the occasion."

"A house party invitation already! See, I told you all society would be atwitter about your match. Who is hosting the event?" Lizzie sat up and her eyes shone with curiosity.

"The invitation is from Lady Frances Pennicott. Are you acquainted?" Hannah had tried to match a face to the name, but couldn't.

The blonde curls framing Lizzie's face swayed when she nodded. "I have met Lady Frances once or twice. She does not much come to London."

"Why not?" Hannah didn't often seek out society herself—she preferred quiet reading and her work. She doubted Lady Frances laboured on some project deep in the countryside that kept her from London.

"Because society is cruel," Lady Loburn said.

Hannah recalled her mother's information about the Earl of Pennicott's being a goblin. "Is that because of her father?"

"Yes, the poor creature is like her father in both form and character. Watch yourself in her company, Hannah. Lady Frances keeps herself entertained by digging out secrets and using them as weapons." Lady Loburn bit out the words in such a way that Hannah wondered if a secret of hers had fallen into the young lady's hands.

"From what I can recollect, Lady Frances's debut did not go well, although I understand she has a close circle of friends who visit her often in the country. Oh, Hannah, did you really ask me to go shopping with you?" Lizzie's blue eyes sparkled with excitement.

Hannah laughed. "Yes, that is why I came for your particular help. We only have a week to prepare. Do you know any seamstresses who might have ready-made garments available for purchase?"

Lady Loburn knitted her long fingers together in her lap and hummed to herself as she thought. Then the fingers unwound and she stabbed at the air. "Miss Amelia Brody."

Lizzie's mouth made an O shape and she nodded in agreement.

Hannah rolled the name around in her mind. "Why is that name familiar? Is she a dressmaker we have discussed?"

Lady Loburn picked up the cushion next to her and gave it a good plumping. "Miss Amelia Brody is not a dressmaker, but rather, a young woman who made a very satisfactory match. Her trousseau was commissioned and I suspect would be nearing completion since the proposed wedding is less than two weeks away."

"I'm not sure how this helps?" Hannah marvelled at how women like Lizzie and her mother managed to keep abreast of everything that seemed to happen in everyone else's lives.

"Just this week we heard the most scandalous news —Miss Brody has run away with a man who is in *trade*." Lizzie screwed up her face on the last word. Nobles and the middle class were not supposed to mix, but sometimes hearts didn't stick to their own class.

Hannah's mind worked through the implications. "I assume she did not take her trousseau when she eloped?"

Lady Loburn readjusted the cushions. "It wasn't finished, I believe. And her parents are now refusing to pay for anything. The runaway is of a size similar to yours, Hannah, and the seamstress might have finished the garments you require."

Lizzie got to her feet and pulled the bell by the door to summon the butler. "Let us make haste, Hannah, lest someone else swoop in on the spoils."

A flurry of activity saw Hannah seated next to her friend in the carriage as they were conveyed to Bond Street. Lizzie was in raptures at being in charge of a shopping expedition for her friend, and Hannah harboured a secret belief that she had been waiting for the opportunity for some time.

"You will need a ball gown, a walking gown, a dinner gown, and a riding habit," Lizzie said, ticking outfits off on her fingers.

"Four new outfits? I cannot." It seemed terribly excessive for a week in the country.

"Four?" Lizzie burst into laughter, a gentle tinkling noise like the soft flow of water over rocks in a stream. "Hannah, you will need two or three of *each*, apart from the riding habit. I know you do not like that activity. And we have not even begun to consider morning and afternoon dresses."

They alighted on the street and Lizzie linked her arm in Hannah's. "Let us find the right shop. While we walk, tell me of married life with Lord Wycliff."

"There is little to report. Life after our wedding is no different to life before it. We continue on our separate ways." Hannah imagined two distinct paths winding through a forest. They walked alone in the wilderness, which meant they would face any adversary alone. That didn't seem right to her. Marriage meant having someone at your side.

"Here it is!" Lizzie tugged on Hannah's arm and pulled her from the forest in her mind.

They stepped over the threshold into a shop bursting with colour, fabric, and feathers, making Hannah long for the less overwhelming, cool grey interior of her father's laboratory.

"Lady Elizabeth." A young woman in a plain black gown and a white apron approached. "How might we help you today?"

Lizzie let go of Hannah and leaned closer to the modiste. "My friend Lady Wycliff requires a number of gowns before next week. I believe she is of a size with Miss Amelia Brody?"

The modiste narrowed her eyes and assessed Hannah. "Yes, I believe your ladyship is of a similar height. We have a few gowns completed. What in particular does your ladyship require?"

"A walking gown, a dinner gown, and a ball gown," Lizzie said. "Morning dresses, afternoon dresses, and a riding habit."

The modiste nodded as if this were not in the least overwhelming. "I shall be back directly, my lady."

Hannah soon found herself the centre of attention as the gowns designed for Amelia Brody were fetched and held up for Lizzie's inspection. The garments were either dismissed with a wave or set aside for further consideration. With relief, Hannah found she and Amelia had something in common—and it wasn't a man with a trade. From the fabrics chosen, it appeared they both preferred a similar autumnal palette of earthy greens and tawny browns, with the occasional orange and yellow. There wasn't a single pink item in sight.

Lizzie kept up a steady stream of one-sided conversation. "How exciting—your first house party as a married woman. We must find you a ball gown in a much bolder colour now that you are a matron. And perhaps a turban with a feather?"

Hannah would rather have a plain gown and a sturdy apron to protect it from stains. A heavy sigh made her shoulders slump. "I don't know how I will endure it."

Seven days in forced proximity with a house full of strangers and a husband known for being abominably rude. Though her curiosity was piqued at the idea of meeting a goblin and his daughter. Knowing that Lady Frances had found a harsh reception in London because of her looks made Hannah more sympathetic to her as yet unknown hostess. Then she remembered Lady Loburn's warning. If their hostess thought to discover a secret about the newlyweds, Hannah would ensure she was disappointed.

"Lady Elizabeth!" an unremarkable young woman called from one side of the shop.

Lizzie looked around and a smile broke over her

face. "Pippa. Do come and be introduced to my dear friend, Lady Hannah Wycliff."

The new acquaintance was of a similar age to Hannah and Lizzie, and entirely ordinary. The sort of woman who disappeared in a crowd. Of average height and average build, she had an average rounded face. The strands of hair that escaped from under her bonnet were neither brown nor blonde but a shade in between. She wasn't pretty, but neither was she plain. Hannah suspected her countenance became more or less attractive depending on the degree of affection held by the beholder.

"Hannah, this is Mrs Philippa Wright-Knowles. We both attended Mrs Granger's Finishing School." Lizzie made the introductions.

Hannah inclined her head with a smile, and Mrs Wright-Knowles bobbed a curtsey. Lizzie had a large circle of friends and acquaintances and at times, Hannah was sure she must know every member of the *ton*. Her friend's gift, which couldn't be magical as there were no mages in her genealogy, was remembering not only names and faces, but pertinent details about each person she met. It was a skill that would be handy in her future role as a duchess, and which always made the listener feel valued due to her friend's attention.

"Pippa married her Mr Wright-Knowles last year and gives me an enigmatic smile whenever I enquire about married life." Playfully, Lizzie tapped her friend's arm.

"There is little to tell about our lives. We are a rather boring married couple, I am sorry to say. Although there is one piece of excitement. Lady Frances Pennicott has invited us to a house party next week." Mrs Wright-Knowles smiled and a marvellous transformation was wrought over her face. Her features came alive with warmth and her brown eyes sparkled.

Lizzie clasped her hands. "Oh, what a coincidence. Hannah and the viscount are also invited. We are here because she simply must have some new outfits for the occasion."

Hannah stared at the toes of her boots sticking out from under her gown and prayed Lizzie would not suggest shoe shopping next. "I bow to Lizzie's superior knowledge of what is required in these situations. But I am relieved to make the acquaintance of someone else who will be attending. I was apprehensive about a week with a house full of strangers."

"I shall be delighted to look after you. Lady Fanny can be a bit sharp, but she means well and simply chafes at life in the country." Philippa's eyes brightened and shimmered with the offered friendship.

"Oh, thank you. I don't know why she even invited us, since we are not acquainted." Hannah was sure etiquette had been breached by extending an invitation to strangers.

Philippa leaned closer and lowered her voice. "Fanny has committed some unpardonable sin and her father refuses to allow her to come to London, despite the fact that they have an invitation to the royal wedding next week. Instead, Lady Fanny is taking slices of society that she can consume in Swindon."

"An unpardonable sin?" Lizzie's eyes widened. "Whatever did she do?"

Philippa looked around and waited for a woman to move on before continuing. "The earl is negotiating the details of her marriage as though it were the merger of two companies, and I hear Fanny is rather impatient to have done with it. Nobody knows for sure yet, but there is speculation it is to do with her marriage contract. I heard it rumoured that she threatened to elope, or even give herself to her fiancé before the wedding night, if her father didn't hurry things along."

Lizzie gasped and fanned her face. "She wouldn't dare, would she? It is the lot of brides-to-be, that we must wait."

"You have met Fanny. What do you think?" Philippa winked.

Lizzie's eyes widened further and then she winked back. "I am surprised her father doesn't have her under lock and key and a man sitting under her bedroom window."

Hannah perked up. The idea of getting to the bottom of a potential scandal and a new acquaintance made the house party seem more tolerable.

THE FOLLOWING week arrived far too soon for Hannah's liking, to the point that she wondered if her mother had been playing with time again. Her luggage was packed and by the rear door, ready to be loaded onto the carriage. There was one last thing to do before she left and, with heavy feet, Hannah took the spiral staircase to her mother's turret.

Sheba jumped from step to step behind her, silken ears flopping as she followed her mistress. At the top of the steps, Hannah scooped the puppy into her arms. "You need to behave—Mother's room is not the place for inquisitive puppies."

Hannah tapped lightly on the door and waited for permission to enter. The light-flooded room was abuzz with heavy magic, like fat bumblebees feasting on flowers. Seraphina sat on the floor, a piece of chalk in her hand as she put the finishing touches to a coffin shape drawn on the bare floorboards.

Over by the east window was a metal pen with a soft blanket in the bottom, into which Hannah deposited the puppy. "Your magic is different today. Are you changing the spell?" she asked her mother.

The muslin veil swayed as Lady Miles nodded and drew another symbol radiating out from the design. "Yes. I am adding a layer of Egyptian elements to strengthen the effect."

Hannah gathered her skirts about her and stepped into the shape. She lay down with her feet pointing east, and crossed her arms over her chest.

Seraphina leaned over and rested one hand on Hannah's forehead. In the other, she clutched a feather from Percy the peacock.

Her mother intoned words in a tongue Hannah did not know. Each syllable cut through Hannah and burrowed into her body until they encircled her heart. With the last word her mother uttered, it seemed a hand squeezed Hannah's heart for a moment and she gasped with the shock of it. Then the sensation dissipated with a buzz and left a tingle running through her limbs.

Seraphina patted Hannah's cheek. "The spell holds, and I sense no deterioration within you. We have another month in which to labour to find a cure."

Hannah stepped out of her chalk coffin and helped her mother back into the bath chair. "Have you had any success with the mummification herbs I gathered from the Chelsea Physic Garden?"

"None as yet." Seraphina gestured to the counter that ran the length of the north-facing windows. Herbs were scattered over the surface in various stages of being dried and ground up. "Egypt is much on my mind. We know Napoleon spent some time there, and I have determined that the mage Cedric Dupré accompanied him. There are many dark rumours swirling around Dupré and I believe his hand created this accursed spell."

Hannah wrapped her arm around her mother's shoulders. "We are close, Mother, I can feel it."

"We peel away the layers to this spell. The heart, and its condition, are pivotal. The Egyptians believed the heart to be the seat of the soul, which is why it remained in the body after mummification. Without a heart, the deceased could not enjoy the afterlife."

"Do you think that is why the Afflicted remain ambulatory? Because their hearts are the last organ to succumb to the rot?" There was one exception. Those recently infected with aged powder experienced the curse in a different way. Instead of the rot attacking the extremities and working inward, it decayed the heart and they dropped to the ground completely dead.

Seraphina wheeled herself toward the door. "Our course feels true now, and if we unlock the secrets of the heart, we will have our answer to this Affliction."

Hannah placed a hand over her own heart. What secret did hers contain?

# 3

HANNAH WHEELED her mother to the shaft that raised and lowered her bath chair to the turret room. "I'll fetch Sheba and see you downstairs."

She collected the puppy and walked down the stairs with a slow tread. The family gathered in the yard, where Old Jim and Frank loaded their luggage onto the back of the large travelling carriage.

Hannah's father had made arrangements for Timmy to spend the week with the aftermage whose magic manifested itself in a medical gift. The lad appeared excited about the change in scenery, until he realised he would be required to travel in the carriage with Hannah and Lord Wycliff. At that point he looked on the brink of rebellion and dug in his heels. "I'll ride behind like a tiger."

"You will not. It looks like rain and I will not have you spending the week in bed with a cold. This is an opportunity for you to learn from another gifted like you." Hannah pointed to the carriage door and gestured for him to get inside.

Frank stood at the horses' heads and rested his own against a starred forehead, whispering words only he and the horse understood. Four horses would pull the carriage to their destination. The sturdy chestnuts had glossy coats and they stomped their feet, impatient to be underway.

Once Timmy had climbed into the carriage, Hannah tapped Frank's arm to attract his attention. "Do look after Mary, please, Frank. I do not want Barnes thinking he can recommence his games with me away. Father is to put him back in his cage if he misbehaves—and you are not to stomp on him."

"Pretty Mary," Frank whispered and a grin pulled his lips tight over his teeth.

"Yes, look out for Mary and keep Barnes away from her," Hannah said.

"Barnes. Bad. Hamster," Frank bit out, narrowing his eerie yellow eyes.

"Barnes can be a naughty Hungarian hamster, but I'm sure he will improve now that he knows his behaviour is unacceptable." Hannah walked back to the carriage and hoped Barnes retained sufficient sense not to battle the Chelsea Monster over Mary.

Inside the carriage, Timmy had wedged himself into the corner, his back to the horses, an anatomy book on his lap. Hannah's father wanted the boy to memorise all the bones, muscles, and organs in the body. While the text was heavy on illustrations, it also aided his reading as he sounded out each word and followed the arrow to where the item resided in the body.

Wycliff joined them, took the front-facing seat next to Hannah, and soon the horses trotted out of the drive and headed west for Swindon. They would break their journey at Reading, the distance being too great to travel with any ease in a single day.

Hannah occupied herself with a book about Egyptian mummification rites. She was convinced that the curse that had created the Afflicted had its origins in that process. If they understood how it was done, it could be undone. The book, unfortunately, was written in Eighteenth Dynasty hieroglyphics.

To aid Hannah's research, her mother had worked an enchantment on a piece of tracing paper. As Hannah pressed the thin sheet to the page of hieroglyphics, the spell translated the symbols underneath. The process was tedious, as first the spell would translate each symbol into a series of more familiar letters, called a *transliteration.* Then the foreign words would dissolve and reorder themselves as the English meaning of the sentence filtered through the paper. At least concentrating on the spidery words let time flow by in the confined space.

Lord Wycliff stared out the window at the passing scenery, but Hannah wondered if he saw anything at all. His attention seemed turned inward and his eyes were unfocused. A book rested in his hands, but he never turned a page in the time Hannah watched him from the corner of her eye.

They stopped at a coaching inn every two to three hours to rest the horses and stretch their legs. Overall, they endured a long day over forty miles of bumpy road to make Reading, where they stopped for the night.

Hannah's body protested as she emerged from the carriage and stretched her arms and legs.

"Is it all right if I sleep in the stables with Old Jim?" Timmy asked.

"If you wish. I'm sure he would appreciate your help with the horses," Hannah said.

The lad glanced sideways at the viscount. "I'm used to being around the horses and I promise I'll do a grand job of rubbing them down after their run today. We don't want them sore tomorrow."

Wycliff nodded to the youngster. "Thank you, Timmy."

Hannah left the youth in Old Jim's capable hands and took Lord Wycliff's offered arm as they walked into the inn. It had a respectable but slightly dishevelled appearance. The whitewash on the walls was faded and needed reapplying, but the timbers all seemed sound. The windows held old-fashioned thick glass with bubbles, but they were clean. The establishment looked aged, but not ignored, like an elderly relative who gave way to the pressure of years, but who remained a much loved part of the family.

Downstairs was a large, open common area with a number of differently shaped tables, from long ones for whole families, to dainty ones for those dining alone. A stairway had a curved end that separated the dining room from the bar.

Hannah stood in the main room and tapped her foot to the music being played on a fiddle, while her husband conducted their business. People crowded around tables and laughter bounced from the thick walls. A few cast curious glances in their direction but most were intent on their own conversations.

One group turned around to stare at her. Three men had vaguely familiar features and were dressed much better than the other patrons. One leaned closer to his companion and said something while still looking in her direction. All three laughed with a cruel edge, as though he had made some jest at her expense.

Hannah clutched her reticule and wished for a wall behind which to hide. When Lord Wycliff returned to her side, Hannah indicated the group with a glance. "Do they look familiar to you?" she whispered.

He made a noise of derision in his throat. "The Devil's Triplets. We shall stay well clear of them."

Hannah gasped and stole another look. She had heard of the three men, notorious for their wild ways. Viscount Charles Stannard, the son of the Marquess of Dolster; the Honourable Ernest Robins; and the Honourable Adam Mowatt were three heirs waiting to inherit titles. They spent their days devising ways to flaunt their wealth and flout society's conventions.

"I have only ever seen them in drawings in the newspaper." Caricatures were rarely flattering, but there was something in the way all three heads bent together that was captured in many drawings.

"Their behaviour has fouled their reputations and most respectable homes are closed to their company. Pay them no heed. Let us hope they are not travelling in the same direction as us." Wycliff took her by the elbow and steered her toward the stairs.

A maid in a dark grey gown with a crisp apron and mob cap waited for them and she gestured for them to follow.

"I have heard they delight in playing cruel jokes on people less fortunate than themselves." A prickle ran down Hannah's spine and she could not dislodge it.

"They are the worst examples of bored heirs with nothing better to occupy their time. Their fathers should have insisted they perform military service. That would at least have given Fate a chance to remove them with a stray bullet." Wycliff's voice rumbled from behind Hannah.

The maid stopped at a door halfway along the corridor and pushed it open. "This is your room, my lord and lady. Would you like supper here or will you come down?"

Hannah wanted to hide in their room, away from the men who laughed at her. Let them find their sport tormenting someone else. But that meant dining alone with her husband in a confined space, and she didn't think she had the courage for that, either.

"Could we have supper downstairs? I did enjoy the music." Music and laughter were more enticing than solemn silence. She would brave the discourteous looks of the Devil's Triplets.

"If you wish," Lord Wycliff said as he waited for her to enter the room first.

Hannah crossed the threshold and stopped in the middle of the room. The reality of their circumstances took their time to sink into her tired mind. "We are to share?"

There was only one bed and not an overly large one at that. Two comfortable-looking chairs were set before a cold fireplace. The window had a view over the courtyard below.

Lord Wycliff crossed to the window and peered out. "I considered securing two rooms, but if you will forgive me, I did not think it advisable for you to be alone. I could not leave you unguarded. I will sleep in the armchair."

*I could not leave you unguarded*, her mind whispered. An invisible force tightened around her heart, but she dismissed it as residue from her mother's spell and nothing to do with his gallant words.

He made a circuit of the room, staring at the ceiling and running a hand over the timbers as though he searched for a hidden door. His inspection stopped at the exit to the hallway. "I will check on the horses and fetch your bag for tonight. Lock the door behind me and admit no one until I return."

"Thank you." A side table held a pitcher with cold, fresh water and Hannah poured it into the shallow basin. She washed her face, hands, and behind her neck and longed to immerse herself in a bath. By the time Wycliff returned with two bags, Hannah felt somewhat revived and refreshed.

With a nervous smile and one hand on her stomach to steady her nerves, she followed him back down to the main room of the inn. They took a table in a quiet corner. Lord Wycliff held out the chair for Hannah as she sat. The fiddler played a mournful tune and conversation became hushed as people listened to the music.

They ate a companionable meal in relative silence. Hannah let the chatter and music wash over her. Lanterns were lit as darkness fell and the circles of yellow light looked like enormous fireflies dotted around the room.

The Devil's Triplets became louder the more ale they consumed. Ernest Robins patted a passing maid on the bottom. The cheer from his friends emboldened him and the next one to pass too close was pulled onto the man's lap. That earned him a slap, but the men laughed as though it were a great jest.

Viscount Stannard stared at Hannah and she dropped her gaze to concentrate on her plate. Though their meal was over, she tore a chunk from the loaf of bread to swipe through the remaining rich gravy.

"Wycliff, you are supposed to leave your horse in the stable, not bring it in for a meal," Stannard called.

His companions hooted with laughter while the other people in the inn cast around, looking from the person who had thrown down the jest to the object of his barb.

Across the table, Lord Wycliff's hands clenched and his shoulders tensed.

Hannah laid a hand over his fist. "They are not worth acknowledging. Besides, I have no issue being compared to a horse—he did not say I resembled a *cart* horse. A thoroughbred is a most elegant and refined creature, beloved by royalty. Your mare is a very fine animal."

He met her gaze with a furrowed brow. "You would turn his cruelty into a compliment?"

"It has been a long day and I am tired. I do not have the energy to be bothered by cruelty and, unfortunately, it is not my first experience with such. If you will excuse me, I shall retire." She rose from her chair and he stood, turning his hand to hold hers before she could pull it away.

"Good night, Lady Wycliff. I will be along to guard your sleep shortly." He kissed her knuckles before releasing her.

Upstairs, Hannah stripped off her gown and stays and left only her chemise. All the time she cast glances at the unlocked door, wondering when her husband would materialise. She climbed into bed and pulled the blankets over her. Sleep crooned to her and she was only dimly aware of the door being opened and the creak of floorboards, before she was swept away by the River Lethe.

Another long day with too few rest breaks saw them reach the sweeping driveway of the Pennicott country estate in Swindon. Since it was a fine day, Timmy had taken up the position of tiger and spent the trip riding at the back of the carriage.

The Pennicott house was of simple Georgian construction and stretched out long and narrow to either side of the enormous portico, big enough to shelter two travelling carriages. The pale stone glowed in the late afternoon sun and the windows all shone like polished diamonds surrounded by golden frames.

"My word," Hannah said as she stepped down. The house was enormous. Even the Loburn family's country home was smaller. A little of her discomfort eased, for in a house of this size, she should have no problems avoiding the other guests. Hopefully it would contain a library, where she could shelter among the books.

A smartly dressed butler in livery of gold and burgundy stepped forward and opened the carriage door. He lowered the steps and held out a hand to assist Hannah.

Either a woman or a small tornado swept down the stairs toward them. "You must be Lord and Lady Wycliff! I have so looked forward to making your acquaintance."

Frances Pennicott was a force of nature with a petite and voluptuous form. Unfortunately, to offset her enviable figure, she had inherited her facial features from her goblin father. A wide, short nose was pinched in the middle as though someone had squeezed the bridge together. A heavy protruding forehead and dark brows gave her the look of a perpetual frown, as though nothing in the world would ever come up to scratch. Her elongated ears with their pointy tips poked through her hair and refused to be concealed.

"Lady Wycliff, I am so pleased to meet you a last." Lady Frances stuck out her hand.

Somewhat bemused by the gentlemanly behaviour instead of a curtsey, Hannah took the proffered hand and shook it.

"Do forgive my being so forward in issuing you an invitation. Father refuses to let me go to London this season, and I am simply dying of boredom out here. Everyone is writing to tell me of your marriage to the viscount and I had to meet you. I have selected a few entertaining guests for the week. I'm sure the conversation will be quite invigorating." She turned to peer up at Lord Wycliff. A sharp tongue darted out and licked her full lips.

Hannah moved closer to her husband, not entirely comfortable with the way her new acquaintance sized him up as though he were breeding stock. Nor did she want to be considered *entertainment* for the other nobles. "It is a pleasure to meet you, Lady Frances, and most kind of you to extend an invitation to us."

Lord Wycliff ignored the exchange and instead appeared to contemplate the architecture of the house.

Lady Frances smiled, but it only made her eyes smaller and narrower. "Oh, do call me Fanny—all my friends do. Now, since everyone is late in arriving, we have decided to bring supper forward to eight o'clock. Once you have refreshed yourselves, there will be drinks in the drawing room. Stewart will show you to your room. She is my companion."

Hannah hadn't even noticed the other woman, and she stood a good head taller than her employer. Lady Frances cast a long shadow.

"Miss Edith Stewart at your service, Lord and Lady Wycliff." She dropped an elegant curtsey. Tall and slender, she had delicate blonde colouring and a serene countenance. A turban in a pale beige silk encircled her hair and complemented her simple gown.

Footmen helped Old Jim unbuckle the straps holding their trunks to the rear of the carriage. More men swarmed around the gleaming black carriage that pulled up behind the rather dusty one they had borrowed from Hannah's parents.

"Do excuse me. Lady St Clair has arrived. I shall see you in the drawing room," Lady Fanny called as she rushed to the next conveyance.

"This way, please." Miss Stewart gestured for them to follow.

Rather than ascending the grand staircase as Hannah expected, Miss Stewart instead turned down a hallway. They passed a number of closed doors and one with double doors that were ajar, revealing a tantalising glimpse of book-lined walls within.

"Have you been Lady Frances's companion for long?" Hannah asked as they walked, curious as to how such a refined woman had failed to make a suitable match. Hannah had assumed she would become Lizzie's companion when her parents could spare her, until unexpected events had led to her marriage to the viscount.

"I have been in her employ these past two years. We both attended Granger's Finishing School, and when I experienced a change in my circumstances, Lady Fanny was quick to offer me a position." A calm smile touched her lips and offered no hint as to what *circumstances* might lead to her becoming a companion.

The walls were lined with portraits of an odd-looking family. Hannah remembered her mother's warning that the earl was descended from a long line of goblins. Hannah didn't know much about goblins, but the paintings could have been taken from any fairy tale featuring the squat and ugly creatures.

The women fared a little better, appearing to mostly take after the maternal (human) line. Though, like Fanny, they all displayed some variant of the wide and squashed nose, prominent forehead, small dark eyes, and pointy ears.

"This is your room, Lord and Lady Wycliff. I will ensure that your luggage is delivered directly. I look forward to seeing you in the drawing room once you have settled in." Miss Stewart opened the door and sympathy flared in her blue eyes before she curtseyed and retreated down the hallway.

Hannah walked into the room with Wycliff behind

her. The footman beat a hasty retreat and as she turned and caught the murderous expression on her husband's face, she understood why the man had scampered like a rabbit flushed from the undergrowth by hounds.

Lord Wycliff had the look of a volcano about to erupt.

# 4

"Is there a problem?" Hannah asked, hoping to defuse the situation.

Wycliff ground his jaw and curled his hands into fists. "They have given us a small room on the first floor. This is an unforgivable slight meant to demean us."

If Hannah had been deeply in love with her new husband, she would have called the room *charming. Intimate. Cozy*. But given that she had to spend a week with a ball of pent-up rage, the best she could muster was *close quarters*.

"This is intolerable. They shall hear of my disgust at their treatment of us." He paced to the window and back again.

The room was smaller than hers back home, but it still contained everything they needed. There was a dresser with a large mirror where she could sit to do her hair. One corner held a small screen that would just be sufficient to conceal her if she didn't flail her arms much while dressing.

A wardrobe stood against the wall that backed on the corridor, and would be more than enough for their clothing for the week. Did matters of propriety extend to clothing? She couldn't see that her gowns would have any objection to hanging next to a gentleman's coats.

A tall, narrow dresser had a mirror where her husband could shave and a gentleman's valet stand next to it was ready to take his waistcoat, coat, and cravats. A sofa stretched in front of the empty fireplace.

Hannah sat on the end of the bed, which seemed rather comfortable. The room was satisfactory for their needs, so long as her mind skirted around the sleeping arrangements. Although, after two long days in the carriage, her body wanted to slumber as though her heart had already stopped. "I don't know how you do it, my lord."

"Do what?" He paused and cast a black glance over her.

On the long trip stuffed in the carriage, Hannah had decided that, as part of her marriage experiment, she would no longer be afraid of her husband. Let him shout and rage, she would let it flow over her like rain on a tiled roof. "How do you profess such complete indifference to what society thinks, and then fly into a rage when they treat you poorly as a consequence? I do not think you can have it both ways—either you care or you don't."

Fire blazed in his eyes and his nostrils flared. Had she overstepped some marital line? Then he tipped back his head and barked a laugh.

He loosened his fists and instead ran his hands through his black hair. "You are right. But how can I let this slight go unremarked? I do not have your gift for turning cruelties into compliments."

Ah. Hannah was an expert in letting slights go unremarked or turning them inside out to find the silver lining. "Imagine, if you will, how such a confrontation will unfold. You will charge out to find our host, while all the other guests gather to watch and whisper. Lord Pennicott will murmur that of course it is an oversight and his lordship will be given a room on the second floor, closer to the family. Then he will ask if you require a room for your valet."

His nostrils flared again. "I do not have a valet."

"Precisely." Hannah rose and walked to the window as she imagined what their host would say next. "What of her ladyship's lady's maid? Where will she be accommodated?"

"You do not have a lady's maid." His dark brows drew close together.

"How very true." Hannah rested one hand on the white painted trim of the window.

He let out a sigh and tormented his hair a little more. "You have made your point. Such a conversation would only further humiliate us and highlight what we lack. What, then, am I supposed to do?"

"Why, nothing. We both suspect that the whole

purpose of our inclusion this week is so that we may be ridiculed and mocked. Lady Frances all but admitted we are the entertainment. Imagine how bereft they will be when we fail to rise to their bait. Besides, if the week becomes too intolerable, from here it will be easy to escape through the window and across the gardens. There is no way down from the rooms higher up." Hannah peered out the window with its low sill. The clipped lawn stretched toward garden beds and some sort of tree-lined walk. It was a rather pleasant view.

Silence hung heavy in the room behind her and she was almost too frightened to turn around. Had she enraged him further? Then she reaffirmed her vow to not be afraid and turned to find her husband staring at her with a quizzical look on his face.

"Each day I find my wife far more than I ever expected," he said in a soft tone.

Warmth rippled over Hannah and emboldened her. "You have raged against the world on your own, but you are alone no longer. We are married, my lord, and while we may not have wed for love, I believe we are both practical people who would seek common ground. If you will allow it, I would walk beside you on the journey we take."

She glanced at him from under half-closed lids, not daring to meet his black gaze. It almost made her hold her breath and she had to command her body to draw air into her lungs. She wasn't one of the Afflicted yet. Breathing was still a required activity.

He crossed the room to join her at the window and

leaned one shoulder on the frame. "It is a hard thing to realise you are not alone when you have spent your life fending for yourself. But you are right—we are in this together. You may call me Wycliff and if you are amenable, I would call you Hannah."

*Hannah.* A weird tingle shot through her body, as though she had walked through a magical barrier. It was rather a familiar way to refer to each other. She had intended to stick with Lord and Lady Wycliff, but it would send an outward message to their detractors that they stood united.

They each had to step from their corners toward the central ground between them. She could agree to his familiar terms. "Very well, Wycliff."

He held out his hand and Hannah placed hers in it. Large, warm fingers curled around hers and they shook.

"There is another matter. I must change for supper." She glanced around the room that wasn't particularly generous. She would seek refuge behind the folded screen, but she baulked at the idea of undressing when she would be able to hear him breathing on the other side of the room. What if he peeked?

His lips quirked in silent mirth as though he read her thoughts. "Of course. I had planned to find the library and see if there was anything diverting to read. How long do you require?"

Hannah did a quick calculation of how long it would take for her to remove her dirty travelling clothes, wash, and put on clean underthings and a dinner gown. "A half hour will suffice. Thank you."

He nodded and left. For a small room, it seemed empty without him in it.

Hannah glanced at the clock on the mantel and began her countdown. With only half an hour, she had to make every minute count. She wasted no time in pulling off her sturdy travelling gown and stays. Next, she rummaged in her trunk until she found a clean chemise and her dinner gown.

She poured water into the basin and washed everything she could reach without removing the chemise. Then she grabbed the clean undergarments and retreated behind the screen. When the dirty garment came off over her head and the fresh air caressed her naked flesh, her heart beat overloud in her chest, as if she expected Wycliff to burst through the door.

Her dinner gown comprised an underdress in deep cream with embroidery around the neckline, and an overgown of forest green. Originally intended for the scandalous Miss Brody, it had needed only minimal alterations to make it fit Hannah as though made specifically for her.

Wycliff returned as she took a seat at the dresser. He flashed her an awkward smile and pulled at his cravat as he walked to his trunk.

Hannah did her best with her hair. They could have asked their host for the use of a lady's maid, but they would be expected to pay a tithe for such a service and she didn't want to draw further on their finances.

Besides, she could manage a basic hairstyle unassisted. She pinned up her hair and then pulled strands free to curl around her face. Next, she took a length of green ribbon with a trail of crystal beads and wound it around her hair to make three distinct bands.

As she worked on her appearance, she caught glances of her husband in the mirror while he changed his shirt. Hannah glimpsed a muscular torso and from her work with her father on cadavers, she recognised a frame that would have little to no fat around the internal organs. Wycliff went behind the screen to remove his trousers and change into breeches and Hannah stopped regarding her husband as an anatomical specimen to be examined.

After a few muttered curses and several minutes, he stepped out from behind the screen. "Do I pass muster?"

Hannah surveyed her husband. He wore black breeches with buttons at the knee and white stockings. A heavy cream waistcoat with a climbing vine embroidered over it lay under his black jacket with tails. When her attention continued upward and reached his silken cravat, she stared at the piece of fabric and resisted the urge to twitch. The knot was uneven.

"May I retie your cravat?" she asked, rising from the padded stool before the mirror.

"Please. I'm always in too damn much of a hurry with the thing." He tugged on the ends and undid the knot, leaving it for Hannah.

"Mother taught me to tie cravats to help Father.

The mathematical tie is his favourite, although I can do a ballroom, waterfall, or barrel knot if you prefer." She made the pleats and passed the fabric behind his neck and back to the front. It conveyed great intimacy as she worked close to him, her fingers grazing his neck as she commanded the stiff fabric into the triangular shape and fastened the ends with a pin.

He held still and even seemed to hold his breath. "Whatever knot you tie is acceptable; they all feel like the hangman's noose to me."

"Perhaps the cravat was invented by a woman as retribution for stays." She stepped back to survey her handiwork and her heart stuttered. He was remarkably handsome when his face was free of frowns and scowls. To think she'd once thought him a wraith or demon intent on sucking the joy from Lizzie's engagement ball. If he smiled, he would be more a heavenly angel, sent to tempt a woman into sin.

He held out his arm. "You look lovely, Hannah. Shall we engage the enemy?"

She rested her hand on his forearm. "Let us undertake a reconnaissance of those who muster against us."

The idea of facing a room full of strangers intent on picking apart her appearance didn't seem quite as frightening with Wycliff at her side. They walked along the hall to the front of the house. A footman stationed by a door bowed, and gestured within.

Hannah and Wycliff paused on the threshold of the drawing room. Decorated in burgundy and gold, the room had a lavish opulence, from the velvet drapes to the enormous circular rug of concentric spirals. A golden-hued pianoforte stood in one corner, where the hostess and three other women flicked through sheet music. Deep gold candelabra were lit with dozens of candles.

Arrayed about the room were a dozen guests, gathered in small groups of two or three. Most of the men wore knee-length breeches and stockings, with tail-coats. One man wore the deep blue uniform of the navy.

The women were mainly dressed in pale hues, making Hannah glad that Lizzie had chosen her gowns. The cut she wore was as fashionable as anything in the room and for once, she didn't feel like the country mouse.

Several turned to stare at them and Hannah's bravery vanished under their scrutiny. Men may have fought charging soldiers during the war, but for a woman, this was another form of battlefield. Reputations were won and lost in the thrust and parry of polite conversation.

One group of men looked familiar. Her fingers tightened on Wycliff's sleeve. The Devil's Triplets.

She couldn't imagine anything worse than a week in close proximity to the horrid Lord Stannard and his two cronies. As Hannah considered bolting back to their room, a large hand enfolded hers and squeezed.

*You are not alone*, he said with his touch, and she stood a little straighter.

Wycliff tilted his head closer to hers. "Whom do

you wish to ignore first? Obviously we will cut Stannard. Or, we could be bold and disregard the entire room and keep to ourselves?"

Hannah cast her eyes downward and bit back a laugh. This glimpse of a mischievous streak in her husband took her by surprise. However, she didn't yet possess his bravery to deliberately antagonise their peers. "There is someone I am already acquainted with. Let me introduce you."

Hannah led him to the corner where Philippa Wright-Knowles, clad in pale green, stood talking to a gentleman. He seemed a fine fellow, who looked at Pippa with such a degree of admiration that Hannah hoped he was the woman's husband and not a paramour.

"Wycliff, may I introduce Mrs Wright-Knowles? Pippa, this is my husband, Lord Wycliff."

Mrs Wright-Knowles dropped a graceful curtsey, then reached out and took Hannah's hand. "Lady Wycliff, how lovely to see you again. This is my husband, Mr Wright-Knowles. Why don't we leave the men to talk business while I introduce you to the other ladies?" Philippa linked her arm through Hannah's and steered her to the group of four women chatting by the pianoforte.

"Ladies, this is Lady Wycliff. I am sure you met Lady Fanny when you arrived." Philippa gestured to Fanny, who wore white trimmed in blood-red velvet, and a blood-red turban dripping a beaded tassel.

"And I met Miss Edith Stewart," Hannah murmured.

Fanny's companion wore a delicate cream gown scattered with embroidered sunflowers and bees. The satin turban wound around her head was adorned with a silk sunflower instead of feathers.

"Then let me introduce Lady St Clair and Mrs Armstrong, wife of the dashing naval hero Captain Armstrong."

Lady St Clair had dark hair, pale skin, and a curvaceous body that reminded Hannah of a fairy-tale heroine on the lookout for a knight. She wore a gown of pale lavender tissue scattered with glittering silver stars and Hannah tried not to stare at her loveliness.

Mrs Armstrong beamed from behind gold-rimmed spectacles. She was a petite woman, with a round face surrounded by light brown hair. Her curtsey was a little too enthusiastic and her curls bobbed frantically. "Lovely to meet you, Lady Wycliff," she gushed.

Hannah glanced to Wycliff and found him in conversation with Captain Armstrong and Mr Wright-Knowles. If her husband could conduct a civil conversation, then so could she.

"How do you like your room, Lady Wycliff?" Lady Frances asked, a glint of anticipation in her dark eyes.

"It is quite charming—so considerate of you to locate us on the first floor, close to the library. My husband and I will enjoy exploring the volumes it holds without having to go constantly up and down stairs."

Hannah beamed, as though being given a first floor room was the greatest privilege.

Lady Frances's smile faltered and dropped away. A tiny frown pressed over the bridge of her nose. "Oh... well...I had heard you were rather fond of books."

"Are many of you proficient on the pianoforte?" Hannah asked. She lacked musical talent herself, but loved to close her eyes and let the music wash over her when a skilled set of hands rested on the keys.

"I enjoy the art," Lady St Clair answered.

A discussion ensued as to pieces to play after dinner and who would sing. Hannah smiled at Mrs Armstrong, who seemed to hover on the constant verge of saying something, but lacked the bravery to jump in.

After a pleasant hour had passed, the doors opened and the butler cleared his throat. "Dinner is served, your ladyship."

Fanny clapped her hands and walked toward the doors. As she passed Lord Stannard, she took his arm.

"If we lined up by fortune, you'd be at the back, Wycliff." Lord Stannard's lip pulled up in a sneer as he cast a look at the assembled guests.

Hannah curled her fingers into Wycliff's sleeve. The strictures of society bound every activity they undertook, even going into dinner. Everyone had to enter the dining room after their hostess in descending order of precedence.

Wycliff, as a viscount and married, walked in behind their hostess and Stannard. Had Lady Fanny deliberately chosen the man who may have shared

Wycliff's rank, but would otherwise have entered behind him? The other guests came in behind them, the captain ranked above Mr and Mrs Wright-Knowles, who brought up the rear.

"If we lined up by wit, Stannard, you wouldn't even be allowed in the house," Wycliff replied.

Hannah bit her lip and looked down at the floor. It was going to be a long week if they had to defend themselves against shots fired by Lord Stannard every time they encountered him.

Stannard snorted and drew himself up, although he was still a good two inches shorter than Wycliff. "Well, if—"

"Save it for dinner, gentlemen. I need a drink in my hand before the entertainment begins," Lady Fanny said, and practically pulled Stannard through to the dining room.

# 5

The long rectangular table dominated the room, draped in a white linen cloth and laid with silverware that glinted in the candlelight. The dinner service was white porcelain with an edge of burgundy and yellow, the earl's colours. The floral arrangements were kept low, so that guests might converse across the table.

Hannah was seated across from Wycliff and next to the empty chair of their host, Lord Pennicott. As his hostess, Lady Frances took the other end of the table, her mother having died a few years before. She had Lord Stannard to her right and Miss Stewart to her left.

A sad air emanated from their hostess's companion, as though she had recently suffered a bereavement. She was a graceful woman with slender limbs and a gentle demeanour, and from their limited acquaintance, Hannah could find no fault in her. Philippa had whispered earlier that Miss Stewart had been set aside by her fiancé and had retired from society. Had that been the change in circumstances that had forced her to become a companion?

Next to Hannah sat the naval officer, Captain Armstrong, and opposite him, his wife, Judith. Philippa and her husband were in the middle of the table and thankfully, Stannard's two companions were at Fanny's end, saving Hannah the necessity of conversing with them. The exotic-looking Lady St Clair also sat toward the middle, as though she hosted her own event with the guests on either side paying her court.

The soup was served and Hannah pondered suitable topics of conversation. While Wycliff might appreciate hearing of the advancements she and her mother had made in finding a cure for the Afflicted, she doubted anyone else wanted to be regaled with the finer details.

Hannah fidgeted with her napkin. Captain Armstrong was a hero of the war with Napoleon. His ship had encountered a French frigate carrying a mage who had English vessels in the grip of a water demon. The captain had swung over to the French warship to engage in close combat and had succeeded in killing the mage, which had saved the English.

Fortunately, the captain opened the conversation. "I am a great admirer of your mother, Lady Wycliff. Lady Miles once saved my vessel by sending a flock of seagulls to tear apart the sails of a French man o' war."

Hannah laughed. "Seagulls? Mother does have a fondness for birds. But tell me, Captain, however did she know you needed assistance?"

The captain was an entertaining storyteller, or he might have been one of those soldiers who appreciated an unsullied audience keen to hear his war stories. Hannah found herself clutching her spoon, waiting to hear if the brave sailors ambushed by the French would survive the terrible sea battle. Who would ever have imagined that seagulls would prove to be their saviours?

Their host, the Earl of Pennicott, joined them late. The men all rose as he took his seat at the head of the table. Short of stature, Lord Pennicott had a bald head and long, pointed ears. He wore gold-rimmed spectacles on the end of his short, broad nose, and his forehead was deeply lined as though he bore many woes.

While startling in appearance, his eyes sparkled as he nodded to Hannah, conveying both warmth and intelligence. "Good evening, Lady Wycliff. How is your mother? Is she still dead?" he asked with a wink as he took his seat.

"Yes, Lord Pennicott. Other than being deceased, Mother is in fine fettle and continues her studies as always." Hannah returned the earl's smile. Now she would have to determine how her mother was associated with him. Did Unnatural creatures hold their own social events?

He picked up a soup spoon and brushed it over the top of the pungent liquid. "If anyone can emerge victorious from a battle with Death himself, it will be Lady Miles. I always thought many peers short-sighted, that they see only her sex and not her ability."

Hannah decided there and then she was going to

like the earl. How enlightened to find a man who considered a woman's abilities! Her mother did say goblins were shrewd and saw things overlooked by others.

"Tell us, Wycliff, what do you do to fill your days?" Lord Stannard asked in a loud tone from the other end of the table. "I hear that you engage in some form of *occupation*."

Hannah cringed as the soup bowls were cleared and the footman began the main service. It was terribly rude to shout down the table. Stannard did seem to like his voice to be heard by everyone in the room.

"I am an investigator for the Ministry of Unnaturals." Wycliff didn't even look up, nor did he increase the volume of his tone, with the result that everyone else strained to catch his words. His attention was on the footman placing slices of beef on his plate.

Laughter erupted around the table, as though Wycliff had told a great joke.

"No noble with any self-respect would stoop to dirty his hands with work," Lord Stannard said. His top lip curled once more in a sneer.

Wycliff took a sip from his wine goblet, then set it down to turn and stare at the man. "I disagree. I believe any man with self-respect should undertake honest labour. I consider myself fortunate that my father frittered away the family fortune. In doing so, he freed me from having to be a similar wastrel, with no purpose in life other than chasing an endless round of vacuous entertainments."

If the conversation were a tennis match, Hannah decided that was a point in Wycliff's favour. Stannard and his friends were notorious for concocting schemes purely to scandalise the *ton* and keep their names in the newspapers.

"Quite so, Wycliff." The earl spoke from his position, his fork waving in the air. "Having an occupation teaches a man the value of a penny—and of himself. Too many of these society popinjays are entirely useless and contribute nothing to the world except twittering nonsense."

Lord Stannard huffed and his cheeks blew in and out.

Mr Robins called, "Why should I care about the value of a penny when my father has thousands of pounds?"

The earl shook his head and pointed his fork at Robins. "See? Foolish idiots. Money will run like water through their hands, you mark my words."

Wycliff turned to their host. "I agree with you, Lord Pennicott. I have an excellent manager on my estate who ensures our labour returns a small profit each year. I have plans to increase our wool production by purchasing breeding stock of a sheep with a far superior fleece. All I need is the capital. Perhaps I might talk to you about becoming an investor?"

The earl sipped his wine. "Later, Wycliff. Dinner is not the time for business conversation. There are ladies present."

"Perhaps if more ladies were exposed to financial

matters, they might be better able to run their households, my lord." Hannah spoke up in her husband's defence. This was the opportunity he sought, and the sooner business was concluded, the sooner they could return home. "I know of ladies who cannot even tally a column of numbers and who are reliant on their household staff to keep the books."

"Indeed!" Philippa joined in. "It's all Greek to me, I have no head for numbers at all. What of you, Lady St Clair? Do you tremble at the sight of an account book?"

The young widow fixed a hard stare on Pippa. "Certainly not. I inherited a sum from my late husband and I intend to manage it myself and not rely on charlatans who might steal the lot and leave me in the gutter."

Philippa paled at the reprimand. But she recovered quickly and turned to their hostess. "Do tell us, Lady Fanny, what entertainments are planned for the week?"

"Ah." Fanny's dark eyes sparkled with mischief. "There will be a ball on our final night, which will be both the culmination of our time together and our own way to celebrate the royal wedding. I have invited what local nobility we think are suitable to mingle with you all. I have a number of sporting events planned for the gentlemen, so they may impress us with their physical prowess." She winked at Stannard, who snorted and raised his glass to her. "And of course, we shall have a hunt before the ball."

*Oh, dear.* Hannah was an inexperienced rider and the idea of charging over rough ground in pursuit of a rabbit or a fox made her stomach flip-flop. Perhaps she could plead a headache on that day and take refuge in the library. Mrs Armstrong also paled at the idea and the loss of colour made her freckles stand out.

"I hope there will be shooting and fishing? I hear you have some fine game on the property, my lord?" Mr Mowatt smiled and elicited a giggle from his hostess.

"The lake is well stocked with trout if you fancy your chances," the earl said.

"He always fancies his chances!" Stannard slapped his friend on the back.

If those three were out in a boat fishing, at least they wouldn't be tormenting Hannah or Wycliff. She pondered how most entertainments for women were designed to amuse those with any artistic talents, but were nightmares to be endured if one was of a more academic bent. No one wanted to hear her sing or abuse a pianoforte.

"One night we shall converse with the dead." Fanny gestured to her companion. "Stewart is an after-mage and can commune with the spirits, if we find one in a talkative mood."

Hannah perked up. That sounded more like an event she would enjoy. It was probably too much to hope that they might start a book club.

Miss Stewart flashed a quick smile. "If they are cooperative, we might indeed be able to speak to someone beyond the veil of death."

Hannah bit her tongue. She spoke to her mother beyond the veil of death several times a day.

Conversation managed to remain civil through the

rest of the meal. At the end, Lady Frances laid her napkin next to her plate. "Ladies, let us adjourn to the drawing room."

All the men rose as the ladies stood. Hannah cast a glance at her husband. She wasn't sure which of them had the worst of it. Wycliff would have to endure the company of the Devil's Triplets as they attempted to make sport at his expense.

And she? What sport would she be required to provide in the elegant burgundy and gold room?

WYCLIFF WATCHED his wife leave with the other women. She had held her own during dinner and he admired her strength of character when she spoke her mind.

"This way, gentlemen." The earl opened a door on the opposite end of the room. Beyond lay the billiards room. The large table took pride of place and a chandelier hung above to illuminate the green felt.

Fat leather armchairs were arrayed around the sides, where a gentleman could sit while he watched the play. A long table was laid with decanters and crystal glasses. A platter held grapes and another a selection of cheeses.

"I leave you to your cigars and brandy, gentlemen. I have work to do." The earl nodded to them.

"Might I have a moment of your time, Lord Pennicott?" Wycliff asked before the noble made his retreat.

The goblin paused and his dark gaze flicked to the empty hall beyond the door. It would seem he didn't want to be marooned with Stannard and his friends, either. "You may make an appointment to see me when I am in London."

Wycliff counted to ten to hold in his burst of temper. If it had been as simple as making an appointment, he would have done so many months ago. "I have tried to do so, but you are a difficult man to pin down. All my requests have been denied or met with silence."

The earl spread his hands and sighed. "I have many impoverished nobles pounding on my door wanting ready cash."

Wycliff took a step closer and pitched his voice low. He despised airing his business with the other men hanging on every word, but it could not be helped. "I'm not asking for ready cash. I have a business proposal that requires capital to make it a viable venture."

Pennicott cocked his head as he made some mental calculation. Perhaps totting up what he knew of Wycliff's net worth. "Very well, but not tonight. I will send Godrich when I have the time to spare to hear your proposal."

With that, the earl excused himself.

Wycliff wished he could do the same. Playing billiards with a group of fops with no intelligent conversation held no appeal. There were a number of things he would rather do, like cut his toenails with a sabre.

Stannard poured himself a drink in a short glass and stared at Wycliff through the amber liquid. "You really don't understand how to be a gentleman, do you? When an estate is bankrupt, you are supposed to find a fat purse to prop it up. The woman you chose is favoured with neither fortune nor beauty."

Robins chortled as he poured a large measure of brandy, but Mowatt held his silence. Wright-Knowles looked uncomfortable and fidgeted, as though he didn't know which side he should take. The captain blanched and busied himself setting up the balls on the felt.

Wycliff held in his anger. Hannah had been proven right—they were invited merely to be made sport of. But he had no intention of being easily blooded prey. He had fangs and would use them. "My wife has several attributes that most women lack. Including a keen mind and an insight into other people. Insult Lady Wycliff again and I will call you out."

So many men were shallow and saw only a pretty exterior. Wycliff looked deeper. The longer their association, the more he discovered about his wife that enthralled him. Hannah was not conventionally beautiful in the way about which poets waxed lyrical. But there was a grace and elegance to her long-limbed body. Intelligence simmered in her eyes and she had a kind heart.

Stannard lit a cigar and took a deep draw before he blew smoke in Wycliff's direction. "You wouldn't dare. Tell us, Wycliff, did the dead mage have to bind you with magic to make you consummate the marriage, or did her father knock you out?"

Wycliff didn't bluff or make empty threats. Nor did

he intend to slap Stannard with a glove. Instead he strode toward him, drew back his arm, and punched him hard in the face. The crunch under his knuckles was eminently satisfying. He embraced the stab of pain in his fist and contemplated adding a second blow. He'd rather see the man on the ground than wobbling on his feet.

"Steady on!" Mowatt exclaimed. He and Robins rushed to their friend. Robins stood guard while Mowatt grabbed Stannard before he toppled over.

Stannard keeled forward, holding both hands to his face. Blood spurted between his fingers. "You've broken my damn nose."

Wycliff shook his fist to relieve the tingle running over the bones. "Tomorrow at dawn. Captain, would you be so good as to be my second, since I have no man here?"

Captain Armstrong took only a moment to decide whose side he wanted to be on. "Of course, my lord."

"There is no need for this, Lord Wycliff. If you intended to draw first blood, you have already succeed-ed," Wright-Knowles said.

"Yes. You have first blood. Let this be the end of it. Unless you want all of society repeating what I said about your wife." Stannard sat in an armchair, took the handkerchief Mowatt offered, and pressed it to his face.

Wycliff clenched and unclenched his fist. Stan-nard's words held him in place. If he pursued the duel, everyone would talk of it and the circumstances that had brought it about. To demand satisfaction, he would have to hold up his wife to further ridicule. The man had wedged him into a near impossible situation.

"Very well, but this matter is not resolved between us," he bit out, and then spun on his heel and left the room.

He had too much energy coursing through his body to sit in the library with a book or even to confine himself to the house. Wycliff returned to the bedroom, untied his cravat, and tossed the crumpled linen over the gentleman's valet. Next, he stripped off his jacket and dropped it over the wooden shoulders.

He wrote a quick note for Hannah, saying he would return via the window at some point during the night and she was not to be alarmed. Then he lifted the sash and climbed out. His wife was right—it was an easy escape from the house. The wide lawn beckoned, draped in the velvet blanket of night. The moon was on the wane and its feeble light did nothing to relieve the gloom.

Assured that he wouldn't be seen, Wycliff closed his eyes and drew a deep breath through his nose. He concentrated on the heat that burned in his gut and allowed it to bloom through his veins and ignite his limbs. The transformation flowed over him and he fell to the ground to land on all fours. The beast shook, reacquainting himself with his changed form, before he loped off into the night.

## 6

Later that evening, Hannah returned to the bedroom to find items of her husband's clothing strewn about and the window standing open. She didn't need the note to confirm that he had escaped across the lawn. She only wondered if he would indeed return, or if she had been abandoned less than a month into their marriage.

Before undressing, she found in her case the small mushroom lamp she had brought from home. Hannah set it on the mantel and tapped the top. The cap emitted a soft amber glow. Satisfied that the small glass fungus would give her husband enough light to see by when he returned, she saw to her own toilette.

Once she had braided her hair and exchanged her dinner dress for a soft cotton nightgown, Hannah climbed into bed. She blew out the candle before settling under the blankets. The mushroom washed the room with its subtle light, and she felt less alone in the strange house with a piece of her mother to watch her sleep.

Exhaustion from the long day and the strange company lapped at her limbs like a gentle ocean at the shore. As she contemplated how she would know it was her husband climbing through the window and not a ruffian—an idea which should have made her sit bolt upright—she nodded off.

Several hours later, Hannah awoke with a start and sat up. She glanced around the room cast in muted hues by the early dawn light. A gentle breeze wafted in from the gap of an inch in the not-quite-closed window.

"Good morning." Wycliff lay on the sofa with his back to the door and stared out the window. A blanket was pulled up to his chest and he wore a linen shirt with the lacing undone at his throat.

Hannah clutched at the bedding and pulled it higher, the thin nightgown not much of a barrier from his intense half-lidded stare. "Good morning. I did not hear you return last night."

"I didn't want to wake you. You appeared to be most deeply asleep." His lips twitched.

"Deeply asleep? Is that a polite way of saying I was snoring?" Preposterous. Ladies didn't snore. Although given that she was asleep, how was she to know what noise she made?

His lips twitched again and a snort became a yawn as he stretched his arms over his head. "Let's agree to call them delicate sleep noises. If you wish, I can find a footman and have a tray brought to our room. Or did you want to brave the breakfast room?"

Hannah felt drained from the effort of being sociable the previous night. How did others do it, night after night? She would need a month alone in the library to recover from the week yet to unfold. "I'd rather stay here, please. No one will remark it in a married woman. Besides, it is far too early for anyone else to be awake. They are probably only now returning to their rooms."

Wycliff grabbed a robe from the floor and shrugged it over his shoulders before standing. "I shall set off in search of breakfast, then."

While her husband was out of the room, Hannah used the chamber pot and then slid it back under the bed before washing her hands. With that pressing matter taken care of, she was more composed by the time he returned. More light filtered through the tall window and it was sufficient for her to read a novel.

Wycliff dug into his leather satchel, pulled out a book, and returned to the sofa. Soon a soft knock at the door heralded a footman carrying a laden tray with silver covers keeping the food warm. Another footman followed with a tea tray.

Hannah was quietly impressed. After the insult of a first-floor room, she worried the staff might feed them stale bread and cold tea. Once the footmen left, they consumed a quiet breakfast in companionable near silence.

"Do you think you will secure an interview with

Lord Pennicott today? He seemed impressed last night that you have an occupation," Hannah said.

"I am hopeful. He said he would send Godrich to find me when he is at leisure." Wycliff sat in a chair by the window, his stocking-clad feet resting on the sill.

Hannah couldn't bring herself to reprimand him for exposing his feet out the window. They were in the privacy of their bedroom, after all, and she appreciated the soft breeze coming in under the lifted sash. The room was warm, as though a roaring fire had burned all night.

"I wonder what activities have been arranged for the ladies. Lord, I hope it's not needlepoint, painting, or calligraphy." If she were at home, Hannah would have chores to undertake in the laboratory. Today was also her father's weekly visit to the Repository of Forgotten Things. What if her mother had made some advancement in the ancient Egyptian potions she brewed? She ought to be there to record it.

Wycliff chuckled. "We are more alike than we appear. I suspect that, like me, you are thinking of all the tasks going undone because we are here."

She flashed him a smile. "Quite so. I enjoy my time in Lady Elizabeth's company, but having to be polite to strangers for hours on end is simply too exhausting. I'm not sure how I will survive an entire week. Do forgive me if I decide to succumb to a fainting fit simply to secure some time alone."

Wycliff barked in laughter and Hannah started at the sound. He was an unusual man and it would take some time to grow accustomed to being in close quarters with him. Although she had noticed that the more time they spent in each other's company, the more he dropped the guarded exterior. His air of suppressed anger dissipated, and she glimpsed a more open and relaxed man in its wake.

"If I secure an interview with the earl early on, we can always pack up and disappear in the middle of the night. We could have Old Jim pull the carriage up by the window and toss our bags through. That would give them all something to talk about." Wycliff wiped a piece of toast over his plate to collect the last of the coddled egg, and then popped it in his mouth.

With breakfast consumed, they tackled the awkward task of dressing. Hannah thought it inconvenient to make her husband leave the room every time she needed to change, which happened a few times a day with such house parties.

She selected her morning gown and then eyed the small screen.

"I promise not to peek. I shall be occupied shaving." Wycliff pointed to the mirror and bowl set atop a dresser. When the footman brought breakfast, the one carrying the tea tray had deposited a pitcher of hot water for Wycliff's use.

"I have every confidence that my husband will conduct himself with honour," she murmured and then scurried behind the screen with a rapidly beating heart.

Once dressed, they left their room to find the drawing room. Hannah and Wycliff chose comfortable corners and took up residence. It was mid-morning before the others began to appear.

"Stannard not here?" Robins asked as he joined them last and cast around the room. "I banged on his door, but he wasn't there. When I peered inside, it didn't look like his bed had been slept in." He chortled at the obvious implication. House parties were notorious for the liaisons of the attendees.

"He will be playing a game for our entertainment, I am sure. Perhaps he started Sardines early. We shall have to hunt for him." Fanny grinned, revealing canines slightly longer than usual.

Before they were sent off to search cupboards for the viscount in hiding, the butler announced his presence by coughing into his hand.

"What is it, Godrich?" Fanny asked.

The man gave a slight bow. "I believe I may be of assistance, my lady. Lord Stannard is in the garden. Or rather, a statue of him can be found there."

"A statue? Whatever do you mean?" Fanny frowned and the crumpled effect made her small eyes all but disappear in her face.

"One of the gardeners reported it this morning. In the ornamental walk, someone has placed a statue of Lord Stannard. The gardeners are most bemused by it, but I instructed them to leave it be until I sought instructions from your ladyship."

Fanny clapped her hands and spun in a circle. "See! I told you Stannard would entertain us. It might be a treasure hunt and the statue our first clue." She gestured for everyone to follow and took Miss Stewart by the hand. "Come along. Let us see what he has conceived."

Hannah and Wycliff trailed the group through the house and outside. While Hannah was curious, she didn't want to play any game that involved the horrid Lord Stannard. He had been nothing but rude to her and Wycliff and she refused to be pulled into his antics.

They walked across the expanse of lawn with its pretty rill of still reflecting water, toward the towering hedge that sheltered the ornamental walk. This garden's beds were laid out in a pattern in which a lady could promenade while admiring the flowers. A large central pond contained bright orange fish that swam among the water lilies.

Sure enough, one pathway was blocked by Lord Stannard.

Or a stone figure of him.

"How clever," Fanny said as she peered closely at the image. "Most lifelike."

The guests circled the statue, admiring the quality of the workmanship. All except Miss Stewart, who appeared pale and shaken by its discovery, to the point that she sat on a stone bench nearby.

"Why, it looks just like him," Pippa said. "But why commission a statue in such a state of undress?"

Hannah examined the statue. The stone Stannard wore neither coat nor cravat. His waistcoat hung unbuttoned and the laces of his shirt were undone at his throat. He looked as though he had dressed hurriedly. What an odd thing to immortalise in granite.

The more she studied the statue, the more she pondered the odd pose the sculptor had chosen, along with the degree of undress. Rather than some heroic stance of hands on hips, the marble Stannard had his arms raised before him.

"Something is not right about this," Hannah said to Wycliff.

"Then let us discover what is niggling at you." He pushed through the other guests and created a path for Hannah.

She stood in front of the statue and set aside her dislike for the subject. It was clearly recognisable as Lord Stannard, down to the shape of his chin and the way his hair was styled.

Hannah followed the protocol established in her family, and spoke aloud as the ideas flowed into her mind. "The fine detail is extraordinary. Even the pupils are dilated and I can see the hint of shadow to his chin. The folds of fabric in the sleeves are expertly cast and look, here, there is something tucked in the waistcoat pocket." Hannah pointed to the statue's left side, where the corner of what could be a visiting card jutted out.

"You can almost see the writing etched upon it." Turning her head sideways revealed the faint trace of script immortalised on the small rectangle. Another object peeked from the purse pocket of the statue's breeches.

"What do you suppose that is—a handkerchief?"

She pointed to an object that appeared to be two inches wide, flat, and destined to spend eternity not quite secured inside the pocket.

Wycliff shrugged. "Why commission a statue dressed like this and in such a pose? People have themselves immortalised in regal and dignified ways. This is ridiculous. Did he intend to mock the observer with his dishevelled appearance?"

The sculptor had captured Lord Stannard with both arms raised, the right extended across his face. His mouth was open as though shouting, the eyes wide. A most unusual pose for a granite form.

Had the artist intended to convey surprise or fear? Hannah wondered. "Why make a statue that appears startled?"

"I would have called his stance defensive. Look how his arms are raised, as though he expects a blow to fall." Wycliff mimicked the gesture and threw up his own arms.

"This will be a marvellous game. I am sure the statue is a clue and we are to hunt him down," Mr Wright-Knowles said. "We need only determine what he is trying to tell us. Perhaps he is pointing at something?"

"How splendid to create an eternal monument to yourself," Mrs Armstrong said from her spot near the back of the group.

Wycliff huffed. "A monument to excess and foolery."

"There is something in his hand." Hannah pointed

to his left hand, curled into a fist and clutching a small object. "Could it be a ball? Or an egg?"

Wycliff leaned closer and heat washed over Hannah. He bent down and looked at it from underneath. "I believe it is a billiard ball. There is a small dot on the bottom."

Hannah tucked that information away, then peered closer. Many of the little details indeed niggled at her mind—one in particular. "The hand that carved it made one mistake. There appears to be something wrong with the nose and eyes of this statue."

Mowatt spoke up. "Lord Wycliff broke his nose last night. His eyes had begun to swell and blacken last I saw him."

Hannah stared at her husband. "You broke his nose?"

Wycliff shrugged. "He deserved it."

She wanted to bombard him with questions as to how *that* had come about, but given the taunts thrown at them yesterday and the day before, she could piece together her own answer. "Your actions aside, how could this statue have been made in advance? Lord Stannard would have had to instruct the sculptor to carve him with a broken nose and black eyes. Then he would have needed to provoke somebody into hitting him, to ensure his appearance matched the statue. It is nonsensical."

"Perhaps not. Given the nature of the man, there would be no end of willing volunteers," Wycliff murmured as he stared at the card in the stone waistcoat pocket.

Hannah was fascinated by the statue. The itch in the back of her mind demanded it be scratched. To satisfy her own curiosity, she placed both her hands on the stone chest and closed her eyes. A weak tingle ran across her palms.

"Oh, dear."

"What is it?" Wycliff asked.

Hannah considered possible reasons for the statue to emit a magical resonance. "I fear magic is at play and this is no ordinary statue. Either it is an ensorcelled object that he managed to create in advance, knowing you would break his nose, or this *is* Lord Stannard."

"You mean he has been coated in stone by some magic?" Wycliff rapped his knuckles on the statue's head. "Sounds hollow to me."

Hannah lowered her hands and searched the stone face for a clue. "I don't know the mechanics of how it occurred, except that magic has been used here. I can sense a weak residue."

"Whatever are you saying, Lady Wycliff?" Lady Fanny pushed forward to stand next to Hannah. "Come, let us be about the game."

Hannah pointed at the statue. "I do not believe Lord Stannard created this as some entertainment. I suspect that this is he, surprised during the early hours of this morning in a state of undress. Most likely as he returned to his rooms."

"Would your mother know for certain?" Wycliff

took her right hand and ran his thumb over the ring on her smallest finger.

"Yes. Ask Lady Miles. Surely she will know if this is a magical spell?" Captain Armstrong suggested.

Wycliff released her hand, and Hannah rubbed the metal peacock feather on her finger. The metal was a rare element called *mage silver* that had a unique affinity with the mage that created it. Her mother knew the location of each piece of metal she crafted. It also allowed the wearer to signal the mage and vice versa.

"Please be free to talk, Mother," Hannah whispered as she kept touching the ring while surveying the garden.

After several long minutes, which saw most of the other guests grow bored and wander off through the garden, a bird flew down from a nearby tree and alighted on the statue's raised arm.

The bird cocked its head and when it opened its beak, Seraphina's voice emerged. "Whatever is the matter, Hannah? Are you well?"

Hannah let out a relieved sigh. The sound of her mother's voice made her feel on more certain ground. "I am perfectly well, Mother. We have a mystery here that requires your expertise. We believe the statue you are sitting on is Viscount Charles Stannard."

The bird flapped its wings and hopped from the statue to Hannah's arm.

"Tell me what you see, Hannah, please," the bird commanded.

Hannah held out her arm at shoulder height, to give

the bird the best view of the statue. "Lord Stannard has not been seen since last night. A search found this statue, which bears a remarkable resemblance to him, standing in the garden. The likeness is too eerie to have been created by a stone mason. Also, the state of undress and pose suggest the subject was caught unawares. I can detect a faint trace of magic and I wonder if the statue is actually the real Lord Stannard, not merely a likeness."

The bird hopped along Hannah's arm as it examined the object. "Most interesting. There are a number of spells and curses that can turn a person, or other objects, into stone. Although I've not heard of any aftermages strong enough to effect such a curse. More likely it may have been a potion that he ingested or that was thrown over him."

Hannah glanced at Wycliff. "There is one aftermage among the guests, although her gift lies in communicating with the dead."

The bird fluttered its wings and then tucked them back along its sides. "I will research such effects and see what I can identify as possible causes. It would help if we knew whether the curse worked from the inside out or vice versa."

Hannah wondered how to ascertain that without breaking off Lord Stannard's arms and examining the structure within. "Timmy is not far away. Perhaps he might have some insight."

"Brilliant idea, dearest. Fetch Timmy, then. We can talk again this afternoon and share what we have learned." The bird chirped, hopped to the tips of Hannah's fingers, and flew back to its brethren in the trees.

"I can ride out for the lad," Wycliff said.

"Take what you need from our stables, Lord Wycliff." Fanny gestured to one side of the house. "Let us pray this is some jest and not some foul spell that has taken Lord Stannard from us."

Hannah rested a hand on her husband's arm. "Thank you, Wycliff. Fetching Timmy will speed matters along. In the interim, I will examine the grounds. It seems unusual for him to be in the garden last night. He may have been struck inside the house and moved here, and there may be some trace."

Wycliff nodded and then strode away.

"Is there anything I can do?" Fanny glanced from the statue to Hannah, anxiety in her eyes for the first time.

There was indeed something her hostess could do. "Perhaps you could ask the staff if anyone saw Lord Stannard last night? It would help if we could identify where and when he was last seen."

"Of course. I shall ask Godrich at once." Fanny took the proffered arm of Captain Armstrong and walked back to the house. The other guests emerged from various parts of the garden and followed their hostess.

Hannah turned to the statue. "Well, Lord Stannard, I assume you will not be going anywhere. I shall return once I have walked the grounds."

# 7

As Hannah paced the grounds staring thoughtfully at the grass, she considered how the statue might have been moved into place. It could have been dragged, placed on a cart, or carried if there had been more than one person to lift it. Any of those methods might have resulted in scuff marks or tracks, yet she found none in the lime chip paths.

She was about to abandon her examination when she found an odd depression in the lawn halfway between the garden and the house.

"A boot heel?" she murmured as she gathered up her skirts to kneel and examine the mark more closely. It was a large, rounded depression. Too big to be a boot heel, and the wrong shape.

Scanning the clipped lawn, she found another. "Curious." They were too far apart to be the strides of a man, particularly if one were carrying something heavy like a solidified Lord Stannard. The shapes might be the edge of the statue if someone had put it down to rest for a moment. Its weight would have made it sink into the grass...though the depression was without the sharp point that a corner would make.

Like a child on a treasure hunt, she moved from imprint to imprint as she neared the house. They had to be man-made and not random like those of a dropped gardening implement, due to the regular spacing and the straight path they took. Soon the pale stone house loomed over her and she looked up, expecting to find patio doors or a side door. Instead she found windows, their sills all at waist height.

A niggle in her mind made her turn around and survey the garden, her back to the house. How familiar the view looked. "No. Impossible."

Hannah spun around and, following the direction of the imprints, headed for one window in particular. A glance inside confirmed her suspicion. It was the bedroom she shared with Wycliff.

The earth under the windows was bare of grass and turned over, as though the gardeners were refreshing the annuals and perennials that would bloom against the warmth of the brick in summer. A black spot caught her eye—another depression in the soil.

Heedless of the damage to her skirts, she knelt. This rounded shape had four more circular depressions around one side.

"A paw," she said the word on an exhale. Then she held her hand over the imprint. "A paw the size of my hand."

She looked up. What creature had a paw of such size? A lion or a bear? There was no menagerie at the Pennicott estate that might explain such an exotic animal's being on the loose.

There was an odd coloration to the earth that wasn't present at any of the other depressions she examined. Hannah wiped a finger through the blackened earth. Paint? She rubbed her thumb and forefinger together, but the substance was gritty and more like soot.

The evidence would suggest a beast with large paws had scorched the earth and run from her bedroom window across the lawn. Yet she did not remember any commotion the previous night. Had the creature peered at her while she slumbered and then run across the garden to encounter Lord Stannard?

"Whatever is afoot in Swindon?" she asked the shrubbery, but there was no reply.

Wycliff borrowed two horses from the stable; it would be quicker and easier for them to both ride, rather than trying to carry the lad pillion. Given that he had been a tiger and worked in stables before he'd become part of the Miles family, he assumed the lad could ride.

He rode with the reins to his mount in his right hand, his left held the reins to the second horse as he cantered down the road toward the house where

Timmy was staying. Doctor Colchester was an associate of Sir Hugh and an aftermage with the ability to discern a person's physical condition. He was teaching the lad how to grow his magical skill.

It was a short half hour's ride to the picturesque cottage. Smoke curled from its two chimneys and there was movement behind the windows.

Wycliff dismounted as a man emerged from the stables. "I'll take them for you, my lord. The doctor is inside."

The door opened as he approached, confirming that someone had been watching from the window. A country doctor was probably accustomed to people riding up at all hours of the day and night, needing help.

An older woman with soft wrinkles and grey hair tucked under a cap smiled at him. "Can we help you, my lord?"

"Forgive the intrusion, madam. I am Wycliff, and we have need of Timmy at the Pennicott estate," he explained as he stood in the hall.

A gentleman of similar vintage as the woman emerged from a side room. "I am Doctor Colchester and this is my wife. You say you need Timmy? It seems I am replaced already," he said with a chuckle.

"Lady Wycliff, the former Miss Hannah Miles, believes Timmy's particular skill will be of assistance," Wycliff said.

"I'll fetch the boy," the doctor's wife said, and bustled along the hallway.

"The lad is quite bright and will make a fine surgeon one day, if he learns to focus on the task at hand." The doctor smiled like a benign grandparent.

"Is milady hurt?" Timmy all but ran down the hall and screeched to a halt before Wycliff.

"She is well, lad. But there is a statue we need you to examine," Wycliff said.

The boy screwed up his face. "A statue?"

"It will be easier to explain when you see it. Can you ride?" he asked.

The youth rolled his eyes. "'Course I can, milord."

Out in the yard, the doctor's man held the two horses. Timmy took the reins of one, placed his hands on the saddle and without the need for a stirrup, nimbly leapt onto the horse.

"Good lad," Wycliff muttered. He could remember being that young and agile.

They made a quick return to the estate and handed the horses over to the earl's grooms. Timmy trotted at his heel as Wycliff strode though the grounds. He found his wife in the garden, on a bench next to the fossilised Lord Stannard. She read from a book as she maintained a silent vigil.

When the crunch of gravel underfoot gave away their arrival, she looked up, placed a silver marker in the book, and set it aside. "Timmy, we have a need of your particular skill." She gestured toward the statue.

"It's a statue," the lad said, a frown pulling down his brows.

Hannah rose from the bench and beckoned the boy

closer to the monument. "Yes, but we believe it used to be a gentleman who has gone missing. I can detect a very faint trace of magic and I was wondering—if this was indeed flesh and blood—whether you could tell us anything more."

"But if it's solid stone, I won't be able to tell you anything." Timmy reached out a tentative hand and poked the hem of Lord Stannard's stone coat.

Hannah wagged a finger at Timmy. "Ah, but even that in itself will tell us something. We do not know if it is solid or not, without breaking it open."

"Why shouldn't you break it, milady?"

"There is a chance Stannard is inside, but coated in granite." Whatever the possibility of that, Wycliff wouldn't be rushing to release the spellbound prisoner.

"I'll try." The youth rolled his shoulders. He stretched out both hands and rested one on the statue's forearm and the other over the breastbone. He closed his eyes and leaned slightly toward the stone man.

Wycliff folded his arms and waited. Whatever the lad was doing, it gave no visible evidence. There were no flashes of light or odd noises. The birds continued to chirp and go about their business.

Timmy's head swung back and forth as though he searched for something in the dark. "It's awfully dense inside, milady."

"All I ask is that you try," Hannah said.

The lad heaved a sigh and the two adults kept quiet vigil.

"Oh! There's a thud. It's faint and far apart. I

almost missed it." The youth leaned closer, pressing his ear to a stone shoulder, since the raised arms made it impossible for him to listen to the chest.

"He has a heartbeat?" Wycliff stepped closer, half expecting to hear the thrum of stone blood through the statue or to see Stannard wink at him.

Timmy looked up with wide eyes. "Blimey slow though, and it's struggling."

Wycliff stared at the broken nose now turned into a work of art. "Hardly surprising that his heart is straining, given it is encased in stone."

Hannah paced back and forth, her hands laced together. "It also means he isn't dead, but perhaps under some spell that could be reversed."

"If his heart still beats, however slowly, do you think he is aware of what has happened to him?" What would it be like—to be encased in stone and able to hear and see what transpired around you, but without any way to interact or communicate with those who stared at you? He couldn't imagine a worse type of torture than to be rendered so completely powerless.

Hannah stopped before the man who thought it good sport to hurl insults at her. "Let us hope not. Most likely he will be unconscious, perhaps in a deep sleep similar to that which struck down Sleeping Beauty in the fairy tale."

Wycliff barked a short laugh. "I won't be kissing him to break this curse."

Timmy moved his hands so they both lay on the

stone torso. "You don't have long, milady. This feels as though it's about to give up."

Hannah tapped a finger on her lip in thought. "Can you sense anything about the curse?"

Timmy closed his eyes and leaned into his hands resting on the cool stone. After a long minute he lowered them and shook out his arms as though they had gone to sleep while he worked. "Whatever it was, it froze him on the spot first, and then it seeped inward, turning him to stone as it went. The heart is the last to go."

Wycliff considered what might have had such an effect. "That sounds like something thrown at him, rather than something he ingested."

"Yes, a potion that he swallowed would have worked the opposite way, from the inside out," Hannah agreed. "Thank you, Timmy, you have been most helpful. One last thing—can you estimate at all how long his heart might struggle on?"

The youth licked his lips, his attention darting from the statue to Hannah. "Oh, milady, he won't last long at all. Maybe an hour at most?"

Hannah pressed the heel of her palm to her forehead. "Oh. I cannot see how we would find a cure in less than an hour. Wycliff, do you think we should gather the rest of the party to mark his passing?"

Despite the grievous insults the blackguard had thrown at her, she still exhibited sympathy for his imminent demise. Wycliff wouldn't be wasting any tears on the man. Unless someone ran from the house, confessed, and pulled an antidote from their pocket, Lord Stannard would mock and belittle others no longer. The Devil's Triplets would lose their leader and he could only think that society would benefit by it.

Hannah placed a hand on his forearm and pulled him from his tally of the unfortunate's sins. "Who would want to murder Lord Stannard in such a way?"

"Given what we know of him, the better question might be, who would not?" Wycliff had found satisfaction in breaking the man's nose. What grudge did someone bear to turn him into stone and squeeze the last beat from his heart? There were so many foul rumours attached to the man, from blackmail to despoiling young women.

"Why did you break his nose?" His wife turned to him with a quizzical expression in her chocolate eyes.

"It seemed the quickest way to silence him." The man was dead, or soon would be. There was no need to repeat the horrid things he'd said.

As they spoke, two liveried footmen approached through the garden beds, weaving their way around leggy lavender that hung over the paths. They stopped before the statue. One raised his eyebrows, but the other had the look of a servant who had seen far worse from his employers than a stone likeness.

"My lord, Lady Frances sent us to stand watch over Lord Stannard," the more stoic footman said.

That would leave him free to prowl the gardens in case the murderer came back to gloat before his victim. "Good. See that no one moves him. This lad will stay here. Timmy, send word when the heart stops—unless by some miracle we are able to reverse the process before then."

Timmy swallowed, a visible lump making his Adam's apple bob up and down. "Yes, milord."

Wycliff took Hannah's hand and pulled her back toward the house.

"We are not going to stay for his final moments?" Hannah looked back over her shoulder as Timmy took her place on the bench.

Wycliff concentrated on the house before them and the tasks he needed to perform. Stannard was the son of a marquess and his father must be satisfied they had done all they could to find the hand responsible. "I need to commence my investigation. As you said, there is little we can do to reverse the spell or impede its progress to the final conclusion."

As they walked back into the house, they encountered the earl in the foyer. "Fanny tells me one of the guests has been turned to stone?"

"Yes—Lord Stannard," Wycliff said.

"No one who will be missed, then." The earl arched one eyebrow and the pointy ear on the same side of his head twitched as though it laughed. "Can the effect be reversed?"

Hannah answered, "Not until we know what spell or potion turned him to stone in the first instance. In any case, I fear we will be too late. My father's apprentice is out in the garden—an aftermage who can sense things about a person's health. The lad says that, while

Lord Stannard's heart still beats, it will soon give up its fight for life."

"Well, if there is nothing to be done for the chap, I assume you want to find out who did this to him?" The earl peered up at Wycliff, keen intellect shining in his small round eyes.

Wycliff nodded. "Yes. Lady Frances was to have assembled the staff. I want to find out who saw him last. I shall talk to Robins and Mowatt and see what transpired last night after I left the billiards room."

"I believe they are all below stairs. You'll find the gentlemen smoking out on the rear terrace, where they are watching the ladies at their painting." The earl gestured down the hall.

Wycliff turned to his wife. "Hannah, could you apprise the ladies of these events while I speak to the other two?"

"Of course," she said.

They headed through the house together and emerged onto a wide stone terrace that led down to the lawn and lake. Robins and Mowatt sat in cane chairs with deep cushions set under the shade of the overhanging roof. Hannah left her husband and walked down the stairs to the women painting in watercolours out on the lawn.

Wycliff leaned on the balustrade. "What did Stannard do after I broke his nose?"

The two men exchanged glances, then Mowatt spoke. "We rang for a footman, who fetched some water and a cloth. We cleaned Stannard up while he kept drinking. He had some rather choice words to say about you, my lord."

Wycliff bit back his retort. He had, after all, had the last laugh. "I can well imagine. Who left first?"

Mowatt shrugged. "We played some billiards, drank some more. The captain and Wright-Knowles didn't last much longer, although they both had warm beds to go to. We retired not long after midnight."

Robins took up the narrative. "Stannard was drunk and leaning to the left when he walked. He kept running into the walls. We helped him up the stairs and dumped him on his bed. Neither of us is his nanny, to undress him and put him to bed, and the earl's valet was occupied."

"Yet he ended up as a statue in the garden. He got there somehow." Blast. If the man was that drunk and had got up to go wandering in the dark, he should have killed himself in a tumble down the stairs. Either he revived quickly, hadn't been as drunk as he made out, or someone had crept into his room and wrought their spell.

Wycliff discounted the last scenario. The man was frozen upright, his arms in front of his face as though warding off a blow. He wasn't on his back with his mouth open in a snore.

"Did either of you leave your rooms again during the night?" Was there a possibility the three of them had got up to some mischief in the early hours of the morning?

"Of course not," Robins said while Mowatt shook his head.

"Milord, the staff are assembled," a footman said as he emerged onto the terrace. "His lordship is waiting also."

"Very well. Thank you, gentlemen." Wycliff followed the footman through the house and down the narrow back stairs.

The staff waited in a large room that served as their dining room and congregation area. Wycliff cast his eye over the assortment of footmen, kitchen maids, upstairs maids, gardeners, and stable hands. The footmen in their burgundy and gold livery, the housemaids in black with crisp white aprons. The staff who laboured out of the view of family and guests were less clean and pressed in appearance. The kitchen staff had stained aprons, and tufts of hair sticking to their faces from the hot work over the ovens.

"Lord Stannard, a guest under this roof, has met with foul play during the night and has been turned into a statue. Did any of you see anything unusual last night?" he asked.

Feet shuffled, some coughed, but none stepped forward.

"Did you see anything, Watkins, when you took Miss Stewart her tray?" the earl spoke to a petite maid hiding between two footmen.

The maid's dark eyes widened and she shook her head vigorously. "No, milord. I didn't see a soul."

"Did anyone see Lord Stannard about the house during the early hours of the morning?" Wycliff asked.

The shuffling of feet increased and many focused on the toes of their boots. House parties were notorious for the nocturnal activities of guests, and any staff they encountered were often paid to remain blind to what they saw.

"No one is in any trouble. We only want to ascertain his movements," the earl said to reassure his staff.

A kitchen maid stepped forward, her apron a dirty grey. "Please, your lordship, I saw him when I was laying the fires."

Wycliff held himself back before he pounced on the terrified lass. He'd get nothing from her if she were scared witless. He gentled his voice. "Do you know what time?"

"I'd not long been up and was cleaning the grate in the drawing room at around four thirty, milord." She spoke with a soft tone and kept her eyes downcast.

It seemed Stannard had revived and gone for a wander. Had the card tucked into his pocket summoned him to a meeting in the garden?

"Did any of you see him after that?" He looked from one maid to the next. They would have been up early, to clean the house before any guests rose.

Heads were shaken and glances shared. Whatever they had seen during the dark hours, or creeping along the hallways moving from one bedroom to another, they kept their silence.

# 8

Hannah had intended to tell her husband about the odd depressions leading from their window to the garden and in particular, the scorched paw mark left in the bare dirt right by the house. But seeing the predatory manner in which he stalked along the path toward her, a small, niggling voice suggested she keep her own counsel for now. It might be two unrelated events, or, more worrying, directly related. A part of her wondered if Wycliff had encountered Stannard in the garden and done this terrible thing. He had admitted to breaking the man's nose. Had he sought him out last night to end their argument with another act of violence?

Hannah didn't think she could live with the knowledge that she was bound beyond death to a murderer.

When Timmy's eyes had flown open and he announced a faint heartbeat, Hannah despaired. What a horrid fate—to be cast in stone. She disliked the man, but no one deserved to be rendered unfeeling or unmoving as their heart was squeezed into stillness.

She placed a hand on her chest. The French affliction was poised within her body, ready to still her own heart when her mother's spell failed. But at least she would be aware when that moment came and would have the comfort of her family around her. Lord Stannard would pass on a spring morning watched only by two footmen, a gifted lad, and an assortment of birds.

A sparrow flew over their heads and left a deposit on Stannard's shoulder.

"You might want to keep the birds from soiling him," she said to the footman, before her husband led her back toward the house.

She had parted ways with him on the terrace. Wycliff began his questioning of Messrs. Robins and Mowatt while she descended to the lawn and considered what to tell the ladies.

They had grown bored once they realised stone Stannard was not a game. Instead, they set up easels on the lawns that faced the lake. Each woman sat under a small tent, with the sides rolled up to stop the pale sunlight from reaching their fair complexions. The lake offered a pretty view, with its narrow jetty and a rowboat tied up, waiting to be taken out. Rushes and lilies dotted the edges and birds swooped over the surface of the water.

"What news? Are you able to cure him?" Lady Fanny asked over her shoulder as Hannah approached.

Fanny's painting was rather good—a man sitting in

the boat, as though he waited for a companion to join him. Hannah wished she could paint. Odd that she found it natural to draw limbs, organs, or cadavers, but a study in anything more beautiful or alive escaped her.

Hannah clasped her hands and considered her next words. Because she was the daughter of a powerful mage, people forgot she was devoid of magic. If only her mother were here—she might have been able to do something. Her failing ate at Hannah. "No, I cannot cure him. We do not know how or what spell was placed upon him. And alas, I fear by the time we do know, it will be too late."

"What do you mean, it will be too late?" Philippa dropped her paintbrush into a jar of water and abandoned her sketch to join them.

The other women all set down their brushes and pencils and gathered around the edges of Fanny's tent.

"I have a lad with Lord Stannard who is an after-mage. Timmy was able to detect a very faint, and struggling, heartbeat within the statue. However, it is not good news," she rushed to say when faces lit up expectantly. "The lad thinks the heart will last only last a few more minutes to an hour at most, before it, too, succumbs to the curse."

The women gasped. Stewart collapsed to the grass, her face losing its colour and taking on a vague grey tinge. The women and the footmen rushed to pick her up and arrange her limp form in a canvas chair.

"I shall be well," Stewart muttered. "I stood too quickly."

A footman poured a glass of water and handed it to Fanny's companion. Her colour improved somewhat as she pressed the cool tumbler to her forehead, but Hannah wondered if something else had caused her to faint. Perhaps it was the shock of learning how Lord Stannard suffered. Some women had such delicate constitutions that the mere mention of unpleasantness brought about a fainting spell.

Philippa clutched at the apron covering her morning dress. "How horrid. You mean he is alive within the stone?"

Fanny stared at Hannah, her small eyes wide. "You mean he has been murdered—or will be once his heart stops—during *my* house party?"

"I am afraid so." This was not the best news to deliver to a hostess seeking entertainment and distraction for the week.

"La! Now I will be the talk of London." A slow smile spread over Fanny's pinched features. "The cream of society will clamour to be included in my next event in case someone else is struck down by a magical assassin."

Hannah was taken aback. She had expected a range of reactions from the ladies. One had fainted as she had anticipated. It never occurred to her that someone would see a horrible death as noteworthy, and able to elevate the status of one's house parties.

"There will be an investigation, of course," she said. "My husband is already questioning the men who were with him last night, as well as the staff, to see if any saw

Lord Stannard. I would ask the same of you, ladies. Did any of you happen upon him last night?"

"Happen upon him?" Fanny tapped Hannah's arm and laughed. "Truly, would any of us admit to creeping along the halls during the night and bumping into him?"

"Oh my. I never left my room all night and I certainly would never wander off in the dark without the captain by my side," Mrs Armstrong sputtered.

"Assuming any lady present encountered Lord Stannard before dawn, it is rather a stretch, you must agree, to imagine that she happened to have a spell upon her person capable of turning him into stone and further, that in the instant of their meeting, she decided to cast it over him," Lady St Clair said.

An excellent point. Even Hannah didn't often carry her mother's immobilisation spell tucked into her stays unless she knew she was about to undertake a dangerous task. But that raised another possibility. What if someone had the spell about their person because they were *seeking* an unguarded moment in which to throw it over Lord Stannard?

"What if it were something he ate? He might have gone for a walk in the garden to relieve the symptoms when he froze." Philippa had recovered from her horror and it seemed ideas were already abuzz in her head.

"I do not think it was a potion. Timmy said the effect froze Lord Stannard instantly and then seeped to his insides." If Hannah had learned one thing in the investigations in which she had assisted her husband, it was that motives were rarely obvious. Everybody hid something. The key was to find the secret that would lead them to the murderer.

"Oh! We shall ask Stewart to contact him tonight. If he is departed, then the easiest way is simply to ask him who did it. What say you, Stewart?" Fanny gestured to her companion.

The colour drained from that lady's face again, although given her sickly pallor to begin with, Hannah couldn't determine if it was the news of Stannard's death or the request from her employer that alarmed Miss Stewart the most.

Miss Stewart took a fortifying drink from the glass in her hand and set it on the table before responding. "Talking to the spirits is not always that straightforward, Lady Fanny. Assuming Lord Stannard departs this earth today, he might move directly to the other side, or if he lingers here, he may be in a state of confusion and unable to disclose who did this to him."

"Do you think we should set up a vigil around him?" Fanny asked. "Light candles or read from scripture until he passes?"

Hannah was saved from answering that question when a footman rushed across the lawn toward them. It was one of the men she had left in the garden, guarding the statue. He stopped before Lady Frances and bowed. "Excuse me, milady, but the lad sent me to tell Lady Wycliff that Lord Stannard's heart has ceased beating."

"Thank you," Hannah murmured. In their short

acquaintance, she hadn't liked Lord Stannard, but he was gone now and would have to account for his sins to a higher authority.

Fanny turned to Hannah and reached for her hands. "Whatever are we to do with him?"

It appeared her role as answerer of questions was to continue. "I'm not sure I understand what you mean."

Fanny fanned herself with one hand and her companion, taking the hint, poured another glass of water and offered it to her employer. "The dead are usually put in coffins and buried, but Stannard is now an ornament in my garden. How am I to return him to his father?"

Ah. Now Hannah understood her predicament. "Assuming his form is no longer required by my husband for his investigation, perhaps Lord Stannard could be laid in a cart and packed in hay? Although there is still a possibility that my mother might know a way to return him to flesh and blood, which will be less distressing to his family."

"If he is trapped inside, could we chip away the stone to reveal him underneath?" Mrs Armstrong rushed her question and then visibly retreated once she had said her piece. She seemed rather timid, compared to her confident and outgoing husband.

"That would merely undress a stone skeleton," Hannah answered without considering her words. In her mind, she saw them at work with little hammers, first removing stone clothing, and then flesh from fossilised bone.

Another gasp and Miss Stewart collapsed back into her chair. She seemed rather nervous, or upset about Lord Stannard's condition.

Hannah flashed an apologetic smile to Fanny. "Please forgive me. I did not mean to startle anyone. I forget not everyone has seen the human body as I have."

Fanny waved a hand and dismissed Hannah's concerns. "Stewart has a delicate constitution, although she doesn't normally faint all over the place like this. But I cannot leave Stannard out in the garden for birds to sit upon. I shall have him moved closer to the house."

Before Hannah could object to the victim's being moved, Fanny held up her hand and winked. "With extreme care, so we don't have bits of him breaking off. Now, if you will excuse me, ladies, I must send an urgent message to the marquess to advise him of his son and heir's passing." Fanny strode off across the lawn to write her sad note.

The ladies removed their aprons and tossed them over their chairs, while Hannah walked away pondering their reactions. Miss Stewart had fainted and Philippa appeared shocked. Did their concern indicate some attachment to the deceased, or fear of being caught for their actions? Lady Frances seemed almost gleeful. Was it purely because her company would be in demand, or was it the reaction of someone who had meted out a horrible death? Lady St Clair had Mrs Armstrong chattering away in her ear.

Hannah walked more slowly and Philippa caught

up to loop an arm through hers as they crossed the lawn. The men emerged from the house and the captain offered an arm to Lady St Clair, ignoring his wife. Mr Wright-Knowles hovered by the captain, bombarding him with questions about life in the navy.

Philippa made a *tsk*ing noise with her tongue as she regarded her spouse. "I feel sorry for the captain. My husband is enamoured of a life at sea. He spends every spare moment building model boats in his study and will not leave the captain alone for a moment."

"Did Mr Wright-Knowles not consider a naval career for himself?" Hannah asked.

Philippa laughed. "Good grief, no. He loves boats, but becomes terribly ill with the *mal du mer*. Why, even if he sat in the rowboat tied to the pier on that lake, he would be violently ill."

"How sad for him. To love something so much but have it cause him such discomfort."

Mrs Armstrong stood on the terrace and stared after her husband and Lady St Clair. She wore a pained expression, as though her shoes were too tight.

"That one is an odd bird," Philippa whispered as she leaned closer. "Or perhaps I should call her a chicken, and a broody hen at that."

"Whatever do you mean?" Hannah studied the woman, but could see no resemblance to a chicken, apart from perhaps a slightly rounded shape.

Philippa lowered her voice as they ascended the wide terrace stairs. "About a month ago we were at a party. The captain and his wife were also in attendance, along with the Devil's Triplets. After dinner, the captain was regaling everyone with his tale of how he killed that French mage. Mrs Armstrong had Stannard cornered and was pecking and scratching at him."

"They had an argument?" Hannah glanced at the subject of Pippa's gossip from the corner of her eye. She didn't seem the type to publicly berate anyone, let alone Lord Stannard.

"Whatever he said to her, it certainly ruffled her feathers. Stannard was quite abrupt in his dismissal of her and he left not long afterward."

"How curious." Gossip or no, Hannah tucked the information away as they entered the house. She would share the details with Wycliff later. Hannah seized the opportunity of the tête-à-tête to ask Philippa a question on her mind. "Do you know how Miss Stewart came to be Lady Fanny's companion? She seems such a gentle and elegant creature." Hannah worried about the woman's health. Fainting could be an indicator of a more serious malady.

Philippa's attention lingered on Miss Stewart, now leaning on the arm of Mr Mowatt. "The Stewarts were a fine family. Then about three years ago, Edith's sister came out, immediately followed by rumours that she was...fast. That changed their circumstances and then two years ago she died. Rumour is there was another scandal attached to her death. Poor Edith suffered for her sister's choices, and the scandal attached to her. Her fiancé cried off and she found herself cut off from society. Fanny took her in, since she had no other prospects."

Could it be at all possible there were hidden layers to that story? Could Lord Stannard have been involved in the scandal that had ruined Edith Stewart's life? Although there did not appear to have been either recognition or resentment between them.

"Thank you, you have been most helpful. But now I must confer with the lad standing vigil over Lord Stannard." Hannah had much to occupy her thoughts as she returned to the garden. Given the few details Philippa had shared, could either Mrs Armstrong or Miss Stewart harbour a motive for foul murder?

# 9

Wycliff concluded his interview with the staff below stairs and thanked them for their time. Then he followed the earl back along the dim and narrow stairway that led to the family's part of the house.

"I'd like to examine Stannard's room," he said as they emerged into the main foyer.

"Of course. I'll have a footman show you which is his, unless you need me in attendance?" The earl waved at a footman who had followed them up the servants' stairway.

"No. I prefer to search for evidence on my own." Wycliff nodded to his host and then followed the footman up the wide and ornate stairs to the family and guest rooms above.

As he walked the plush hall runner, he wondered who had ordered that he and Hannah be given a room on the first floor. It seemed unlikely to have been the earl, and most likely the staff followed directions given by Lady Frances. What drove some to torment others, simply because their position gave them the latitude to do so?

"This is Lord Stannard's room, milord." The footman stopped at dark panelled door close to the end of the hall.

"I shall summon you if I require anything else." Wycliff dismissed the man, then turned the brass knob. He stepped over the threshold and stopped, allowing himself time to take in the disarray and the last moments of Lord Stannard's life.

The room was easily twice the size of the room Wycliff shared with Hannah. Even the screen in the corner was constructed on a more generous scale and could have concealed a well-endowed opera singer with her arms flung wide.

The substantial bed had four barley-twist posts that reached up nearly six feet, where they held aloft a green velvet canopy. Two armchairs and a sofa sat before the cold fireplace. A writing desk was placed under the window, with its view to the front of the house and the sweeping driveway. Another door led to a dressing room and a small bed for the man's valet, should he have brought one.

The room was in disarray, with clothing strewn over the chairs and furniture. A blank piece of paper sat in the centre of the desk, with the desk set pulled forward as though he had intended to write a letter. The bedding was crumpled, but still pulled up to the pillows as though no one had slept in it. Stannard had been deposited on top of the blankets when his friends returned him to his room last night.

Wycliff wasn't sure what clues he would find in the dead man's room, but rifling through Stannard's possessions seemed as good a starting point as any to determine who wanted him dead. Interesting that the murderer had chosen a magical means. Did they want Stannard to suffer, or was there some deeper meaning in turning him into a statue?

If he were formulating an unpleasant death to dispatch an enemy, he would choose a stab to the stomach that wasn't outright fatal, but that would fester over time. Gut wounds caused excruciating agony as they killed a man. At least, that would have been his preferred method, until the disastrous campaign on the Peninsula had taught him what it was to gaze into the abyss of despair and suffering.

He began his search by looking under the bed, in case the occupant sought to hide anything from a cursory glance. That revealed the chamber pot, containing a quantity of vomit. Now he knew why Stannard was up and about after his night of drinking. He'd spilled his guts. Perhaps he'd wandered off in search of something to eat when he met his end, but that didn't explain his placement in the garden.

As Wycliff slid the chamber pot back under the bed, a small leather satchel attracted his attention. He grabbed the strap and pulled it out. Within the bag were letters and notes. A tin the size of his hand contained three French letters made of sheep's intestines. Had Stannard prepared in advance for assignations during his stay, or did he always travel with a tin of preventative measures?

A feature of the statue sprang to Wycliff's mind—the flat, rectangular shape escaping his pocket. A hurriedly grabbed condom? The things were too valuable to discard and were washed and dried for re-use.

Wycliff closed the lid on the tin and dropped it back into the bag. He pulled out a handful of letters and scanned the contents. Many were from Stannard's father, the marquess, castigating his son as a ne'er-do-well and a wastrel. He instructed his son to marry immediately and settle down if he ever wanted to inherit.

Other letters were expressions of affection from a variety of women. God only knew why women would throw themselves at the feet of such a cruel and insufferable man. Surely London was not experiencing a lack of suitable bachelors?

Two letters caught his attention. One was a flirtatious verse that offered a reward if Stannard dared to reach for it, but it was the initials at the bottom that made him clutch the letter tight—*LStC*.

*Lily St Clair*. The lovely and exceedingly wealthy widow.

"Well, well. Perhaps Stannard took his father's advice to heart and sought to snag the widow. Even he would have trouble running through her fortune." He tucked the letter into his coat pocket and determined to speak to the widow forthwith.

Perhaps she'd met Stannard in the garden but changed her mind about an assignation. It wasn't unheard of for a woman to carry a protective spell, if she could afford one. Hannah had used one to immobilise the two Afflicted responsible for three hideous murders.

Wycliff read the next letter. It was a scant line demanding that Stannard hand over a letter in his possession or *suffer the consequences*. Most interesting. What correspondence did Stannard have that warranted such a dire warning? Lady St Clair's? The man certainly suffered consequences, but had they been at the hand of whoever had penned the note? How could he determine the author?

He went back through the letters and notes, comparing the handwriting of the threat to the signed letters in Stannard's satchel. None matched the unknown writer. Shame. He pocketed the note next to the one from Lady St Clair and would discuss it with Hannah later. His wife might know of some means of conjuring up the author.

He finished his search of the room and then headed downstairs to the drawing room. Within was a dim, sombre atmosphere and to his eyes, the only bright point was Hannah, seated before the window. Lady Frances appeared intent on having a fine time, despite the news circulating that Stannard had passed. The Pennicotts were certainly practically minded. No point in ruining the party just because one guest had been murdered.

Robins and Mowatt were subdued and muttered darkly about the disrespect done to their friend. Lord Stannard now graced the entrance foyer and as he had passed by, Wycliff fought the urge to hang an umbrella from a granite arm.

"The marquess has been informed of his son's... passing," Lady Frances announced. "I have asked what he wishes us to do with his remains. It would be of assistance, Lady Wycliff, if your mother knew of some way to turn him back into a body his family could bury."

"I will ask my mother when next she contacts me," Hannah replied. "But I fear that unless we know the process by which he was turned into stone, we will be unable to reverse it."

Afternoon lengthened into an equally sombre evening, and a quiet dinner was served accompanied by muted conversation. Hannah excused herself early, pleading a headache. Wycliff took the opportunity to leave with her.

"Do you suspect it was one of the houseguests?" Hannah murmured as they walked to their room.

"I am open to any possibility, but I will begin with those closest to him." He would speak further with what was now the Devil's *Duo* tomorrow. They had been closest to the dead man and Wycliff needed to dig into their sordid memories to see what they knew, particularly of the letter that someone sought to retrieve from Stannard.

"Did you discover anything in Lord Stannard's

room?" Hannah pressed a hand to her temple and tired lines pulled the corners of her eyes.

He narrowed his gaze, scanning her features for signs of fatigue, or worse, signs that the French curse was about to snatch her life. "I found two notes of interest. One was from Lady St Clair. I intend to talk to her about her association."

"And the other?" Fatigue was replaced by a flare of curiosity in her dark eyes.

As he held her stare, he realised there were tiny flecks of amber close to the pupil. What else would he discover if he held her gaze long enough?

Then he shook his head to dispel such foolish notions. "A note from an unknown author demanding the return of a letter and threatening consequences if it were not."

Hannah's eyes widened. "Do you think whoever wrote that note is the murderer?"

"It is the most substantial clue I have found so far, but keep in mind many people issue empty threats—few follow up with action." Robins and Mowatt would be the most likely to have some knowledge of the subject. Nothing in Stannard's room seemed to warrant his being murdered, which meant he must have stashed that letter somewhere else. "Do you recognise the writing?"

He passed the note to Hannah, who squinted at the tidy writing. "No, but then I am not familiar with the hand of everyone in the house. One of the grooms has returned Timmy to Doctor Colchester, since there is nothing more he can do here. Mother has not reported back to me yet, but her research could take some time. I do have one snippet to share." Hannah leaned closer to Wycliff and lowered her voice to a whisper, as though she thought someone might be listening at the keyhole. "Mrs Wright-Knowles recollected a party last month where Mrs Armstrong had a heated conversation with Lord Stannard."

"Mrs Armstrong? That is most curious." The timid creature didn't look the sort to get into an argument with anyone, let alone a man of Stannard's reputation. It could be nothing, but given the way the man liked to hurl insults, perhaps he had thrown one that rankled the captain's wife. Or her disagreement might have another cause. He would find out, either way.

With the kitchen maid's information shared, Wycliff gave his wife privacy in which to conduct her toilette while he slipped out the window and strolled in the fresh air. He had believed the cool breeze would aid his thoughts, but he returned to the room with unresolved turmoil swirling inside him.

The next morning, they slept late and followed their noses to the breakfast room, where an enticing buffet had been laid out. Wycliff's plan of a quiet conversation with his wife was interrupted by the arrival of the other guests. He held his temper in check.

Was it too much to ask for a small amount of privacy in which to converse with one's spouse?

"Today we shall take our entertainment out by the lake," Lady Fanny announced once everyone had eaten their fill. "The staff have set up chairs, blankets, umbrellas, and a refreshment table. Some fresh air might do us all good."

"Someone in this room murdered Charles Stannard and you want us to all frolic in the sunshine?" Robins blocked the door and crossed his arms over his chest.

"It hasn't been determined yet that the responsible person is in this room. It could have been a member of staff or, most likely, someone who came onto the estate under the cover of darkness and departed once the deed was done," Lady Fanny retorted.

The problem, Wycliff thought, was that Stannard had too many enemies to narrow it down to someone in the room, even if that was his starting point for the investigation.

"The local authorities should be called and everyone questioned." Robins seemed determined to see justice for his friend.

Wycliff glared at the man. "No one is stopping you, if you want to bring in the magistrate. I will tell you now that he will simply hand the matter over to me, since it involves a death by Unnatural means." He had the matter in hand and two potential leads in his pocket.

"Come on, Robins. We can make our own enquiries." Mowatt gave his friend a push out the door.

The other guests trickled out after them, leaving Wycliff and Hannah alone for a brief moment. He held out his arm to his wife. "Shall we join the excursion outside and see what other snippets we can ferret out about our fellow houseguests?"

As they walked outside, he considered how his view of marriage had changed in a few short weeks. Instinct had made him offer the protection of his name and body, but now he wondered if there was a deeper purpose in their being joined. He found Hannah good company and more frequently, he sought her opinion.

He even found himself wishing her parents success in discovering a cure for the Affliction. An odd sensation settled in his gut when he tried to imagine what would happen if Lady Miles's magic failed and Hannah's heart ceased to beat. Once she arose as one of the Afflicted, she would have to subsist on brain matter. Or, as it was euphemistically called, *pickled cauliflower*.

He no longer thought of the undead Afflicted with disgust. His association with Hannah and her mother had made him see that he held the wrong opinion and people should be judged by their actions. Could he ask the same of his wife? If he unburdened himself of his secret, would she recoil from him in horror, or accept him for the broken creature he was?

Instinct pushed him toward making that revelation. The restlessness within him calmed around his wife, and he found himself pondering Lady Miles's advice to him—to find an anchor before he became lost on a stormy ocean. He glanced at his wife's profile. The curve of her jaw and the strands of loose hair brushing her cheek made him want to take her face in his hands and ask, *Would you be my safe harbour, if I dared share my burden?*

"You are very thoughtful," Hannah said as they crossed the lawn to where rugs and tables were arranged close to the water's edge. For those needing more physical entertainment, croquet hoops were dotted through the grass and a collection of mallets waited next to balls painted in red, blue, and yellow.

"I have much to occupy my mind of late." He had stared death in the face and yet his throat constricted at the thought of exposing his secret to his wife. Like a coward, he wanted to be sure of the outcome before he took the irrevocable step.

"If you ever need a good listener, I'm sure you know where to find me." She squeezed his arm and then let him go to gather up her skirts as she knelt on a rug.

He knew where to find her. He just hadn't made up his mind yet whether or not to add to her already heavy burden.

# 10

HANNAH ENJOYED the warmth of the sun on her skin as the others played croquet. She preferred to observe from the side than be a participant. It gave her a chance to watch how the houseguests interacted with each other. Wycliff also stood to one side, talking to Captain Armstrong, with Mr Wright-Knowles bouncing on his toes and hanging on every word.

Mrs Armstrong tapped her ball around the outside of the hoops and no shot ever seemed to go her way. Miss Stewart commiserated with her and tried to offer advice. Fanny laughed loudly and often, with Mr Robins at her side. Mr Mowatt's ball always strayed toward Pippa and she playfully fended it off with her mallet. Lady St Clair had a most determined glint in her eye as she won the game.

They had a pleasant light repast after the match. Conversation stayed on neutral topics. No one mentioned the death of Lord Stannard and who might have been responsible. Not until the butler appeared carrying a silver tray bearing a letter, which he offered to Fanny.

"Thank you, Godrich," she said as she ripped open the missive. She read it through and then turned to Hannah. "The marquess is sending a party to retrieve Stannard. Amongst their number will be Mage Tomlin, who has consented to ascertain how his son died."

"I'm sure we would welcome Mage Tomlin's opinion." Hannah kept her tone light. She knew something of him and, like her mother, did not hold the mage in high regard. He had chosen to let his daughter die in an impoverished state and had refused to acknowledge Timmy as his grandson.

"I'm sure Lord Tomlin will get to the bottom of this," Mr Robins said.

"Yes, I imagine that with a simple truth spell, he could have everybody's secrets aired out to find the particular one that ended in Stannard's death." Wycliff selected two apples from a basket on the table.

Everyone fell silent and many averted their eyes—perhaps contemplating the secrets they would rather keep hidden from inspection. Wycliff returned to the rug he shared with Hannah and pulled the knife from his Hessian boot. With deft moves, he sliced the apple and offered the pieces to Hannah.

He handled a blade with skill, which made her think of her father and his delicacy with a scalpel. She missed her parents, but at the same time, found she rather enjoyed the time with her husband and the opportunity to know him better.

Her fear and distrust of him had turned into curiosity...and something else. A deeper, warmer feeling crept through her as she glanced at him from under her lashes. How had she ever thought him a terrible wraith? When the tension eased from his features and he smiled, he quite stole her breath.

Laughter made her turn. Lady St Clair tossed pieces of fruit at the captain, who tried to catch them in his mouth. His wife sat apart under the shade of a tree, where she leaned against the trunk.

A pang of empathy burst through Hannah. It could be no easy thing to watch a beautiful and wealthy woman flirt with your husband. As Hannah cast her mind back over recent days, she couldn't recall any demonstrations of affection or even friendship between the Armstrongs. Was theirs an unhappy marriage, or could it be as simple as the captain wanting some time apart while at the Pennicott estate?

Miss Stewart fussed around Fanny and bustled to carry out any orders her employer issued. She walked among the guests, ensuring everyone had enough to eat and drink.

"Lady Wycliff, do you require a glass of lemonade, or a cup of tea?" the gently spoken woman asked as she reached the Wycliff rug.

"Do not trouble yourself on my account, Miss Stewart. I'm quite capable of walking to the table if I require anything else," Hannah said.

"It's no bother. I find satisfaction in ensuring the happiness of others." Her smile seemed tight and something flashed behind her blue eyes.

A glint of gold at the other woman's throat caught Hannah's attention. She wore a locket with ornate carving over its tiny surface. "That is a beautiful locket. What an unusual pattern to the engraving."

"Thank you." Miss Stewart fingered the pendant. "The carving is a remembrance spell."

When Hannah peered at the piece of jewellery, she saw tiny forget-me-nots surrounded by Celtic knots. "What a lovely idea. It must contain a token of someone you loved very much."

"My sister," the companion whispered. She slid a fingernail into the side of the locket and it sprang open. Within was a miniature of a dark-haired girl with laughing eyes.

Hannah recalled Philippa's story of how the girl died with scandal attached to her name. There was no hint of oncoming tragedy in the painted face, only a joy for life. "She was beautiful."

"Celeste much resembled our mother, whereas I favour our father." Miss Stewart snapped the locket shut and let the pendant drop. "Now if you will excuse me, I must see if Lady Fanny requires anything."

"Who wants to take the boat out for a row?" Mowatt jumped to his feet and walked down to the small pier. "To take our minds off Stannard, what if we had a gentlemanly competition? Each man could row a companion out to the middle of the lake and back again. Since we have the esteemed captain in our midst, perhaps he would be the judge of our command of this vessel?"

Philippa clapped her hands. "Oh yes, what fun. I'd love a turn about the lake."

Mr Wright-Knowles turned green, even though he was still on *terra firma*. "You know I get terribly sick on the water, Philippa."

His wife's shoulders slumped and her smile fell away. "I only wanted to join in the fun."

"With your permission, Mr Wright-Knowles, I am willing to stand in your stead, if you would entrust your lovely wife to me?" Mowatt bowed to Philippa and cast a questioning look to the woman's husband.

The other man beamed. "Oh, indeed you can. Perhaps the captain and I could judge together? I have some familiarity with boats, too, you know, even if it is only an academic knowledge."

The captain stood and brushed his trousers. "We can confer, Mr Wright-Knowles, which will be handy in the event of a tie. I will tell you now, gentlemen, my sailors say I am an exacting master."

"Shall we go first, Mrs Wright-Knowles?" Mowatt offered his hand to Philippa and helped her rise.

Her husband handed her a parasol and then he joined the captain at the water's edge.

Mr Mowatt and Philippa walked to the end of the jetty, where the small boat was moored. He stepped down and then placed his hands on Philippa's waist to lift her into the boat. She laughed and rested her hands on his shoulders, the two them standing close and quiet as the boat rocked.

The woman seemed to bloom under Mowatt's touch and a faint blush tinged her cheeks. Then she took her seat and opened the parasol, blocking her face from view.

"Cast us off, would you, Robins?" Mowatt called to his friend.

The other man undid the rope and threw it into the boat as Mowatt took up the oars and in just a dozen strokes, carried the couple out to the middle of the lake.

"I say, he has good form, don't you think, Captain?" Wright-Knowles ventured closer to the water and watched the boat take a leisurely circle.

"Indeed. He would pull his weight rowing the tender to shore," the captain replied.

A smirk broke over Robins's face. "We have an unfair advantage over you gentlemen. Mowatt and I rowed for Cambridge in our youth."

Hannah got up to stretch her legs and walked over to Fanny, who sat in a chair facing the water. She took the chair next to her hostess as Philippa's laughter carried over the lake. "Mrs Wright-Knowles seems to enjoy the company of Mr Mowatt."

Fanny glanced at her, then returned her attention to the couple circling the lake. "They have known each other since childhood. When we were at Mrs Granger's Finishing School together, Pippa used to live or die by whether she received a letter from Mowatt. She was such a gloomy thing if he failed to write every week."

"And yet she did not marry him." Hannah considered Mr Wright-Knowles, who conducted an animated conversation with the captain. While he didn't have a dashing figure or a handsome face, he nonetheless projected a robust, jovial air.

Fanny leaned closer to Hannah and dropped her tone. "They wanted to. Pippa's father disapproved of the match and instructed her to marry Wright-Knowles instead. I never saw a more unhappy bride than she on her wedding day."

"Yet her husband seems an amiable man." It seemed the lot of dutiful women to set aside the desires of their hearts to follow the instructions of their parents. Hannah's gaze wandered over the lean figure and stern countenance of her husband, and her heart fluttered.

In some instances, being dutiful could have unexpected rewards.

Fanny turned to stare at the man in question, who blushed like a schoolgirl every time the captain spoke to him. "Wright-Knowles is kind, malleable, and with an even temper. Hardly the sort to incite a grand passion."

Hannah watched the couple out on the water. A degree of comfort seemed to lie between them as they conversed and laughed. How sad for Philippa, to love one man but be wed to another. What obstacle had her father seen, that he had prevented their match? Had his reputation as one of the Devil's Triplets been known even back then?

Fanny turned her shrewd gaze to Hannah. "What

of you, Lady Wycliff—how did you come to marry the viscount? Society abounds with rumours, particularly given the haste of your match."

Hannah bit the inside of her cheek. Lady Frances might delight in collecting secrets, but she would never be privy to Hannah's. She certainly wasn't going to blurt out that they had married so that she and her mother would have the viscount's protection when her heart stopped. "I'm sure our marriage is no different than many others. We have developed a mutual regard and when Wycliff made his offer, I accepted. Since we are both of a practical disposition, we did not see the point in a long engagement. And of course, we are often working together on Unnatural investigations, such as the strange death of Lord Stannard."

"But what of love? I cannot imagine that Wycliff would be an easy person to live with unless you had a great affection for him. He has a reputation for being a rather...intense individual." Fanny's piercing stare drilled into Hannah.

"We have been married less than a month. I am given to understand that feelings change once a couple are better acquainted." Hannah had moved to sit next to Fanny to confirm her suspicions about Pippa and Mr Mowatt. Not to have to her own marriage placed under scrutiny.

Wycliff approached and saved Hannah from further questions. "Might I interrupt, if you would care for a turn about the lake, Hannah?"

She placed her hand in his. "Only if you promise that I will not get wet. I cannot swim."

Philippa and Mr Mowatt had finished their excursion and walked back to the company. Hannah marvelled at the lightness to the other woman's step and the joy in her eyes. As they drew near, a visible change came over Philippa. The joy vanished from her face and her smile faded away.

Mr Mowatt bent over her bare hand and kissed her knuckles. "A pleasure to captain your vessel, Mrs Wright-Knowles."

Sadness took up residence in her gaze as she sat on the rug close to her husband.

Thoughts swirled in Hannah's mind. Did her husband know of the prior attachment? Even the most mild-mannered and amiable man might have a breaking point.

"You had the look of someone being interrogated. I thought you might need rescue," Wycliff said as he led her out on the jetty.

Hannah watched a dragonfly skim the surface. "Yes, thank you. Lady Frances was prying for intimate details of our marriage."

He grimaced. "We did suspect that was the reason for our inclusion this week. What did you tell her?"

Her hand tightened on his arm. "I told the truth. That we have a mutual regard and we did not see the point in a long engagement."

For a moment, something flared behind Wycliff's

eyes and then it was gone. “Exactly so. Let us hope that is the end of her questions.”

Wycliff helped Hannah into the little boat and it rocked under her. She gasped and sat down hard to grip the wooden sides. It had seemed such a pleasant idea when he offered, but now she found herself wondering at the depth of the water and trying to recollect how long it took a person to drown.

“You are safe with me. I hardly think there are any monsters lurking in the depths, nor will a rogue wave capsize us. Fortunately, I grew up by the ocean and could swim long before I could run or ride.” Wycliff took up the oars and rowed them away from the jetty.

Some people were afraid of mice, or spiders, or the dark. Hannah had no qualms about any of those things. But the ocean drove a cold spike of fear through her very centre. The sea was vast and tumultuous and history was filled with tales of sailors and ordinary folk dragged to their deaths in its cold embrace.

The water of the lake had barely a ripple upon its surface, except where the oars dipped in and out. Hannah could almost become accustomed to a quiet body of water such as this one, as long as she could touch the bottom should she fall in. “I cannot fathom what it must have been like, growing up near the ocean. Did you not fear it would crash over the shore one night and drag everyone into the depths?”

He narrowed his eyes and then the edges crinkled in a smile. “People usually fear what they do not understand or cannot control. Do you think you would still be afraid if you could swim with some confidence?"

"Does skill at swimming help if you are in a boat torn to pieces by a raging sea miles from shore?" Her fear probably seemed silly. If, or when, the Affliction stilled her heart, she could never drown, as she would no longer breathe. Perhaps then she might go walking along the bottom of the ocean and explore a whole new world.

This time he did laugh. "I do believe that is the first time I have heard you make an overly dramatic statement. But point taken. I shall endeavour to ensure we are never in a ship during a fierce storm."

Her husband proved a satisfactory seaman as he navigated their way around the lake. Hannah's fears eased a little, to the point she could trail a hand in the water and watch the eddies and swirls around her fingers.

All too soon their private time came to an end and the boat bumped against the jetty. Wycliff hopped over and lashed the rope to the bollard, and then leaned down to help Hannah climb out.

"I enjoyed that, thank you," Hannah murmured as they walked back to the others.

He ran his thumb over the backs her knuckles in an unconscious manner. "As did I. Now I need to question Lady St Clair and Mrs Armstrong."

But Lady St Clair seemed intent on evading Wycliff's questions. She twirled her parasol over her shoulder and walked out on the jetty. "Will you give us a demonstration of your skill, Captain? I am more than willing to put myself in your capable hands."

"How can I refuse the offer of such divine company?" He strode along the jetty and jumped into the boat. Then he made a show of bowing and assisting Lady St Clair down and to her seat.

He saluted, before taking his seat in the middle and grabbing hold of the oars. Hannah didn't think he was much of a rower. Wycliff performed far better, but Mowatt had put them all to shame with the economy of his movements and the way he powered the little rowboat around the lake.

The captain was rather red in the face and sweating when they returned to the jetty. "I must confess I am more used to sitting in the bow and commanding than I am at pulling an oar."

Lady St Clair laughed and tapped his arm. "You are a man used to command, not manual labour. Never make apology for that."

Next to Hannah, Mrs Armstrong huffed. She recalled Philippa's words when she described the captain's wife as a broody hen. Her feathers did appear to be ruffled by Lady St Clair's flirting. Did the house party have *two* mismatched marriages, crumbling under the strain of company?

The feather ring on Hannah's finger tingled and interrupted her thoughts. She looked to Wycliff. "Mother is trying to contact me. Let us see what news she has."

Hannah looked up at the surrounding trees, trying

to locate her mother's messenger. She held out her arm to create a perch for whatever bird would be the vessel for the mage's voice. Seraphina had two ways of communicating; her preferred method was a bird, but she could also use stained glass or a painting, if Hannah or her father were inside.

A fat little chaffinch was a blur of wings as it propelled itself from its perch and landed on Hannah's hand. It ruffled its wings and shook its body before it hopped around to face her.

"You go first, dearest. What did Timmy discover?" the bird chirped.

"Timmy detected a very faint and weak heartbeat, but Lord Stannard passed yesterday, less than an hour after our discovering him." Hannah fell silent and the bird bowed its head. Hannah imagined her father would be scribbling away to determine a formula for the rate at which human flesh turned into stone.

"That tells us that the spell is not immediately fatal. Do you know how long it took to claim his life?" The bird cocked its head.

"He was seen at around four thirty in the morning by a maid laying the fires in the drawing room. It was after eleven when Timmy sent word that the heart had ceased beating. That gives us a little over six hours." During that time the person responsible had never felt sufficient remorse to release the viscount from his stone prison. "Timmy found that the spell or potion was cast upon Stannard and seeped through to the inside, turning his heart to stone last."

The chaffinch ruffled its feathers and scratched its head with a claw. "Most curious. I had thought only a potion could bring about such a death, but it could have been a thrown liquid or a spell spoken at him. I have not yet discovered anything that works in such a way without having to be cast by a mage, but I shall keep searching."

"Thank you, Mother. The Marquess of Dolster has been informed of his son's strange demise and has asked Mage Tomlin to investigate."

The bird made a short chirp that sounded like a snort. "He may discern something that aids your investigation. Keep an open mind, Hannah, and any dissenting opinions to yourself."

Hannah knew of Lord Tomlin's reputation. Unlike her mother, who invited intelligent discourse, the other mage was known to be rigid in his views and rather full of his own self-importance. "I shall keep my ears open and my mouth shut, Mother. Shall we reconvene tomorrow?"

The bird hopped to sit on her wrist. "Please tell Wycliff that I have informed Sir Manly that a death by magical means has occurred. He has confirmed that Wycliff is to investigate. Tomlin cannot supersede that authority, despite what he might claim."

The bird took flight, released from the magic that allowed Seraphina to speak through its small form.

"Oh, dear," Hannah murmured.

While her mother had promised to turn Wycliff into a carp should he prove an unsuitable husband,

Mage Tomlin might actually do it if the viscount disagreed with him or made a point of asserting his authority in the matter. Hannah was growing accustomed to her husband's figure and didn't want a cold fish sharing her room. She would have to ensure she smoothed any ruffled feathers when the mage appeared to claim Lord Stannard.

Being a wife was rather more challenging than she had expected.

# 11

As the afternoon air began to cool, Wycliff considered whom to question first. His wife's subtle approach had appeared to rub off on him, when he decided against throwing out his questions where everyone could hear and hang on every word. He needed a quiet moment with each lady who had a prior association with Stannard.

Mrs Armstrong picked up a load of shawls and rugs and scurried away like a mouse when a lamp flared. Bother. He would corner her later.

Lady St Clair wandered away from the group and Wycliff took the opportunity to follow. "Lady St Clair, might I have a private word?"

She arched a refined eyebrow but inclined her head. They walked farther away, to a stand of birches. "In the course of investigating Lord Stannard's murder, I searched his room and found your note to him. Did he go to your room the night before last?"

In the dappled light of the birches she closed her parasol and rested the tip in the grass. "Yes. He knocked on my door at around three in the morning."

There was no need to ask what they had done behind her closed door. A man didn't sneak to a woman's room in the early hours to play chess. "Did he stay long?"

She ran her thumb over the silver handle of the parasol and turned to gaze back at the others. They formed a loose group as they headed toward the house. "We dallied for a little more than an hour and then I asked him to leave. A woman needs her beauty sleep."

Wycliff recalled the maid's words that she had seen Stannard walk past the drawing-room door at approximately four thirty. Was the widow telling the truth and someone else had waylaid Stannard after he left? Or had she lured him out to the garden to immortalise him as a bird perch?

The greater mystery was what appeal Stannard could have had for the widow. Wycliff couldn't imagine any woman wanting to be alone with the braggart. "Were you engaged?"

"Certainly not!" She laughed and turned away.

"Yet your note hinted at a reward to be had." Wycliff wondered at the woman's motives. He supposed society considered Viscount Stannard, with his future prospects as a marquess, a *good catch*. But in ascertaining a person's worth, Wycliff looked to more than the state of their pocketbook. The Marquess of Dolster might be wealthy, but his son had relied on his allowance. How many people would bang on the marquess's door now, demanding payment of overdue invoices incurred by his wayward son?

Lady St Clair opened the cream parasol and placed it over her shoulder to protect her porcelain skin from the sun's touch. "I am young, widowed, and wealthy. While my position gives me an enviable amount of freedom, I have no intention of living the rest of my life alone. I am searching for the right companion, but in the meantime I keep myself...shall we say...*entertained*."

He arched a brow but swallowed a retort. He had always chafed against society's double standards and now Lady St Clair raised another. If a married man could openly keep a mistress, why shouldn't a widow be allowed to discreetly entertain a lover? "I don't suppose anyone saw Stannard leave your room this morning?"

She twirled the parasol and the tassels hanging from the end of each rib swung through the air. "As a matter of fact, yes. I just don't know who. There was a woman in the hallway. She must have hidden when she heard my door open, perhaps not wanting to be seen returning from her own assignation. But from the light spilling from my room I saw her shadow, thrown from behind an Egyptian statue."

Another woman roaming the halls? There weren't many houseguests present. That narrowed his enquiries further. "How did you know it was a woman?"

"She held a hood over her face, but a woman's hands are rather easy to distinguish from those of a man." She made a gesture of pulling a hood across her cheek.

"Lady St Clair?" Captain Armstrong called as he approached across the lawn. "Do you feel up to a hand or two of whist? A few of us are going to start a game."

"Thank you, you have been most helpful." Wycliff bowed and left the widow to the captain's care. He caught up with Hannah, who was taking her time crossing the lawn.

"I am going to walk the route from Stannard's room to that of Lady St Clair. They did indeed have an assignation that night," he said as he took her hand.

Hannah paused and glanced toward the house. "I will take a book to the drawing room while the others play cards. I may hear something that will assist your investigation."

He nodded and released her. Inside the mansion, Wycliff prowled the second floor corridor and found the statue Lady St Clair had mentioned. At seven feet tall, it occupied the space opposite the door and provided ample room to shelter someone who didn't want to be seen.

A rattle made him look around the edifice and down the hall.

Mrs Armstrong jiggled the door to Stannard's room.

He had his mouse, cornered.

He advanced down the hall on silent feet, placing

each foot with care. As he neared, he caught her muttering under her breath, as though she did not expect the door to be locked.

"Is there any reason you are trying to gain entry to Lord Stannard's room, Mrs Armstrong?" he murmured as he stood at her back.

The woman yelped and flung herself against the wall. Her face turned a deep red and she puffed in and out. "Lord S-Stannard's room?" she stuttered. She pressed a hand to her forehead. "How silly of me. I must have got turned around and thought it was ours." She pointed to the opposite end of the hall and the door that was the mirror of Stannard's.

Wycliff didn't believe her for a moment. He might have a dim view of her intellect, but if the woman couldn't even find her own room, she had serious problems. More likely, she was trying to conduct her own search and he only needed to find out why.

He crossed his arms and blocked her exit. "Did you have a previous acquaintance with Lord Stannard?"

Her eyes widened and she edged a step away from the door. "No, I did not know the man."

*Liar*, he thought. "And yet, I am informed that not so long ago, you had a heated conversation with him at a party."

She screwed up her eyes and he thought steam might emerge from her ears. Here was a woman unused to being put on the spot.

She opened her eyes again but didn't meet his stare. "Oh, I recollect that evening now. He stood on my train in what I am sure was deliberate attempt to trip me up. I castigated him for his cruel behaviour, nothing more." Mrs Armstrong fidgeted under his gaze and peered around him as though plotting an escape.

"Had you spoken to Stannard at all between then and his death yesterday?"

She shook her head and then nodded, confusing both of them. "I made some small talk in the parlour the day we arrived. Or rather, he spoke to the captain. He had no apology for me and seemed to not even remember my dressing-down."

He leaned left as she moved that way. He had his mouse by the tail and wasn't going to let her go yet. "Did you leave your room that night, after you retired?"

"No. Not at all. Now, if you don't mind, I am quite exhausted after this afternoon and would like to lie down before dinner." She edged around him and scuttled straight down the hallway.

Wycliff kept his eye on her until she hurried through her bedroom door. She glanced at him briefly from around it, before slamming it shut. She turned the key on the other side with an audible click.

Most odd. She had lied to him, of that he was certain. On this occasion, he would defer to his wife's gentler nature. His gut suggested Hannah might elicit the truth from the woman where he had failed. He trotted back down the curving stairs and along the corridor, only to find their room empty. Hannah had said she was going to select a book. That suggested where his wife might be found—the library.

Sure enough, when he pushed open the double doors, he found Hannah prowling the rows of books, her lips moving as she read the titles.

She smiled on seeing him and he stopped in his tracks. The effect of one happy glance from his wife rooted him to the spot as, for a moment, he relished the awareness that she was pleased to see him and to have his company.

"If you seek diversion, I am afraid it is rather dry offerings here. I have found a bounty of economics, politics and mathematics, but little in the way of history, philosophy or literature." Hannah pulled a volume halfway out and then pushed it back in. "I had hoped a goblin would possess some intriguing books on Unnaturals, hidden away."

He scanned the shelves that stretched up for nearly fifteen feet. A ladder attached to a brass rail could be wheeled along the wall. "Perhaps they are hidden among the more mundane? If I possessed rare and unusual tomes unsuitable for most folk, I would place them where they would escape a cursory look."

Wycliff pushed the ladder along the rail and nudged it close to a corner. He flicked the lever to lock the wheels in place. As he ascended, he scanned titles. It became a mission of honour to find a book that would bring a smile to his wife's face.

Higher and higher he climbed, looking to the left and right.

Her voice drifted up from beneath him. "Do be careful, Wycliff. I have other books to read. It was silly of me to think there might be more unusual books here."

A book with a deep green cover and gold lettering called his hand. He wiggled the book free without even looking at the title, some instinct inside him compelling him to choose it. One glance at the spine and he huffed with satisfaction.

He held it in one hand as he descended the ladder. When he reached the ground, he placed the slender volume in Hannah's hands. "Would *A History of the Fae* be of interest to you?"

She gasped and stared, looking from him to the book as though she didn't quite believe it. With one finger she traced the title. Then she kissed his cheek. "Thank you."

Two simple words made a rare wave of happiness crash over him. Despite the old saying, *marry in haste, repent at leisure*, he found that every day his satisfaction with his match increased. With each quiet moment in Hannah's company, his belief grew that their marriage had the potential to bring joy to them both. Yet how could true affection flourish if he didn't unburden himself of his secret? A plant could not grow if one poisoned its roots, and surely what he left unsaid between them would seep into the soil of their relationship.

"Do you make any progress with your enquiries?" Hannah walked toward one of the leather sofas, cradling the book to her chest.

He set aside his secret to tackle another day. The

greater priority was ferreting out whatever secret had resulted in Stannard's being turned to stone. "A few minutes ago I surprised Mrs Armstrong trying to enter Stannard's room. She said she was confused and thought it was hers. She also claims her previous conversation with Stannard was about his standing on her train and trying to trip her up."

Hannah watched him pace. "But you don't believe her."

He stopped. This was where he needed his wife's assistance. "I am highly skeptical, yes. Could you broach the topic with her in a subtle way? I think she might open up to you where she stays closed to me."

"I shall seek out a quiet moment for a chat with her. I fear she is a woman much used to being overlooked." Sadness tinged Hannah's eyes and she looked down at the book in her hands.

His wife would no longer be overlooked if Wycliff had anything to say about it. He saw her and he intended to draw her from the shadows. "My other interesting conversation was with Lady St Clair. Stannard went to her room the night he died, and left not long before the kitchen maid saw him."

Hannah swallowed that news without so much as a raised eyebrow. "The maid saw him alone, correct? So, either our unknown murderer did not follow Stannard from the house; they followed at a distance and were unseen by the staff; or someone met him out in the garden. There is the card in his pocket, but we cannot discern the writing upon it."

"Lady St Clair said there was a woman in the hallway when he left, hiding behind the Egyptian statue. Could you see if any of the women might let slip it was she? I would like to confirm that Stannard left Lady St Clair at the time she says, and the unknown woman did not follow." Given the woman had concealed her face, he doubted he would have any success in asking them which one was conducting an affair. If nothing else, he had learned to trust his wife's discretion in such matters.

Hannah leaned back on the sofa and worried at her bottom lip with white teeth. "I will ask, discreetly, but the woman concerned might wish to remain anonymous to protect her reputation...to say nothing of her secrets."

Blast. A shame not all women were as honest as Hannah. If one were conducting an affair, then lies might flow easily to the tongue. Should the other women in residence all deny being the woman hiding in the shadows, then how would he discover who it was?

"Find out who it was first. We'll worry about what secret she is concealing after that."

Someone wanted Stannard either dead or incapacitated, and he would find out who. He still needed to dig deeper with Robins and Mowatt. As Stannard's closest friends, they would know if he'd ever spoken of anyone wanting to harm him...other than the usual parade of people, like Wycliff, who fought the urge to punch him in the nose.

# 12

Hannah was sitting on the stool before the dresser mirror, arranging her hair for the evening, when the ring on her pinkie finger tingled. “Mother is summoning me.”

She glanced around the room, but the walls were hung with painted landscapes that would not give her mother a means by which to communicate.

“I need to find a bird.” Hannah walked to the window and raised the sash. Outside, the day edged into evening and birds rustled and chatted in the trees as they found a roost for the night.

“You’re going out the window?” An amused twitch pulled at the edges of Wycliff’s lips as he buttoned his waistcoat.

“Of course. It’s far quicker than going all the way through the house.” She would have to gather up her skirts and hope she didn’t expose too much of her legs as she scrambled over.

"At least let me go first, to help you through." Her husband tossed his cravat to the top of his dresser. With his long legs, he hopped over the ledge and stood in the garden beneath the window.

Hannah nearly called out for him to be careful of the scorched paw prints, but they were obliterated under his boot heel. *Bother. An accidental action or a deliberate one?*

She had no time to ponder that question, as the ring tingled again. Hannah took Wycliff's proffered hand as he steadied her escape out the window. She kept hold of his hand as she stepped out of the garden bed and onto the grass in her satin evening slippers.

Birds flew overhead, heading for their treetop roosts. One peeled away from its flock and dived toward the ground. Hannah held out her hand and the little sparrow alighted on her wrist.

"Mother?" Hannah addressed the mottled brown bird. "Can you hear me?"

It chirped and fluffed out its feathers. "Yes, dearest."

"Lady Frances asks whether it is possible to reverse the spell on Lord Stannard," Hannah said. "The marquess would rather inter his son than add him to the garden as an ornament."

The bird tilted its head from one side to the other. "Anything is possible, once we discover the method. I have found one spell and one potion capable of turning a man to stone. The potion must be ingested, so I think we can strike that from consideration given what we learned from Timmy. The spell takes a large amount of magic and I cannot see anyone less than a mage performing it."

There were no mages in the region. Besides, it was forbidden for a mage to use their magic to kill someone unless it were in a time of war or dire need. Hurling insults and being a cad were hardly grounds for murder. "Could the spell be written down and used by another, such as your immobilisation spell that I use?"

The bird shook its head. "Not the one I have found. It needs to be incanted. But I will keep searching. I might yet locate a potion that can be thrown over someone."

"There is another possibility, Lady Miles. What of Medusa?" Wycliff spoke up from beside Hannah and, startled, the bird hopped on her hand.

The bird let out a low trill. "Yes, Medusa did indeed turn men into stone with a glance. But she was a most fearsome creature. Is there a guest or servant there with a writhing bed of snakes instead of hair, fangs, the grey mottled complexion of stone, and a serpent's tail?"

"No. None." Hannah could recall the hair colour of each lady and gentleman staying at the Pennicotts' and none even resembled snakes. Nor could any be described as fearsome, unless they rose from bed in such a state and a careful toilette made them civilised.

"I shall continue my studies. How are you faring, Hannah?" The bird hopped a step closer. Its gaze flicked to Wycliff and then back to her.

Hannah decoded the subtle message—her mother was enquiring how she was coping with her married state. "I seem to be holding my own, thank you, Mother."

"Summon me, if you require help. Your father and I do worry." The bird closed its eyelids as though it fought the urge to fall asleep.

"I shall. But now I must finish dressing for dinner. Good evening, Mother." Hannah threw the bird into the sky and it flew toward the closest tree. "What made you suggest Medusa?" Hannah asked as Wycliff boosted her back through the window.

His hand lingered on hers as she found her footing. "Your mother gave me a book of Greek myths recently, and Medusa's tale was one of those in the volume."

"If she were among the guests, Medusa would indeed be the most likely culprit. Is it possible she might be hidden elsewhere, perhaps as a statue in the garden that we have not noticed?" They hadn't spent much time examining the other statues; Stannard's had claimed all their attention.

Wycliff let go of her hand and picked up his cravat. "A possibility. Tomorrow we shall roam the grounds and investigate the statues and the monuments in the family cemetery."

Hannah took the length of silk from Wycliff and stepped closer to tie his cravat. They both fell silent as she worked, and she found heat creeping over her skin from the proximity. When her work was done, she stepped backward and smiled at him. "You are quite dashing in your evening finery."

"And you are captivating," he murmured.

She blushed at his words and dropped her gaze to the toes of her slippers. For that evening, Hannah had chosen an overgown in a bright blue, with a golden embroidered edge that covered the plainer cream undergown. Lizzie had suggested the overgowns as an easy way to change the look of her outfit, without needing an entirely new dress. The outer gown dropped to the floor at the back, but the front was cut short and fastened under her bust with an enamelled brooch.

"Thank you," Hannah said.

Wycliff flung open their door and escorted her along the hall. The houseguests had once again assembled in the drawing room. Fanny and Miss Stewart sat on a sofa and Hannah was relieved to note the latter had regained the faint pink tone to her skin and no longer looked in danger of fainting away.

They made polite small talk, with no opportunity for Hannah to enquire who among the women was conducting an affair. Nor could she corner Mrs Armstrong, who hovered close to her husband.

Lord Pennicott was absent from dinner, lending the room a sombre air with the host's place empty at the end of the table. Mowatt and Robins muttered between themselves and cast sidelong glances at the other guests.

Tonight, Hannah was seated next to Mr Wright-Knowles, who regaled her with tales of the toy ships he constructed. Captain Armstrong was deep in conversation with Lady St Clair, who wore a gown of deep red with a low neckline that revealed the curve of her bosom. The captain's gaze kept straying to her décolleté as though he were keeping a weather eye on a swell at sea.

"Will the ball still go ahead?" Philippa asked Fanny.

"Oh, yes. Stannard would have wanted that. Besides, everything is prepared and the invitations were sent out last week," their hostess replied.

Hannah glanced across at Wycliff. Would her husband dance with her at the ball? The thought created an odd flutter in her stomach. The ball would signal the end of their stay and, she hoped, by then they might have found who had murdered Lord Stannard.

Wycliff arched a dark eyebrow as he folded his napkin and draped it on the table when the last plate was cleared.

Fanny rose, and all the gentlemen pushed back their chairs to stand. "If you could all join me in the drawing room, please. We will return here in one hour. Stewart will attempt to contact Stannard, and then Wycliff can ask who turned him to stone."

In Hannah's limited experience, talking to the spirits was a frustrating effort and often, the aftermage merely spouted comforting words that grieving ladies wanted to hear. She wondered if death snatched away some of a person's common sense, leaving their shade only able to talk in riddles. Or were the dead deliberately obtuse so as not to reveal too much about the afterlife?

Not that death had affected either her mother's wit or intelligence. Her mother rarely touched on the changes in her perception since her assassination, and even the Afflicted ladies Hannah had questioned saw no difference in their sensibilities before or after death.

The larger question hung uppermost in Hannah's mind—what marked the change from an existence in this world to one in the afterlife? That those with no heartbeat continued to move among society proved that death alone was not sufficient cause. *There* was a conversation she would like to conduct with a ghost.

In the parlour, Captain Armstrong stood by the pianoforte and regaled an enraptured Philippa with the tale of how he had killed the French mage. He glanced at Hannah and paused in his narrative. For an instant she thought she glimpsed embarrassment in his gaze, then Philippa pressed her hand upon his arm and urged him to continue.

Hannah moved to examine the paintings on the wall. She didn't want to hear how the mage had been struck down, even if he was French. She imagined that somewhere in France an agent might even now be recounting how he had assisted in the poisoning of the mage Lady Seraphina Miles and delivered a blow against England.

Wycliff appeared at her elbow and presented her with a delicate crystal glass of sherry. “I’m going to talk to Stannard’s cronies, if you can lie in wait for the women as the opportunity presents itself?”

“Of course.” As Hannah watched him stroll over to where Robins and Mowatt talked, she remembered something her mother had once said about the viscount. That he would embolden Hannah, even as she smoothed off his rough edges. It might only have been her imagination, but he seemed to be far more civilised now than when she’d first spied him at a ball, demanding that the Afflicted women reveal themselves in public.

She drifted over to where Mrs Armstrong chatted with Edith Stewart and joined their conversation about knitting. Not that Hannah had any great opinion to venture about yarn. Her moment arrived when Fanny grabbed Miss Stewart and ushered her out to prepare for the evening’s entertainment.

Silence fell over the corner they occupied by the window. “I have a most delicate question to ask of you, Mrs Armstrong. I can assure you of my utmost discretion, whatever your reply.”

The lady’s eyes widened behind her spectacles. “Oh? I am most curious as to what you would ask of me.”

“A lady has revealed that Lord Stannard was in her room the night he died. She confided that another lady saw him leave. We simply wish to confirm that sequence of events. Were you, by any chance, in the hall in the early hours of that morning?" Hannah kept her language as diplomatic as possible. No need to assert that the lady had concealed her face because she was between rooms following some clandestine affair.

Mrs Armstrong's eyes became unblinking as those of an owl. Then she chuckled to herself. "How scandalous! Two secret assignations that night? But no, I can declare that my life is not nearly so exciting. I slept soundly all night long in my own bed."

Hannah detected no artifice in the woman's reply. Her face remained open and honest. That left three possibilities—Philippa, Fanny, or Edith Stewart. Philippa was married—surely she wouldn't have been sneaking around with her identity concealed by a hood?

Laughter drew her attention; Philippa had moved to converse with Mr Mowatt. She leaned into him and placed her hand on his arm while she beamed up into his rugged face. Hannah turned to find Mr Wright-Knowles, and located him by the bookcase, wearing a heavy scowl.

*Oh, dear.* Was he aware of his wife's previous attachment to Mr Mowatt? An inescapable question tumbled through Hannah's mind—what if the other woman hiding in the shadows had been Philippa? Not waiting to waylay Lord Stannard, but on her way to Mr Mowatt?

Soon they were all called back to the dining room, which had now been dressed for the event. Blood-red velvet covered the table and flowed down over its sides.

Many of the candles had been blown out, dimming the light and increasing the depth of the shadows. The chairs were placed closer together, gathered at one end of the table.

Miss Stewart seated herself at the head of the table now, with Fanny on her right. A thick red veil covered Miss Stewart's hair and features and her head was bowed. Her hands rested in her lap, clasped together as she whispered to herself.

Fanny gestured for them to take their seats. "If you could all be silent, please. Stewart will cast out with her gift and see who is available to converse with us."

The captain fidgeted in his seat and his gaze went from side to side, as though expecting some enemy to materialise from the wood panelling. Would the French mage have a few words to say to his killer?

"Lord Stannard," Miss Stewart intoned in a clear voice, "if you still linger in this realm, we ask that you come forward and identify your killer."

Wycliff's shoulders heaved and Hannah imagined him wanting to blurt, *If only it were so easy!*

If the ghost arose from the table and pointed his finger at someone, what then? There was no legal precedent for using the testimony of a ghost at a trial. They should have thought ahead and laid out paper and a pencil so he could write his account of events.

Miss Stewart's head nodded toward her chest. "Lord Stannard, we beseech you to make yourself known."

Only the tick of the clock broke the silence. Miss

Stewart looked up and the red veil swung. "I am sorry, Lady Fanny. Often the recently deceased are confused by their state and he might not know how to reach out to me."

Fanny sighed and threw up her hands. Lord Stannard had ruined the entertainment for the evening. "That is a shame. Are there any other ghosts in the room who wish to communicate?"

"I shall try." Miss Stewart bowed her head again. After a long minute, her head snapped up and she pointed across the table to Lady St Clair.

"Where is your honour and modesty? You shame me with your behaviour." The voice issued from Miss Stewart's form, but it was thick and masculine. Apparently, just as Lady Miles could speak through a bird, the dead used Edith Stewart's form.

Lady St Clair sucked in a breath. "I have done nothing to bring dishonour to your name."

"Even the dead see the parade of men through your bedroom." The words were sharp, spat out against the covering veil.

The accused woman pulled her spine tall, and struck back. "I am no longer a marionette, dancing as you pull my strings. Death has freed me from your control and I do not answer to you."

Hannah would need to start a new notebook to keep track of all the revelations about each guest. If Fanny collected secrets, she must possess several volumes with all the titbits recorded.

Miss Stewart muttered and her head swung back and forth. The words turned indistinct, as the tone changed. It became more nasal, with short clipped words. "Coward!" she yelled in a booming voice. Everyone at the table reacted to the single word. Some jumped, others twitched, or sat bolt upright. The unknown accuser snapped, "Tell the truth of what you did during the war! You watched me die and I name you coward for it."

Wycliff and the captain both leapt to their feet on opposite sides of the table. Chairs were thrust back—the one behind the captain keeled over like a felled tree.

"That is enough of this nonsense," Wycliff said.

"Quite so, my lord." The captain bent down and righted his chair. "Shall we leave the ladies to such tricks and adjourn for a brandy?"

The clatter of chairs and raised voices seemed to break the connection between Miss Stewart and the dead. She moaned and slumped back in her chair.

"Stewart is not responsible for what she says. It is the spirits who use her as a conduit." Fanny rose from her seat and poured a glass of water. She lifted her companion's veil and offered the refreshment.

"Death does not make a spirit tell the truth. They can be malicious and delight in spreading harm." Wycliff extended his arm to Hannah.

Hannah was perplexed by this unexpected turn of events and wanted to interrogate this new spirit, although it appeared the person had vanished into the panelling. Only two men at the table had served their country—Wycliff and Captain Armstrong. Both men had reacted to the accusation of cowardice. Did that mean anything, or was it merely the response of any military man who felt his honour was besmirched?

# 13

WYCLIFF CLENCHED his hand into a fist and dug his nails into his flesh. He wanted to grab the woman, tear the veil from her face, and demand to know the name of his accuser. For there were many to choose from. The spirit could be any one of the men in his regiment who had been slaughtered. When he closed his eyes, he could still hear his men begging for his help.

No good could come of dredging up long-ago deeds. Lord knew he had paid for the choices he made that day. His soul was consigned to the pits of hell and his physical presence shunned by society.

"I do not think the accusation was levelled at you." Hannah's voice pulled him from his thoughts.

He had forgotten he prowled the halls, dragging his wife along beside him. She had remained silent until they were well clear of the others. He slowed his pace. "What makes you say that?"

She flashed him a grateful glance that they no

longer marched at double time. "You said spirits could be malicious. Accusing men who fought of cowardice seems a cruel taunt to throw. I would imagine every single man who saw action must doubt himself at some point."

He halted and took Hannah's hands in both of his. Her skin seemed cool to his touch and he wondered if the curse frozen in her body affected her temperature. Not that she ever complained of being cold. "You are right. The captain also seemed affronted by the charge. It is a low blow to call into question a man's honour during war."

Her attention dropped to their joined hands. "One among us has been killed and we are all a little on edge. I found a moment to ask Mrs Armstrong if she had wandered from her room last night. She said in most emphatic terms that she stayed in her bed the entire time."

"That leaves us three possible players for the role of Concealed Woman." He let her hands go and tucked his own behind his back as they took a more leisurely pace along the hall.

Hannah stopped by their door. "Or it could have been someone else entirely. What if one of the men had summoned a woman from below stairs to his chamber?"

Wycliff swung open the door. "Mowatt and Robins are the only single men. I shall talk to them again and see if they had company. That is, if you do not mind being left alone?"

"I am perfectly at ease with my own company and

after today's events, solitude will give me time to contemplate what we have discovered so far." She stepped into the room and dropped her shawl over the arm of the sofa.

"I'll not be long." He nodded and closed the door behind him.

Wycliff found the men, as before, in the billiards room. The captain took his shot while Wright-Knowles hovered behind him. The admirer narrowed missed getting a cue in his gut, so close did he stand. Robins leaned on his cue, waiting, while Mowatt poured drinks at the buffet.

Wycliff stood between Robins and Mowatt and directed his question at them. "Did either of you two have company the night Stannard was murdered?"

Robins glanced to his friend and snorted. "*I* was alone the entire night."

Wycliff turned to Mowatt. "By inference, I assume you were not?"

The man hardened his jaw and shot a look of pure vitriol at his friend. "No. But I will not compromise the lady."

It didn't take a genius to conjure a name, but Wycliff wouldn't say it out loud with the cuckold in the room. He inclined his head in Wright-Knowles's direction and arched one eyebrow.

Anger flared in Mowatt's eyes and he stepped close to Wycliff. "Do not drag her into this. Pippa has suffered enough."

Laughter burst from behind them, where Wright-

Knowles congratulated the captain on a well-played shot. It would be rude to allow the man to overhear them discussing his wife's nocturnal activities.

"Does he know?" As soon as Wycliff said the words, he knew the answer. The man was affable, but not overly endowed with intelligence. He appeared oblivious to the unhappiness of his spouse and his sort would sleep soundly, never knowing his wife slipped from one bed to warm another.

"No." Mowatt clenched his hands into fists and ground his teeth.

Wycliff stared at the man, bemused by his concern for the woman's reputation—very much at odds with the reputation of the Devil's Triplets. "I'll not reveal your affair. I'm merely trying to ascertain who saw Stannard leave another lady's room."

Mowatt nodded and snatched up his glass to down the brandy in a single gulp.

Wycliff took his leave of the men and returned to his room.

Hannah sat at the dressing table, brushing her long dark hair. The sight made a knot form in his gut and he kept his hands busy untying his cravat. "Mowatt had Philippa Wright-Knowles in his bed the night Stannard was killed."

The brush paused in its toils and she met his gaze in the mirror. "There is a tragedy unfolding in full view. I cannot see their plight ending happily for anyone involved. But that aside, I shall find out if she is our mysterious woman hiding in the shadows."

"Thank you." He tossed the cravat to the dresser and his jacket followed. The air seemed close in their room, so Wycliff pushed the window open and sat on the ledge. Sweat trickled between his shoulder blades and his skin pulled tight over his muscles.

Working alongside his wife was proving more beneficial than he had imagined. Hannah's quiet way elicited information from the women that would have been refused to him. As he watched Hannah work her hair into a loose plait, the knot inside him unfurled a little and he rubbed at his chest.

He needed to occupy himself before he did something foolish to ruin their fledgling accord. "I'm going to have another look at the garden."

She rose from the stool and walked to the bed. "Now? In the dark?"

He watched her turn back the coverlet from under half-lidded eyes. "Yes. I want to see how much is visible by the light of the moon and try to ascertain if Stannard would have recognised his attacker. Will you be all right here on your own?"

She smiled and patted a book on the bedside table. "I will be perfectly well. A most excellent book that my husband found in the library will keep me entertained."

He hopped through the window and landed in the garden below. Earlier, he had scuffed up the paw prints in the soft earth before Hannah caught sight of them. He wasn't ready to answer questions about the scorch marks beneath the window where he came and went.

Wycliff walked across the moonlit lawn to a yew hedge. In the dark embrace of the towering hedge, he let the heat flow through his veins as it reshaped his form. He let out a long sigh as the world shifted around him. The moon shone as brightly as the sun. A faint green mist exuded from the trees as Nature breathed. The bricks of the large house were smudged at the edges, as though it became something indistinct and impermanent in the landscape.

He glanced back to the house to ensure no curious eyes stared out the windows. Then he set off across the lawn. A faint tinge of guilt shot through his long form, for he hadn't been truthful with Hannah. Not that he could tell her what quarry he sought.

He didn't want to search the garden for clues. He was looking for Stannard.

If Miss Stewart was correct, Stannard had already passed to the other side and there would be nothing to find. A part of him wanted to prove her false. If she had misled them about Stannard, then the veracity of everything she said was called into question.

*Tell the truth of what you did during the war! You watched me die and I name you coward for it.*

Hannah had said it was an easy accusation to cast at any man who had served. Except it rang true for him. Wycliff didn't need a spectral accuser to name him coward—he had already done that for himself. While his men were slaughtered, he had done nothing. Sheer hopelessness at their situation had pressed him into the dirt, where he watched them die.

Why had he survived? Or had he? The skin at the juncture of his left shoulder and neck itched. Most days he thought his survival a punishment for his inaction.

He shook his head to clear old memories and concentrated on the task at hand.

A wisp floated across his path and he snapped his jaws at it to hurry it along. Such things had died long ago, but for whatever reason, they remained attached to this plane. Over a period of decades, their forms dissolved until they seemed to be no more than clouds of heavy fog with no distinguishable features. Nor were they capable of conversation. This wisp would be no help to his investigation.

Wycliff peered through an opening in the hedge to ensure no one wandered the paths in the dark, before he trod over the gravel to where Stannard had died. He sniffed the air. A faint, sharp tang lingered in one spot.

Words muttered softly attracted his attention. Wycliff crouched low and crept through another opening cut in the hedge. The small garden beyond contained a central fountain and on either side, benches had been placed under vine-covered arches. A man sat on a bench, his forearms resting on his thighs. His head was slumped forward as he rolled something from one hand to another and whispered to himself.

Wycliff padded closer and sat between fountain and bench. Sensing his presence, the man looked up. Even in spirit form, Stannard had retained his broken nose.

*Curious*, Wycliff thought, *why did Miss Stewart*

*lie?* She said Stannard had already passed to the other side.

"Women. Damned women," the spectre said upon seeing Wycliff. The movement of Stannard's hands paused. He held something clutched in one fist.

This is where things got difficult. Most spirits were confused and focused on the heightened emotions of the moment they died. Meaningful conversation was difficult to elicit and often cryptic.

"What woman?" Wycliff asked. Had the killer been a woman, or was Stannard referring to women in general?

Stannard pushed off his thighs and sat up. A ghostly hand jabbed at the air with the object it clutched. Small, round, and white, like a billiard ball. "She did this."

Well, that narrowed down his suspects. Wycliff was looking for a woman. "Who?"

Stannard dropped the ball and it rolled along the path before it disappeared with a puff. He wrapped his arms around his body and rocked back and forth. "So cold. Can't breathe."

"Who did this to you, Stannard?" Wycliff crept closer. All he needed was a name.

The air next to the bench shimmered. It sucked the faint mist rising off the grass and trees and the shape grew as it swallowed. Soon it hung a foot from the ground and spread until it was seven feet tall and three feet wide. It tore down the middle and the two sides peeled apart to reveal inky, starless darkness.

*Bugger.* Wycliff had seen the rift before. His time with Stannard was about to be cut short.

The ghost seemed unaware of the pulsating void hanging next to where he sat. "Hurts. She hurt me. I'll hurt her. The witch will get what she deserves!" He banged a fist on his chest.

"What is her name?" Wycliff barked out the words, hoping to jolt Stannard into a moment of coherence before his time was gone forever.

"Whores. All of them. They tease us. Inflame us. Then the trollops say no. They deserve what they get." Stannard gasped each word, slamming one fist into the other as he spoke.

Anger coursed through Wycliff. He knew the stories attached to Stannard. Rumours that he and his friends despoiled as many young, innocent women as they could get their greedy hands on. There were darker rumours—that the girls were unwilling and Stannard was little more than a rapist. But no gently bred young lady could level such an accusation without ruining her reputation and pulling her family down as she tumbled from grace. Society would punish the victim, not the perpetrator.

The void sang to Wycliff. The words were soft and seductive as it urged him to feed it the evil, worthless soul before him. Shadows moved within the inky shape, and whispered that they would ensure Stannard was tormented for all of eternity for his crimes. The creatures promised to dispense the punishment society was too afraid to mete out to one of its own.

It took mere seconds for Wycliff to make his decision. In life, Stannard had delighted in tormenting others and he had been particularly cruel about Hannah. Let him answer for his crimes to a higher power, one who would not be swayed by rank or money.

He lunged and grabbed the ghost between his jaws. Stannard let out a yell and struck out at Wycliff. Ghostly arms batted him about the head and snout but he tightened his grip as he dragged him sideways and off the bench.

Wycliff bunched his muscles—spirits were surprisingly heavy—and tossed his captive at the void. The suspended shape caught Stannard. His arms flailed and he clawed at the air, but there was nothing to halt his tumble as he screamed. The void swallowed the spirit form like a snake devouring prey. Bit by bit, Stannard vanished into its maw. The ear-piercing wail made Wycliff cringe and cover his ears.

It cut off and silence fell over the garden. When he looked up, Stannard had gone. The shimmering void curled into itself, smaller and smaller, until it winked out.

Wycliff sat on the path and stared at where the rift had been. Was this his purpose in life now—to dispatch foul souls straight to Hell? If he could cull the likes of Stannard from society, he might yet become accustomed to the task.

With nothing more to be discovered in the garden, Wycliff crept back to the tall hedge. He drew a deep breath, and, gathering the heat from his veins, he locked it away inside him. Fire was replaced by ice and a chill took hold of him. He rubbed his hands up his arms as he crossed the lawn, but the cold was lodged deep within.

Wycliff climbed over the sill and pulled the sash down behind him. He stopped and leaned against the wall. Hannah had fallen asleep while reading. The ensorcelled light cast a soft golden glow over her face and the book about the Fae rested across her chest. Her dark plait curved over the pillow.

Instinct urged him to gather her up in his arms and hold on tight. The voices from the void still whispered in his mind and he needed someone to remind him of his humanity so he didn't stare too long into the abyss. He needed Hannah pressed against his skin to remind him that he still walked this earth and that he was more than a servant of Hades.

Now at last he understood what Lady Miles had meant when she told him to find an anchor in this world. Part of him had enjoyed sending Stannard's soul to Hell. How easy it would be to lose himself to the hellhound. To spend more time in that form, seeking out miscreants deserving of punishment, or hunting the unnatural creatures and demons who had escaped from the underworld.

As he walked past the sofa, he picked up a blanket. He wouldn't wake Hannah or disturb her sleep, but he needed to be close. Wycliff eased himself down on the mattress and stretched out next to his wife. He lifted the book from her limp fingers and placed it on the side table. Then he draped the blanket over himself and laid his head on the pillow.

Soft breathing came from the woman next to him and he fell asleep wondering what it would be like to hold her in his arms.

# 14

THE NEXT MORNING, Hannah awoke when the mattress shifted next to her. She opened her eyes to find a man on her bed. Wycliff was stretched out atop the blankets with one arm flung over his head and the other across his chest. She took a moment to study his profile. His features were softened by the early light and the relaxation of slumber.

He was a striking man, firm of both feature and opinion, and her stomach fluttered as her mind called him *husband*.

As she stirred, he opened one eye. "Good morning. Forgive my presence beside you, but the sofa is damned uncomfortable."

"I wondered how you were managing; you are taller than the sofa is long." Hannah managed a shy smile and clutched the blanket tight to her chest. She used the bedding as a shield against the unexpected intimacy.

Her husband was on the bed beside her. Whatever

would be next? Before she knew it, he would be *under* the blankets. For some reason, her imagination conjured the image of them both in bed but without their nightgowns. Heat rushed up her neck and over her cheeks.

She was a married woman and shouldn't be having such fanciful thoughts. Yet a new yearning stretched inside her as she studied the planes of Wycliff's face. She had been married for nearly a month and hadn't even kissed her husband. Not properly. The chaste peck at the end of the ceremony didn't count. That made her mind whirl. Did she really want to kiss him?

He sat up and lowered his feet over the side of the bed, revealing that he was still clothed in his shirt and trousers. "I shall order a breakfast tray, since you are awake."

"Yes. Thank you. That would be lovely." What Hannah needed was to return to her scientific studies with her father. Jaunting around the countryside and attending house parties was filling her mind with silly romantic nonsense.

By the time Wycliff returned, Hannah had relieved herself and reclaimed the book about the Fae. The glimpse into a world she thought only a fairy tale was fascinating, and she wondered how she might find a Fae in England to study.

"Did you discover anything in the garden last night?" she asked as Wycliff sat on the end of the bed.

He ran his hands through his hair and tugged a lock

back behind his ear. "No. But after consideration, I believe Stannard's killer is a woman."

Hannah closed the book and reluctantly set it aside. Fairy folk could wait—they had a murderer to catch. "What brings you to that conclusion?"

Wycliff leaned back against the corner post. "The method used. However his transformation to stone was wrought, it strikes me that it might not have required physical contact with Stannard. Nor is it a particularly violent end. When a man commits a murder, it is more...*brutal*, for want of a better word."

Hannah pondered the idea. Men did seem more direct in their dealings with one another. Such as breaking a man's nose immediately following a hurled insult. Women tended to plot and then act. Being physically weaker, they took precautions to protect themselves and often employed spells or potions.

"But who among us has the motive?" Assuming it was one of the nobles, that made five possible suspects.

"That is what we need to determine. There are still many questions that need answers. Why did Lady Frances invite Stannard this week? Perhaps it was to seek revenge. We only have Lady St Clair's word that Stannard left her room and she did not follow. What if they argued, or he spurned her? Then we still need to find who penned that note demanding the return of a certain letter. On that head, I suspect Mrs Armstrong, given her attempt to enter his room." Wycliff's hands moved from tormenting his hair to scratching at the stubble on his chin.

There was a knock at the door and Wycliff rose to admit the footmen carrying the breakfast trays. Her back against the pillows, Hannah hugged her knees to her chest as she waited for them to depart. Ideas swirled in her mind as she tried to imagine who among the ladies was capable of taking a man's life. She didn't think any of them looked the sort. Yet women were masters of hiding behind masks. They were taught from a young age to smile despite any torment they endured on the inside.

Any one of them could have been so injured by Stannard that she felt death the only suitable way to ease her pain. Hannah needed to draw on all her skills to discover which woman nursed a fatal secret.

Wycliff carried a tray to the bed for her. She picked up the cup of hot chocolate and took a sip while she considered which strand in her mind to tug on first. She decided on the one thing that had stood out for her during the picnic the previous day.

"We have learned that Mrs Wright-Knowles was with Mr Mowatt the night Lord Stannard died. But did you know that they have quite a history together? Lady Frances told me they grew up together and were expected to marry, but her father forbade the match." Hannah sought the words to voice her concerns. Pippa glowed and laughed when she was with Mowatt, but became wan and flat near her husband.

Wycliff sat at the dressing table, but slid his chair around so he could face Hannah. "I had noticed the familiarity between them, which is why it wasn't difficult to guess whom Mowatt entertained in his room. Do you think Stannard might have held something over the couple?"

Hannah put down the cup and picked up a piece of toast to nibble. It didn't seem right to discuss another woman's infidelity, not even in the privacy of the bedroom. "That would imply there was some evidence for him to manipulate. Besides, Stannard and Mr Mowatt were friends. Surely one of the Devil's Triplets would not blackmail the others?"

"Or they appeared to be friends. I shall find an opportunity to ask Mowatt why the marriage was not permitted." Wycliff picked up half a kipper on his fork and devoured the small fish.

Hannah mentally ran through the other noble ladies staying under the Pennicott roof. "I will endeavour to seek a private moment with Mrs Armstrong. There are also the circumstances surrounding the fall from grace of Miss Edith Stewart's family. Is it possible that Stannard was involved in her sister's scandal?"

Wycliff swallowed before answering. "He had been known to ruin women for sport. See what you can find out. I'm going to talk to Robins and see which of the women Stannard knew before arriving here."

In only a few days, Hannah had grown accustomed to Wycliff's presence in the room as he went about his routine. She no longer dreaded the coming years, since they had found a way to work together. If only there were a cure for the Affliction frozen within her. Could they have a happy future, if the death sentence were removed from over her head?

As usual, they assembled in the drawing room to await the announcement from Lady Frances of the day's activities. Hannah played cards with Philippa and Miss Stewart.

When at length Fanny swept into the room, the men jumped to their feet. "Good morning, everyone. Lord Wycliff, have you discovered yet who murdered my guest?"

"No, I am still conducting my enquiries." Wycliff spoke to their hostess but his gaze went to the other women in the room.

Robins snorted. "You don't seem to be making any haste, sir."

"A charge of murder requires evidence. If you possess evidence that would speed along my investigation, then do share." Wycliff glared at the other man.

Hannah thought Mr Robins impertinent. She could understand he grieved for his friend, but they could not charge an innocent person. Justice had a process to be followed. Nor did they have any compelling evidence to suggest a culprit.

"I don't know of anyone who would want to harm him," Mr Robins said.

Wycliff's eyebrows shot up and he inhaled, but his retort was never voiced.

"What do you have planned for today, Lady Fanny?" Miss Stewart asked.

Fanny's dark eyes gleamed. "Today is a most

exciting day! After nuncheon, we shall go off on a hunt!"

The others gasped and smiled at the news, while dread plunged through Hannah. Mrs Armstrong paled even as her husband cheered.

At midday, the party assembled at the rear of the house, in the cobbled yard before the stables. The grooms held the reins of a large number of horses in a range of sizes and colours. Some of the animals pawed at the ground, impatient to be underway, while others stood with their heads lowered, as though they slept in the sun.

The women were all attired in subdued hues—green, navy, grey. Their veiled top hats sported ribbons that matched their habits and the strands hung down their backs, but would fly out behind them once the horses picked up their pace.

Lady St Clair wore a jacket so tight that Hannah wondered how she managed to fasten the buttons. Philippa wore navy and looked very stylish. Poor Mrs Armstrong wore a pale grey that made her look like an apparition, not helped by the grim look on her face.

Hannah wore a riding habit of darker grey with black military trim on the jacket, a style that was all the rage since the war. At least she looked the part, but it did nothing to melt the cold lump in her stomach. She didn't view the afternoon's activity with the same excitement as the others.

"Oh, do buck up, Judith," the captain said in a loud tone to his wife before striding off to talk to the other men.

Mrs Armstrong dropped her chin and wiped a tear from the corner of her eye.

*Oh, dear*. Hannah wondered what trouble brewed between the two.

Lady Frances wore deep green that seemed to accentuate her goblin features, although she was in a fine mood and wore a huge smile. "We all need a good ride to blow away the cobwebs and melancholy of the last few days. Lord Stannard loved a hunt. I am sure he will join us in spirit."

Everyone turned to stare at Miss Stewart, expecting some sort of confirmation that Lord Stannard was among them, mounted on a spectral horse. When she didn't point to an empty spot and cry, "There he is!" everyone turned back to Lady Frances.

Fanny wielded her crop like a conductor's baton as she directed the assignment of animals. She pointed to a horse and then to a gentleman or a lady. Hannah hoped to be given one of the sedate-looking horses. The ones prancing at the ends of their reins were akin to fire-breathing dragons in her mind.

"How do you feel about a spirited mount, Lord Wycliff?" Lady Frances indicated a dark brown horse with long limbs that stamped its foot and tossed its mane.

Wycliff studied the horse for a moment and then nodded. "I'm sure after a hard ride we will understand each other."

Fanny smiled and cast a sideways glance to Robins, who snorted. Then her beady eyes turned to Hannah. "What of you, Lady Wycliff? Do you prefer a fast or slow ride?"

Mowatt laughed out loud and Robins's shoulders heaved as he sniggered. Hannah had no time to ponder why that question should be so amusing. "A slow, sedate ride, please."

"For me also, please," Mrs Armstrong called. She moved closer to Hannah, as though she sensed a kindred spirit in their dislike of flighty horses.

"How odd—two wives who prefer a sedate ride when their husbands much prefer spirited mounts," Fanny murmured with downcast lashes. For some reason, that sent Robins and Mowatt into fits of laughter.

Wycliff glared at her and emitted a half cough, half growl. Fanny visibly wilted and for a second, embarrassment flashed over her face. Then she smiled at Hannah as she pointed to two small and sturdy types and adopted a more businesslike tone. "The cobs will look after you both. You won't be able to keep up with the rest of us, but you will be safe upon them."

A groom approached Hannah with the placid horse. Wycliff stepped to her side to assist. Hannah whispered to her husband under her breath, "Must we all undertake a mad dash across the countryside?

Perhaps the hares and foxes do not want to be disturbed today."

Wycliff lifted Hannah into the sidesaddle and placed her foot in the stirrup. "Do you not want to go for a gallop?"

"No. I would much rather go for a ramble." She had considered lying about her ability, but that seemed foolish when they were about to dash over uncertain terrain.

"We don't have to follow the pack. I can stay with you—perhaps we might ride over the estate instead?" He cast a glance at his horse, who jumped to one side and snorted at an invisible demon.

Her husband stared at the horse with such a look of longing that Hannah simply couldn't understand. But if he wanted to tear over the fields, she wouldn't be an impediment to his enjoyment. "I will be perfectly well. I believe Mrs Armstrong would also rather take a slower pace, and it will give us an opportunity to talk in private."

Hannah thought she was ungainly in the saddle, but Mrs Armstrong appeared to be having difficulty keeping her seat even at a standstill.

"What do you say, Mrs Armstrong—shall we set our own pace, and leave the others to gallop off?" she called to the other woman.

Relief washed over Mrs Armstrong's face and she clung to the reins. "Oh, yes, please."

Hannah smiled at her husband. "See?"

Wycliff patted her horse's neck. "Very well. Thank you."

The others all mounted up and trotted out of the yard after Lady Frances. A groom blew on a trumpet and the dogs all barked and yapped, before taking off. The canines seemed oblivious to the horses as they scented the ground and scattered, only to reform behind one who appeared to be the leader.

Wycliff took the reins from the groom and leapt into the saddle. The horse danced sideways and he crooned to it softly. The horse's ears twitched backward as it listened to him, then it blew out a snort and settled under his calming influence. Wycliff pointed his crop at one of the grooms. "Stay with Lady Wycliff and Mrs Armstrong."

As the riders cleared the courtyard and entered the fields, the riders put heel to their horses and they leapt forward in a canter. Lady Frances and Philippa laughed from the front. Lady St Clair bent over her mount and urged the horse on faster. Miss Stewart cantered along behind them, riding with an elegant ease that Hannah envied. The men took off like hounds in pursuit of a rabbit as the women took the lead.

Hannah shuddered. "I don't know how they can do that. I find the idea quite terrifying."

"I also prefer a more sedate pace. Do you mind terribly if we just walk?" Mrs Armstrong said as she edged her horse closer.

"I have no objection at all," Hannah said as she

nudged her horse in the same direction the others had taken.

The groom followed, reins in one hand and a bored expression on his face.

Fortunately, the two cobs had no desire to race after the other horses and were content to amble through the countryside. The women chatted of inconsequential things. A prickle between Hannah's shoulder blades reminded her of the groom, who had nothing to do but listen to every word. They needed to lose him—a rather difficult prospect when neither woman was a proficient rider.

They reached a large, flat, open field. It ended in a gentle rise, where they could see the other riders as tiny shapes hurtling up the hill. The dogs were white and brown spots zigging and zagging between the horses.

"Do you feel up to a wee trot or possibly a canter?" Hannah asked. She would never improve her horsemanship if she kept to a walk.

Worry flashed over Mrs Armstrong's face and then she swallowed and tightened her hold on the reins. "Let us give it a go. Nothing ventured, nothing gained, as they say."

Hannah settled herself in the saddle and tapped the placid horse with her left heel. It blew a snort, then broke into an easy trot. Hannah remembered her instruction and pressed her right foot into the beast's shoulder. The gait threw her up and down and with effort, she let out a breath and relaxed her spine. When she did that, the trot didn't seem so horrid.

Mrs Armstrong bounced next to Hannah, her face flushed. The large horse the groom rode barely trotted at all and only needed an energetic walk to keep pace with the shorter-legged cobs.

"Could we try a canter?" Hannah called to the groom. She wasn't sure how to make her horse go any faster, and hoped it might follow the lead of another.

"Of course, milady." The groom didn't seem to move at all and yet his mount popped into a slow canter.

The cob trotted faster and just as Hannah worried about a compression injury to her spine, the animal broke into a canter. Hannah held her breath and then reminded herself to breathe. She hadn't fallen off! In fact, the slow rocking motion was far easier to sit and more comfortable than the trot.

A smile broke over her face. Not only was she cantering across the field, she was enjoying the sensation. But life had a way of striking you down when you least expected it. Her happiness couldn't last.

# 15

The startled shriek broke Hannah's enjoyment of cantering through the wildflowers. She glanced at her companion, whose placid cob had decided to enliven his task.

"Oh, dear!" Mrs Armstrong screeched as her horse put his nose to the ground and gave a small hop with his back legs.

It wasn't really a buck—the quiet horse put no real effort into the motion—but it was enough to unseat Mrs Armstrong. She veered from one side to another for several agonising moments as the horse made a valiant effort to catch his unbalanced rider.

Hannah could only watch, helpless to assist. The groom had cantered ahead and swung his horse around when Mrs Armstrong called out. He cantered toward them as the captain's wife disappeared over the side and her skirts ballooned up like a sail blowing in the wind.

"Are you all right, ma'am?" The groom pulled his horse to a halt and leapt to the ground. He rushed to Mrs Armstrong's assistance.

Hannah had to take a longer route to dismount since she didn't want a speedy drop like Mrs Armstrong's. Fortunately, her horse had already halted and used the opportunity to crop the grass tickling his nose. Hannah had to gather her skirts up as she flung her right leg over the upright pommel and wiggled sideways on the seat.

With the lad preoccupied, Hannah was left balanced on her mount but with no help to reach the ground. Gritting her teeth, she propelled herself off the saddle. She hit the grass and nearly buckled at the knees. Only the hand she kept on the horse's neck kept her upright.

She rushed around the horse to where Mrs Armstrong lay on the ground. The groom knelt beside her, his hands hovering over the woman, but he didn't dare touch her.

"Are you hurt?" Hannah knelt in the grass and did a visual check for any broken bones or signs of blood.

Mrs Armstrong grabbed Hannah's hand and sat up. Her hat had been knocked off by the fall and rolled to a stop in the grass. She held her head and silent tears rolled down her face.

Hannah waved the groom away. "See to the horses, please, while I ensure Mrs Armstrong is unharmed." The other woman needed a little privacy in which to cry.

"Luckily I landed on my posterior, which provides ample padding." The lady drew in a ragged sob.

"Are you sure nothing is broken? I am going to examine your legs." Hannah ran her hands down each limb and noted both the straightness of the bones and the lack of reaction in Mrs Armstrong. "You don't appear to have sustained any serious injury."

"Only to my dignity." Mrs Armstrong wiped the tears from her face and patted the grass, looking for her hat.

Hannah picked it up and placed it in her hands. "There are only two witnesses, and we won't tell anyone, if you'd rather the others didn't know."

She looked to the groom, now holding three horses contentedly grazing the lush grass. Hannah silently willed him to hold his tongue.

"I won't tell, milady," he said at length.

There was no doubt he would tell the other grooms that one of his charges had taken a tumble, but Hannah suspected Mrs Armstrong was more concerned about her husband's finding out.

"Do you want to mount again, or would you rather walk?" Hannah asked as she helped the other woman to her feet.

"Do you mind terribly if we walked? My bottom is ever so sore and I can't face climbing back on that brute." She adjusted her spectacles, which had miraculously stayed put on the end of her nose, and managed a weak smile.

"Of course I don't mind." Hannah gestured to the

groom. "You may join the others. Mrs Armstrong and I will proceed on foot back to the house. I'm sure we can cope on our own."

"Are you sure, milady? Lord Wycliff asked me to stay with you." He glanced over the fields, where tiny toy horses cantered off toward the horizon. He had the same look of longing that Wycliff had worn.

Hannah took the reins of the two cobs. "Quite sure. If my husband asks, tell him we are on foot and I dismissed you."

The groom touched the brim of his cloth cap, swung himself into the saddle, and was galloping over the fields before he even had his feet in the stirrups.

"Well, he was in a hurry to leave." Hannah brushed grass from her companion's habit. "There is a small stain, but I'm sure no one will notice. If they do, we shall say we rested for a while in the damp grass, which is entirely true."

Mrs Armstrong gathered up the train of her habit, took the reins to her horse, and drew a deep, sobbing breath. "Thank you, Lady Wycliff, for keeping this incident to yourself."

Skirts over their arms, the two women headed back the way they had come toward the house in the distance.

"I apologise if I am prying, but I think you don't want Captain Armstrong to know about your fall. Are you sure that is wise? Some injuries are not immediately apparent, and he is in the best position to observe you." Hannah worried about the other woman. Head injuries could take a few days to manifest, and her husband should be alert to any change in her condition.

Another ragged sigh tore through Mrs Armstrong. "Oh, Lady Wycliff, the captain will be ever so disappointed in me. He is quite a skilled rider and views my complete lack of any aptitude with some disdain. I do not wish to give him further reason to be disappointed in me."

"But a married couple cannot be equally matched in all things. Everybody has different strengths and weaknesses. As you saw, my husband charged off on a fire-breathing steed." Hannah never received any censure from Wycliff for her lack of equestrian accomplishments, and heaven knew he was vocal enough in his opinions if he thought a person deficient in some area. Rather than criticising Hannah, he had seemed more concerned that she not be left alone.

Mrs Armstrong picked a strand of grass and waved it through the air. "Differences may be charming at first, but over time, they can transform into barriers. It is difficult to be married to a dashing war hero known for his feats of bravery."

"Wycliff does not talk of the war. I think he prefers it be left in the past." Hannah was married to a man who had suffered a disastrous campaign before returning to England in disgrace. If he were renowned for a heroic act, would that put pressure on him in peacetime to continue to live up to such heroism?

Hannah plucked a cornflower and threaded it

through the trim on her jacket. The bright blue was a sharp contrast to the grey.

"I have not been married long, but I hope we can solve any issues that arise in the future." Hannah was not so naive as to believe all marriages produced a happily ever after. Problems would rear up and it was how you dealt with them that mattered. It bolstered her confidence in dealing with Wycliff, knowing that her mother would smite the man if he treated her abominably.

Mrs Armstrong let out a loud sigh. "I do try to be worthy of the captain."

Hannah reached out and stopped the other woman, resting a hand on her arm. "I am sure he values and respects you just as you are. After all, is that not why he married you in the first instance?"

Mrs Armstrong looked away. "I fell in love with and married a newly made lieutenant with nothing to his name. It was only with the passage of time that he rose in rank and reputation. Now, I think he wishes for a graceful and witty wife who mirrors his accomplishments. I do what I can to prove my support, but I do not think it is enough to retain his love."

"Oh," Hannah whispered.

"And yet...he will always retain mine." The other woman's heartbreak was etched on her face and fresh tears rolled down her cheeks. Hannah wished there was a spell her mother could cast on inconstant men. Better yet, perhaps she could ask Wycliff to box some common sense into the captain.

"Many men returned from the war changed, and the captain has been much in demand to relate his feats. I am sure with a little time and patience, he will remember his love and affection for you." It was a rare thing to slay a mage, and many people clamoured to hear Captain Armstrong's account.

Mrs Armstrong patted her hand. "You are a kind soul, Lady Wycliff. Unlike some others."

"Lord Stannard possessed a cruel streak. Were you acquainted with him?" Hannah used the direction of the conversation to ask the question that niggled in her mind.

Mrs Armstrong didn't answer for a long time, letting her horse amble through the wildflowers. "I will not mourn his death. He was not a good man," she said at length in a soft voice. "But nor will I speak ill of the dead."

*Bother*. Hannah was hoping to elicit details of her argument with the deceased. What would Wycliff do? He would hurl the evidence at the poor woman and demand to know the truth. No, Hannah couldn't take such an approach. She needed to pick gently at the edges.

"I only knew Lord Stannard by reputation until recently. Wycliff and I encountered him and the others in an inn, in Reading. He made some particularly horrid remarks about me." Perhaps if Hannah offered up her tale, Mrs Armstrong would counter with hers.

The other woman's lips thinned into a grimace. "You are fortunate if words were the only offensive matter he threw at you. He was capable of more appalling acts."

"The man has been murdered, Mrs Armstrong, and my husband will be unrelenting in unearthing any motives that a guest might harbour. I can assure you of the greatest discretion if there is something you would confess to me. But I cannot intervene with my husband unless you tell me why you were trying to enter Lord Stannard's room." Hannah tried to prise the woman's secret loose. Wycliff would be a dog with a bone once he had it confirmed she hid a motive.

"I am such a fool. Daniel would set me aside if he knew what a mess I have made." Her voice wavered and broke and she pressed one hand to her temple.

"Nothing is irreparable, I am sure." Hannah couldn't see what grievous crime the woman could have committed. Nor did the timid Mrs Armstrong strike her as a murderess.

Mrs Armstrong gripped Hannah's hand and her eyes were bright behind her spectacles. "You cannot breathe a word of it to anyone. Promise me. I cannot risk a hint of my foolish actions getting back to my husband."

"On my honour, I shall keep your secret. Do you seek to protect yourself?" Hannah expected the woman to confess to an affair with Lord Stannard. That line of thought made her wonder how such a thing could possibly have come to pass.

Mrs Armstrong laughed. "Protect myself? No."

Realisation washed over Hannah. Not an affair.

Now the glances and words made sense. "The captain. You are protecting your husband."

A sigh heaved through Mrs Armstrong and her shoulders slumped. "After he returned from the war, Daniel fell ill with a terrible fever. He hovered near death for nearly two weeks. I sat by his bed the entire time, wiping his brow and giving him sips of water."

"As any good wife would." The woman was a most devoted wife. How did the captain not see that?

"The fever had control of his mind, and in its grip... he said things. He unburdened a most terrible secret. No one knows. When he recovered, he had no knowledge of his ramblings, but it consumed me." Mrs Armstrong rested a hand on the horse's neck and stared up at the sky. After a long moment, she continued, "I confessed my husband's secret to a friend in a letter. I sought her counsel as to what I should do."

"How did Lord Stannard become involved?" Hannah couldn't hold back her question. How could a letter penned by Mrs Armstrong to a confidante have fallen into his hands?

"She never said, and denied all knowledge of it, perhaps to conceal her own shame at what she had done. It was Lord Stannard who told me he had removed it from her bedroom." Mrs Armstrong glanced at Hannah and then looked away.

Here was another ugly aspect of the dead lord's character revealed—searching a woman's room for letters he could use to his advantage. He would never have had the opportunity if so many married women weren't unhappy and seeking diversion elsewhere. Imagine if women were allowed to marry for love, instead of where it was most advantageous for their families! Such things might not occur so often.

"You sought to retrieve the letter from Lord Stannard, to protect your husband."

Mrs Armstrong nodded. "The rogue said he was going to make it public and humiliate him. I could not let him do that. We would be ruined."

Humiliated and ruined. How far would Mrs Armstrong go to protect her husband? Had she murdered Stannard, thinking she could then retrieve the letter and destroy it?

"Wycliff searched Lord Stannard's room, but did not find the letter. I am sorry. He only found your note demanding its return." Stannard might be dead, but the letter revealing the captain's secret was out there, somewhere.

Hannah recalled the spirit speaking through Miss Stewart, and its accusation of cowardice. Wycliff thought it referred to him, but what if it had been meant for the captain? For only one act had made him famous and elevated his standing in society—killing the French mage.

# 16

Wycliff's heart felt lighter in his chest as they rode back to the house, and he even allowed a smile to break free. Lady Frances had chosen a hot and opinionated mare for him. Once they had the measure of each other, he allowed the mare her head and she galloped faster than any of the other horses.

"Well done, Lord Wycliff. She is a difficult horse, but you seem to have reached an agreement with her." Lady Frances trotted alongside Wycliff as they clattered into the yard.

He patted the mare's neck. She was covered in sweat and would need a good slow walk and a rubdown. "The difficult ones often bring the greatest rewards."

"When you take such enjoyment in a feisty ride, why did you choose such a placid wife?" Robins called as he dismounted and tossed the reins to a waiting groom.

The smile vanished from Wycliff's face and he fixed the man with a hard stare. How foolish of him to think the barbs tossed at Hannah would cease on Stannard's death. Robins needed to be taught a lesson, and Wycliff saw no difficulty in breaking another nose. "An intellectual challenge is as invigorating as a physical one. Only a fool would judge a person by what they see on the surface. It's not your fault you are incapable of perceiving deeper intelligence—I suspect you were dropped on your head as a babe."

Wycliff turned his back on the man and dug into his pocket. He found a sugar cube for the mare, who snuffled it from his outstretched hand. "Give her a good walk to help her cool," he said to the groom.

As he cast around for Hannah, he spotted the two cobs already in the stables being rubbed down. "Where is Lady Wycliff?" he asked a stable boy.

"Lady Wycliff and Mrs Armstrong went that way, milord." The lad pointed to the garden gate.

Wycliff walked in that direction and found his wife and Mrs Armstrong deep in conversation as they strolled among the flower beds.

"Wycliff!" Hannah called on seeing him, a smile on her dusky lips. "Did you have a good ride?"

"Yes. The dogs flushed out two rabbits. Were you all right on your own? I was worried when you sent on the groom." The ache reappeared in his chest and he rubbed over the knot.

Hannah grimaced at the fate of the rabbits, and then waved a long-stemmed daisy at him. "Mrs

Armstrong and I needed to walk. The sidesaddle is quite a strain when you are not used to it. Although I did manage a canter and I must say, I rather enjoyed it."

"I am pleased to hear you had an enjoyable time." He held out his arm to her. "Shall I escort you back to our room?"

Hannah excused herself to Mrs Armstrong and then took his arm. Once they were alone on the stretch of lawn before the house, she tipped her head closer to his.

"Mrs Armstrong did indeed pen the note you found in Lord Stannard's room. He possesses an indiscreet letter she wrote, detailing a confession her husband made while in the grips of a fever. He threatened to use the letter to ruin the captain and she sought its return."

Wycliff let out a long breath. "It's always the quiet ones who harbour the deepest motives."

Hannah tapped his arm and frowned up at him. "I do not think she is a murderer. It would make no sense to kill Stannard before she secured the letter. Now she does not know where it is."

That didn't mean she wasn't a murderer, merely an incompetent one. It would make sense to have your hands on the letter before doing away with the blackmailer. "I found no letters in Stannard's room of an incriminating nature concerning the captain. Did Mrs Armstrong reveal the nature of the secret?"

Hannah glanced around at the other guests

wandering up from the stables and dropped her voice. "No. But I would hazard a guess it might have to do with the mage he killed. He has derived a certain amount of fame from that."

Only two men had witnessed the captain's battle with the mage and one of them was dead. Was there a different version of events than those with which the captain had regaled many a party? "I cannot remove Mrs Armstrong as a suspect," he said. "Indeed, she has the only strong motive of any of the women."

Hannah ran her fingertip along her bottom lip as she thought, an action he found most disconcerting. "Stannard might have had it on his person, which means it has now been immortalised in stone. I will find a moment to ask Pippa if she saw him the night he died. Then at least we will know if Lady St Clair or someone else followed him to the garden."

"That leaves us two women with secrets to unravel. What resulted in Miss Stewart's fall from society, and why did Lady Frances invite Stannard this week?" One by one, they would scrutinise and discard the pasts of each guest.

Wycliff found a certain amount of enjoyment in working with his wife, and the results her gentler approach yielded for his investigation.

WYCLIFF SPENT a pleasant few hours with his wife in

companionable silence in the library. He sat at the ornately carved desk by the window and wrote out his notes on each guest and their possible motives. Hannah explored the books, seeking another hidden treasure about Unnatural creatures.

As the afternoon lengthened, and once the ladies had recovered from the day's exertions, Lady Frances had arranged pistol shooting for the men. Chairs and linen-draped tables were set out for the women under a row of trees by the lake. The women were far enough away from the targets that they were in no danger of a stray shot.

A sheet had been tied around the huge trunk of a spreading oak. Concentric circles in red, white, and blue were painted on it, with numbers inked at each circle. Lady Frances stood by a table covered with a white cloth that revealed only lumps and shapes underneath. Once the men had gathered, she pulled away the tablecloth with a theatrical flourish.

Beneath were pistols, shot, and gunpowder.

"I have a number of single- and double-barrelled flintlocks for your use, gentlemen. You are permitted two shots. The ladies and I shall keep score, and there will be a prize for the man with the greatest number of points. You see there the numbers painted in the circles, the highest in the centre." Lady Frances waved toward the target and then retreated to her chair.

Miss Stewart held a sheet of paper and a pencil clutched in her long fingers.

"Shall we, gentlemen?" The captain rubbed his hands as he surveyed the weapons.

"Oh my, it's not real shot, is it?" Mr Wright-Knowles edged away from the table as he eyed the pistols.

Robins laughed as he reached for a weapon. "Of course it's real shot. What did you think we would use —spun sugar?"

The other man paled. Apparently, just as he preferred toy boats to real ones, he also preferred wooden pistols over their more deadly metal counterparts. Wycliff wondered if that was why his wife sought entertainment in another man's bed—were other things about Wright-Knowles childlike or toy-sized?

"I never was any good with a pistol. More of a sword man, myself. I shall sit this one out, gentlemen." Mowatt stalked over to the ladies and took a seat beside Mrs Wright-Knowles.

Wycliff selected a single shot pistol and took his time loading the powder and shot as he watched the captain and Robins take their shots. The captain had good aim and hit near the centre circle. Robins shot wide and only clipped the edge of the target. Lady Frances called out a number, denoting which ring the shots had hit, and Miss Stewart scribbled on her piece of paper.

Wycliff walked to the yellow ribbon pinned on the grass. The bright strip created a line the men were not allowed to cross. He raised his arm and took aim. The shot rang out and the pistol bucked in his hand. A puff of smoke curled away from the barrel and vanished like a wisp.

"Twenty points for Lord Wycliff!" Lady Frances called. His shot had dug in only two inches from the centre of the target.

The men returned to the table to reload. Robins picked up a flask and poured gunpowder down the muzzle. Next, he loaded the shot into a double flint-lock. "Something needs to be done about Stannard's murder. No one has been brought to account. You seem more intent on enjoying yourself, Lord Wycliff, than on discovering who killed my friend."

Wycliff took the gunpowder flask and measured out the load for his weapon. "Someone will be held accountable, but it takes time to ascertain the guilty party and gather sufficient evidence."

Robins used the ramrod with short, hard actions as he tamped in the ball. "I don't see you doing much investigating or gathering evidence."

"I have spent the last two days questioning people, determining motives, and trying to ascertain who was in the garden with Stannard that night." Wycliff didn't have to answer to this man. The process of finding who had cast the spell or curse would be quicker if everyone were honest and not hiding so many secrets.

Robins barked a laugh. "Have you questioned yourself? Need I remind you, my lord, that you were the one who broke Stannard's nose and called him out? No one else argued with him that night."

"Steady on," the captain said. "Lord Wycliff agreed after that punch that first blood had been drawn and honour satisfied."

Robins waved the pistol and the captain ducked. "What if he were *not* satisfied? I think he did it to defend his mousey wife."

Wycliff stepped closer to Robins and placed a hand on his pistol so that it pointed at the grass. "You will cease your remarks about my wife or I will break *your* nose."

Robins refused to back down. "Your mother-in-law is a powerful mage. You probably had some spell in your pocket that you cast on him. Tell me, Lord Wycliff, have you failed to find the murderer because you have not yet looked in the mirror?"

Wycliff tossed his pistol to the table and drew back his arm. Captain Armstrong grabbed hold of his elbow. "He's mourning a friend. Let him cool off. Mage Tomlin will be here soon, and with his abilities, he may be able to discover more."

Wycliff nodded and wrenched his arm free before stalking off to the refreshment table. Captain Armstrong was right. The mage might discern something in the stone Stannard that Timmy did not yet have the skill to discover. He might even be able to determine the spell used and reverse it. Wycliff poured from the pitcher on the table and drank down the tart lemonade.

Robins stalked to the ribbon, but when he extended his arm, he shook visibly. He took his shot and went wide.

"Oh, bad luck, Mr Robins," Lady Frances said.

"Your turn, Captain Armstrong," Lady St Clair called.

"It is all his doing," Robins shouted and gestured to Wycliff with the pistol. The gunshot made people jump.

But not Wycliff.

He looked down as pain bloomed in his chest. His hand went to his jacket and, pulling it away, he found his fingers covered in blood.

Pippa screamed. "You shot him!"

The ladies leapt to their feet, Hannah the first to rush to his side.

Robins stared at the pistol in his hand. "It was an accident. I didn't know it still had a second shot. You all saw." Robins cast around and Mowatt and Wright-Knowles nodded their heads in agreement.

"Let me see." White as bleached linen, Hannah reached for him.

Wycliff swiped her hands away. "Leave me be! It's not the first time I have been shot. I can deal with it."

He turned on his heel and stalked across the lawn as loud voices drifted after him.

"You must believe me, Lady Wycliff—it was an accident," Robins called.

Wycliff gritted his teeth as fire spread through his right shoulder. He slowed his pace to hear his wife's retort. "You shot my husband, Mr Robins. I need to tend his wound, not pander to your guilt."

Wycliff laughed, only for it to turn into a cough. He pressed the heel of his hand to the wound, to stem the flow of blood. Damned fool had shot him. But was it a deliberate act in retaliation for Stannard, or a genuine accident?

# 17

WYCLIFF STRODE off across the lawn while Hannah struggled to remove Mr Robins's importunate hand from her arm.

"I didn't mean to do it! I've not handled a double flintlock before and didn't know it would go off again. You must believe me, Lady Wycliff—it was an accident." His fingers wrapped around her wrist stopped her from running after her husband.

Honestly, how could some people think only of themselves? Her immediate concern was the injury to her husband, not the circumstances of how it had happened. "You shot my husband, Mr Robins. I need to tend his wound, not pander to your guilt." She wrenched her arm out of his grip, picked up her skirts, and ran.

Wycliff had disappeared inside the house. At least he hadn't keeled over or collapsed on the grass, and appeared well enough to make his exit.

As Hannah entered the house, she scanned tiles and carpets for blood. She found none, so the wound could not be bleeding too much. By the time she burst into their room, Wycliff was seated before the fire, his torn and bloody shirt tossed to the floor, where it made a sad bundle. He peered at the wound and prodded it with his fingertips.

Hannah poured water from the ewer into the basin and picked up a clean cloth before carrying them to the table by the sofa. She didn't know which aspect of the scene before her to comment on first.

Wycliff's torso was carved in ways far superior to any she had seen before—and she had studied a few bare chests. Unlike many other gently bred young women, Hannah had seen a number of human specimens, even naked ones. Although they were usually dead and not in such remarkable physical condition as her husband.

What caught her eye more than the bullet hole in his chest, was the wound at the juncture of his neck and left shoulder. It appeared as though something with a large jaw had tried to take a bite out of him, yet the scar tissue had the distinctive, smooth silver look of a burn.

"We need to remove the ball." Hannah focused her mind on her task.

Wycliff's hand dropped from the wound. "I'd rather not seek out a surgeon. Although I could ride to Doctor Colchester if I could be certain this wouldn't open more on the way."

"You don't have to, if you can tolerate my doing the work," she said.

Surprise was a fleeting thing in his black eyes. Then he smiled. "Yes, thank you."

Amongst Hannah's luggage was a rather unusual item. She fetched a small box that went everywhere with her. Made of a dark wood, the edges were gilt and a complex pattern of interlocking shapes picked out in shell and bronze adorned the top.

She lifted the lid and removed the tray. Within, the box was stuffed with medical supplies. Needles, thread, bandages, and tiny vials that only contained a single mouthful of liquid each. She pulled out a long, narrow case that contained scalpels and tweezers.

Wycliff peered inside. "I thought that was a jewellery case."

Hannah glanced at him and huffed. "I don't require a case for the small quantity of jewellery I possess. A pocket would suffice."

Hannah cut a length of thread, pushed the end through the eye of the needle and then set it aside. Next, she removed the scalpel from its leather sheath. "This will hurt, and I need you to hold still. Do you require alcohol or something stronger to deaden the pain?"

He sat up straight and tightened his jaw. "No. I will not move."

She stood so close to him that their breath mingled. Hannah placed her left hand on his collarbone, just above the wound. She splayed her fingers, ready to pull the sides open. His skin heated her palm. "I need to make the wound larger so I can remove the ball. I could use the tweezers, but I cannot feel my way as well."

"Do what you think best."

She pushed the scalpel against his flesh and sliced. He sucked in a sharp breath. Hannah froze and glanced up.

"Continue," he said through gritted teeth.

"I will be as quick as possible, but I need to make the path larger so I can find the ball." She concentrated on the job and not his reactions. With the wound enlarged, she drew a steadying breath and then inserted her fingers into his flesh. Using thumb and forefinger, she probed the hole until she found the small projectile. Grasping it firmly between her nails, she drew her fingers out.

Wycliff grunted but held still. Hannah dropped the bloody shot into the bowl and picked up the cloth. She worked quickly to clean the wound with the contents of one of the vials, and washed her hands in the water. Satisfied that the wound was clean, she switched to needle and thread.

"I will apologise in advance that I am not my father. He does a stitch so neat that a seamstress would weep with envy, which means he can minimise scarring. I am a poor substitute, but can do as good a job as any country surgeon." Hannah worked with quiet concentration as she ensured each stitch was the exact size as the others and her line neat.

Even as she stitched, she couldn't stop her gaze

from darting to the scar at Wycliff's neck. The silvery tissue had what appeared to be depressions around the edges. Like...teeth marks. In all the books she had read, the only similar wound she could recollect was one given by a lycanthrope during a process they called *the bite*. But this bite seemed to have resulted in a burn. No lycanthrope had a flaming mouth.

"Have you never thought of pursuing the same career as your father?" His question whispered over the skin of her neck and sent a shiver down her spine at the ghostly touch.

Hannah looped the thread and made the next stitch, concentrating on pushing the needle through his skin. "Society struggled to accept a female mage. I think a female doctor would be asking too much. But I have assisted Papa for years and believe myself an entirely adequate nurse." She paused. "Do you believe this was an accident?"

"If it wasn't, he made a far bigger mistake by not killing me." He spoke in short bursts, his breaths timed for when she eased the thread through the punctures.

Hannah was still getting used to being married. The idea of being widowed so soon roused deeper emotions than she expected to find within herself. "I am glad that this is merely a flesh wound. The ball struck neither bone nor organ. But I agree, killing you would seem an overreaction, no matter how strongly he dislikes your investigative process."

Wycliff grunted.

"There, all done." She placed the needle in the

bowl to be cleaned, and picked up the cloth. She dabbed at the last few specks of blood that marred her line of stitches. "It is an awkward spot to bandage, but I have something that will work."

Hannah stepped away from his warmth and dug into her wooden box. She pulled out a rolled bandage and cut a rectangle that would fit over the stitches. The crepe bandage had a cotton layer which she removed, before pressing the cloth against his skin. With a fingertip, she smoothed out the edges.

"That tickles. What is it?" He looked down at the cream shape adhering to his skin.

Hannah pressed gently over the whole with her palm. "My father found that spiderwebs are excellent for stopping wounds from becoming infected, and they have the added benefit of being sticky. Mother makes these adhesive bandages—there are rather large spiders in the garden that she asks to spin their webs over the cloth."

He took her hand and rubbed his thumb over her palm. "I have a most skilled wife."

Hannah stared at her hand, amazed that a small touch from Wycliff could create such a large reaction that rippled over her skin. "Most wives stitch shirts for their husbands. I stitch my husband. Fortunately, my parents thought I should be able to sew both."

She withdrew her hand and gave the bandage one last pat, to ensure the magical web would hold cloth to skin.

"Thank you," he rasped as he stood. With one

hand, he cupped her cheek and turned her face upward to look at him.

His head bent until his lips were a mere inch from hers. Hannah closed her eyes as a heat wave rolled over her and coursed through her bones. She placed her hands flat on his bare chest as his lips touched hers. Wycliff's hand moved from her cheek to her nape, holding her in place as he kissed her with a gentle touch.

A sigh worked its way upward through her body even as she wanted to buckle at the knees. Hannah had never known that kissing could be quite this delicious. She leaned closer until her body pressed against Wycliff's and she tilted her head, seeking more of the marvellous experience.

Then her sigh turned into a squawk as in an instant, the bedroom door burst open and Wycliff thrust her out of the way and behind him.

Hannah caught her breath and peered around Wycliff. A crowd tried to rush through the door at once, but only succeeded in wedging themselves in the opening. Mr Wright-Knowles and Lady Frances were at the forefront, with Mr Mowatt and Pippa peering over their shoulders.

"Get out!" Wycliff barked. He kept one hand at Hannah's side, keeping her behind him.

"Lord Wycliff! How marvellous to see you erect!" Mr Wright-Knowles called as he struggled to break through the doorway.

Lady Frances burst into laughter and Philippa said

from behind her husband, "He means *upright*. We are so relieved to find you *standing*."

"Hannah has tended the wound and any decent man would have knocked before bursting into another man's bedroom." Wycliff's voice was rough and low, almost bordering on a growl.

While staring at her husband's broad, naked back, Hannah observed a strange phenomenon. Heat wafted off his skin, like steam from a hot bath. A ridge appeared along his spine and sprouted what she could only call *phantom fur*. Of an inky black, the ends were tipped in red and swayed like fire. When she touched a furry flame with a finger, it passed through it as though it were made of smoke, and dissipated to reform again.

If her husband had been a dog, she would have said his hackles were well and truly up.

Philippa shouldered past Lady Frances and stood next to her husband. "It's all my fault. Do forgive our terrible intrusion, Lady Wycliff. I was so concerned that Lord Wycliff might be fatally shot and that we would find you sobbing over his lifeless body."

"My husband is in no danger of dying, but thank you for your concern." Hannah couldn't move, Wycliff kept his arm snaked around her, holding her to his back. Whatever would the others think?

Some instinct pulled at Hannah and she laid her hands flat on either side of his spine. She worried she might be burned, but the heat shimmer rolled along her arms. While warm, it wasn't unpleasantly so. Then she rested her cheek against his vertebrae, where the fur was soft and insubstantial and dissolved under her touch.

"Let them go," she whispered against his skin.

The moment she said the words, the heat shimmer dissipated and the ridge sank back into his body.

"I am well. You should be more concerned about Robins. The man is a danger to those around him." Wycliff released Hannah and lowered his hands to his sides.

"I'm sure we can discuss the matter over a drink in the parlour later?" Hannah stepped away from Wycliff and addressed Lady Frances, whose gaze appeared to be fixed on Wycliff's naked torso.

"A drink? Marvellous idea. I'm feeling quite parched and overheated for some reason." Fanny licked her lips.

Hannah gestured toward the door and took Philippa's arm to turn her toward the exit. "I have removed the shot and stitched the wound, so there is nothing for anyone to do. I'm sure Wycliff would appreciate some quiet time to dress and recover." Removing the others from their room was akin to moving along the chickens at home. Hannah flapped her hands and drove them to the open doorway.

One by one, they slipped back into the hall, where they huddled and peered around one another.

"Did you see the scar on his neck?" Philippa said as Hannah closed the door.

"His neck? Who was looking at his neck?" Lady Frances laughed.

Hannah turned the key, in case any of them thought about barging back in for a second look at her half-naked husband.

Wycliff walked to the wardrobe and pulled out a clean shirt. He dropped it over his head and tugged at it to cover the pale scar.

"That is a nasty burn. How did you acquire it?" Hannah laid a hand along the side of her neck to demonstrate its location.

Wycliff tucked the shirt into his trousers and retrieved his waistcoat. "A burning timber struck me. I don't remember the details. So many things during the war are locked away in my mind. I could do with a drink, if you feel like braving company."

"Of course. I need a moment to tidy away my supplies first." Hannah emptied the bowl out the window and packed away her medical supplies.

Ideas swirled in her mind as she fitted together snippets of information about her husband. *A burning timber?* She doubted that. Not unless the timber had jaws and teeth.

# 18

Wycliff finished dressing as Hannah cleaned the scalpel and needle and packed them away in the wooden box. A number of emotions swirled within his head creating a maelstrom, and he wasn't sure which one to battle first.

Anger at the fool Robins, who had shot him, whether accidentally or not.

Gratitude toward his wife, who had so ably removed the ball and stitched him up.

Fascination, as another facet of the woman who now shared his life was revealed.

Hunger to repeat the kiss that had been so rudely interrupted.

Then a tinge of shame washed over all the roiling emotion—had Hannah glimpsed his secret? The beast had surged to the surface to protect her. But astonishingly, her hands on his spine had soothed it back under control.

"Let us hope I don't require my supplies again," she announced, and broke through the storm in his mind.

She had changed her bloodstained afternoon dress while he was struggling with his revelations. He held out his arm and they walked through the quiet house to the drawing room. Within, he was greeted by a rousing cry of *Huzzah!* from the other guests, as though he had performed an act of merit. At least...most of the guests were pleased to see him ambulatory. Robins stared at his drink and appeared sullen.

Lady Frances rushed over and pressed her hand to his arm. "We are so pleased to see there is no permanent harm from this afternoon's misadventure."

"I will recover. Thank you for your concern." Wycliff bowed and turned so that her hand fell away.

"You must have thought you had left the days of being shot at behind you," the captain joked.

"It is unfortunate when one is shot by one's own side," he murmured. *Traitors*, they called such men, or *cowards*. He narrowed his gaze at Robins. Was the man so dim he didn't realise a double flintlock had two shots? Wycliff had watched the man load the pistol and tamp down both barrels. The more he thought on it, the more he believed that Robins had acted deliberately. The only question was, how ought he to respond?

The earl appeared in the parlour and made directly for Wycliff. "Wycliff, I hear Robins put a hole in you."

Wycliff touched a fingertip to his collarbone. "Yes. I am fortunate to have a skilled wife, who took care of the wound and patched me up."

The earl's eyebrows shot up and when he grinned, his eyes disappeared into deep creases in his face. "I would expect the daughter of Lady Miles to be resourceful. Do you have a moment? I am willing to hear your business proposal now."

"That would be most convenient." He turned to Hannah and nodded to her, before leaving with the earl.

He followed the goblin across the grand foyer and around behind the curved stairwell. Lord Pennicott pressed on an area of wainscoting and a hidden door swung open. Wycliff had expected to be ushered into a lush and opulent study befitting the wealthy creature. Instead, he found himself in a room that could have been a wine cellar.

"An interesting choice of room for a study," he murmured as he surveyed it.

"I appreciate my privacy." Lord Pennicott pushed the door closed.

The room had no windows and the door closed behind Wycliff with a solid thud that hinted at steel behind the wood. Ensorcelled lamps hung from the ceiling and burst into life to emit a soft yellow glow. A desk sat opposite the door, its green leather blotter clear of any papers.

One wall was covered in small wooden drawers, each approximately eight inches square and each with a gleaming brass keyhole in the centre. The other wall held a bookcase crammed with ledgers. Two plain brown leather wing chairs were placed before the bookcase. It was the sort of room where a man might hide any number of secrets. Probably in the locked drawers.

Lord Pennicott gestured to the chairs and took the one closest to the desk. "Your father inherited a sum adequate enough to maintain your family estate." He leaned back in the chair and tented his fingers in front of his nose. His beady and knowing eyes seemed ready to dissect Wycliff's finances.

Wycliff settled in the warm leather and rested his arm on the curved side. "Yes. Had he shown any form of restraint or care for the title, I would not be in my current predicament. Instead, Father indulged his own selfish habits and desires, and frittered the money away."

"You inherited nothing but debt." The earl's features gave nothing away. Was he raking over past events to humiliate Wycliff, or to take his measure?

Wycliff clenched his fist. Anger surged through him at how his father had thought only of himself and never spared a moment to consider his wife, son, or the community that depended on them. He let his hand relax. What was done, was done. He had the chance before him to make reparations. "I have spent the last five years selling what I can afford to lose and using every penny that comes my way to pay off his creditors. I have a good man running the farm and we return a small profit. I want to grow that, so I can repair the house and rebuild our undertakings."

The earl tapped his fingertips together. His fingernails were long, yellow, and thick, tapering to sharp points. "And your proposal?"

"I require a modest sum for breeding stock. There is a new breed of sheep called the Merino that I wish to breed for its much finer fleece. I have done some calculations and believe I can repay you, with interest, within five years." Wycliff drew a creased and battered sheet of paper from his pocket. He had spent weeks agonising over the sums and kept the page on him constantly, in case such an opportunity as this presented itself.

He handed the sheet to Lord Pennicott and waited. It was like handing in an examination sheet to one's tutor and trying to stand still while it was marked. Would he pass or fail?

Mutterings came from behind the paper and occasionally a finger tapped a number. Then it dropped and a steady glare fixed him to the spot. "This *is* a modest amount. Did you not approach your mother-in-law about funding your enterprise?"

Wycliff clenched his jaw. "There are already those who mutter under their breaths that the mage compelled me to marry Hannah, which is utterly false. I'll not add fuel to that particular fire by seeking money from Lady Miles and have them say that I was not only ensorcelled, but paid. I will recover my estate through my own efforts." *So that I can support my family*, a low whisper rang through the back of his mind.

The earl folded up the page and handed it back. A

rare smile pulled his lips into a thin line. "I appreciate a man who is not afraid to get his hands dirty through honest labour. I will advance the money to you, at my usual interest rate."

He rose and went to the wall of drawers, pausing before one on the left-hand side. The earl extended the index finger on his left hand. The nail twisted and elongated as it neared the drawer. The goblin inserted his nail into the lock and turned. Then he extracted two pieces of paper, one a large sheet covered in writing, the other smaller and more rectangular. With one hand he pushed the drawer closed as he turned to the desk.

Once seated, the goblin plucked a silver nib quill from its holder and dipped it into the ink. The sound of nib scratching paper filled the small room. Then the quill was returned to the holder and the page held out to Wycliff. "These are my standard terms and conditions. I have specified the repayments to be made and the loan will, of course, be secured by your estate. If you agree, then you have only to sign and I will give you a note that you can take to your banker."

Wycliff walked back to the armchair and sat while he read the neat script. The repayments were achievable, barely. He would need every penny from future livestock sales of cattle and fleece to make them. But each year would give him a little more breathing room as the herds grew. "I am surprised, and relieved, at how quickly you agreed to my proposal, sir."

The earl laced his fingers over the rectangle of paper as though he shielded it from view. "From my association with Lady Miles, I have come to believe she would not allow a fool to marry her daughter. You would have been disposed of—either quietly, or dramatically—if she wanted to send a warning to like-minded suitors. That and my own enquiries satisfy me that you are a man of your word who will honour our agreement. And as you said, it is a modest sum."

It was a modest sum to a man with vast coffers. It was a life-changing amount to a man with none. "I agree to your terms."

"If you sign the agreement, I shall draft the bank note." Lord Pennicott gestured to a second quill standing at attention in the holder.

Wycliff took up the quill and signed his name to the paper. As he did so, he vowed to see the money repaid and his estate brought back to life. Unbidden, an image came to his mind of Hannah standing on the front lawn, looking out over the rolling hills toward the sea, watching for his return at the end of the day.

"If I might enquire, sir—why did Lady Frances invite Stannard and his friends this week? I have the impression theirs is not the sort of company you prefer."

The earl looked up, rolled his eyes, and sighed. "That man and his ilk are a waste of flesh and blood. It certainly wasn't my idea to have them underfoot. Stannard, Mowatt, and Robins were much around Granger's Finishing School when Frances attended and she was quite taken with them. Stannard attempted to court her once, but I quashed any romantic notions before they could develop. It's one thing for her to be entertained by the fellow, quite another to expect me to leave my fortune to a wastrel. We all know how that turns out."

Wycliff huffed a laugh. Had he lived, Stannard faced being cut off by his own father due to his extravagant and scandalous lifestyle. The marquess would be inundated with creditors' demands now that his son had died.

The earl took the agreement and added his own signature. "My daughter did not have an easy upbringing. Due to our heritage, there were those who treated her badly. Some think her cruel, but Frances protects herself from their barbs by firing first. I know her life here is not what she would prefer, but I try to protect her from the worst of society. Ironic, I know, that we invited it here instead."

Wycliff wondered how far Lady Frances's fascination with Stannard went. Would she have conducted an affair with the man under her father's nose, and while her marriage contract to another was finalised? "Whatever her motive for inviting Lady Wycliff and I, I am grateful that it gave me the opportunity to have this conversation with you."

"One other thing, Wycliff. Mage Tomlin will be here in the morning to collect Stannard and return him to his father. He may yet provide a critical insight to aid your investigation." The earl rose from the desk and handed the bank note to Wycliff.

"Let us see what developments the morning

brings." He took the paper and tucked it into his jacket pocket before bowing his gratitude. At long last, the tide of his fortune was on the turn.

After Wycliff's departure, Hannah cast about the drawing room. Lady Frances, Lady St Clair, Mr Robins, and Mr Mowatt sat at the green felt table to play cards. Mrs Wright-Knowles wandered to the window and gazed out over the garden. Hannah took the opportunity to approach.

She stood next to the other woman. Outside, the shadows fell over the garden and turned the hedges into a barrier encircling the house. Soon the night predators would emerge to stalk their prey. But were they all outside, or were some prowling within? The thought made a chill wash over her and Hannah rubbed at her arms.

"I have a rather delicate question to put to you, while the others cannot hear," Hannah murmured as they stood side by side.

Philippa turned her head and a smile glistened in her eyes. "Oh? I am intrigued."

Hannah dropped her attention to the curtain tie, unable to meet Philippa's warm gaze. "I am aware that the night Lord Stannard was killed, you were not in your bedchamber. By chance, did you see anyone in the hall that night? We are trying to determine whether anyone followed him out to the garden."

Silence fell between them and Hannah dared a glance sideways. The other woman clutched her evening shawl, her fingers working at the silk. "You must think me a terrible person, but in truth, my heart has always belonged to Mowatt. I betray him when I must consort with Mr Wright-Knowles."

The confession only deepened Hannah's desire to know why Philippa's father had refused Mr Mowatt as a suitor. "It is not my place to cast judgement. My husband has determined that a woman saw Lord Stannard in the early hours. We seek only to identify her, to learn what she saw."

Philippa turned her back to the garden to survey the guests. Her attention lingered over Mr Mowatt before going to her oblivious husband. "I saw no one. I was most careful of that."

"Thank you." Hannah took Philippa's hand. One by one, women were removed from their short list. Assuming everyone had been truthful, Hannah was left with Lady Frances and Miss Stewart.

Philippa squeezed Hannah's fingers and when she looked up, she found the other woman's eyes shining with unshed tears. "Beneath it all, he is a good man who was led astray and did some terrible things. He paid the price for his actions when my father refused his offer for my hand. Mowatt has tried to rebuild his reputation outside of Stannard's influence, but he had a way of pulling him back in."

*Curiosity satisfied.* Perhaps now, with Stannard dead, Mr Mowatt could rebuild his reputation. Too late, however, to win the woman he loved. How tragic.

"Why don't you play for us, Mrs Wright-Knowles? You have a lovely singing voice," Lady Frances called.

The women drifted to the pianoforte and Hannah turned the pages of the music as Philippa performed a plaintive air that matched her mood.

Wycliff rejoined the party as dinner was announced. He took Hannah's hand and drew her close. "I have been successful. The earl will fund my business venture. If there wasn't a murder to solve, we could have slipped out the window with our bags after dinner."

"That is marvellous news." At least there was one bright point to the week. Even more satisfying was that he had told her immediately. Such a small act blew on the spark inside her.

Throughout dinner, Mr Robins avoided any eye contact with Wycliff and, as though by some prior mutual agreement, no one at the table mentioned the shooting incident.

Hannah barely joined in the conversation, instead studying the other guests. She could imagine Philippa's pain at not being allowed to marry the man she loved. Mr Wright-Knowles seemed a genial enough chap, but rather blind to his wife's unhappiness. Despite his obsession with boats, didn't he also deserve to be loved? Hannah would never reveal what she knew, yet she wondered that in continuing their affair, Philippa was making not two, but three people unhappy.

Lady St Clair hung on the captain's words—and his arm—whenever she had the opportunity. Mrs Armstrong sighed beside Hannah, her pain palpable. Which situation was worse—to be oblivious to your spouse's infidelity or to be in the audience while it was played out over dinner?

"How are you feeling, Mrs Armstrong?" Hannah whispered. She worried the woman might have hit her head when she'd fallen from the horse.

"A little sore, but none the worse for the experience. I wish I could say the same for my battered heart." She poked at her fish with her fork, pulling flesh from the tiny bones.

Hannah re-evaluated her previous question. It was far worse to watch your spouse flirt with someone else. She only hoped for Mrs Armstrong's sake it was merely a brief flirtation. For some men, a beautiful woman's company was akin to a piece of steak dangling in front of a hungry dog, and they completely forgot their manners and good sense. "I'm sure your husband is merely flattered by the attention. He will recover his senses when you return home."

That elicited a brief smile. "Let us hope so."

After dinner, instead of the men and women retiring to separate rooms, they all returned to the drawing room. The laughter seemed louder and grated against Hannah's ears. The smoke from the cigars tickled her nose. She brushed a hand across her brow and wondered about pleading a headache so that she might retire early.

Wycliff approached and leaned close. "I am going to leave. My tolerance for civility has worn off and I'm fighting the urge to knock Robins's teeth down his throat."

Hannah took her husband at his word. "It will give me a chance to check your dressing and ensure you're not bleeding."

They made their good-nights and returned to their room. Hannah was relieved to see the bandage still adhered to Wycliff's skin and there was no sign of blood or infection. She also stole another look at the old burn, supposedly made by a burning timber. A supposition that made her snort.

She disrobed, climbed into bed, and picked up her book. Wycliff paced in front of the fire and ran a hand through his hair. He appeared unable to settle.

"I have no objection if you wish to stretch out on the bed. Above the blankets, of course," she murmured as she opened the volume.

Hannah kept her eyes on the page detailing the lush Fae court as Wycliff stalked toward her. He snatched the blanket from the foot of the bed and paused at the bedside.

Hannah turned another page and refused to show the nervous tremble that shook her dinner inside her.

Wycliff added an extra pillow and then took his assigned place. He reminded her of Sheba, the puppy. The little spaniel turned around a number of times before she could settle. Wycliff played with the pillows at his back and then seemed to spend a large amount of time spreading the blanket and tucking it in under his feet. At last, he let out a sigh and took up his book.

Marriage might not be so terrible after all, if it involved reading in companionable silence. Though the part of her that trembled could not help but long for a good-night kiss.

# 19

THE KNOCK at the door awoke Hannah. She rubbed her eyes to find the faintest trace of dawn light creeping into their room. Wycliff was already alert, and glanced at her before he flung off the blanket and padded to the door in his bare feet.

"So sorry, milord, but the earl said to fetch you." The voice of a footman came from behind the door. "There has been another one."

Those words galvanised Hannah into action. She hurried out of bed and snatched up her robe, pulling the tie tight. She passed Wycliff as he threw on his deep blue velvet robe and they set off after the footman.

Up the grand staircase they went, to the second floor, where the family and other guests resided. They trod the hall with light feet, as though no one wanted to break the silence with a heavy tread.

The Earl of Pennicott stood by a partially open door with Godrich the butler next to him. Farther down the hall, a small cluster of maids gathered, one clutching her feather duster as though it were a sword or magic wand and she would defend the others.

"Ah, Wycliff. One of the staff discovered him this morning." Lord Pennicott gestured to the door that stood ajar, stone fingers still curled around the timber. A face peeked through the gap between door and frame, a permanent expression of surprise carved in stone.

Mr Robins. The Devil's Triplets were now down to one.

"From the look on his face, he didn't expect his visitor." Wycliff crouched and peered through the gap.

"It could also have been an arranged meeting, but when he opened the door it wasn't the person he expected." Hannah wondered how many secret assignations were taking place under the earl's roof. With so many people creeping along the halls at night, how were they not bumping into one another?

"How long has he been like this?" Wycliff asked.

The earl shrugged. "No one knows. With the door only cracked open, no one noticed until dawn, when the light coming through the windows illuminated the situation. The maid found him."

A grandfather clock on the landing chimed seven times. Hannah did a rough calculation in her head, from what they had learned about Stannard's demise. It had taken six hours for his heart to turn to solid rock.

"If this happened before one o'clock this morning, we are already too late to help Mr Robins, even if we could reverse the effect." Hannah kept her tone low, for what if stone ears could still hear? How terrible to know your life was ebbing away while those around you were unable to save you.

Wycliff made a grunting noise that Hannah took as agreement. "I'll fetch Timmy anyway. Better to be sure. The bigger concern is the murderer among your guests, Lord Pennicott."

The earl arched one eyebrow and peered up at Wycliff. "So it would appear. Although some will point out that you had a disagreement with both victims only hours before they were turned to stone."

Wycliff ground his teeth. "I am no murderer."

"And which of our guests does not also make that claim?" Lord Pennicott said. "Yet someone must be."

Hannah laid a hand on Wycliff's arm. "We need to fetch Timmy and ascertain how long Mr Robins has been like this. Then we must question the guests and staff again. Someone is hiding the truth, and time is of the essence."

"Where is the maid who found him?" Wycliff asked.

"'Twas I, milord." A young woman stepped away from the small group of staff. She wore a dark grey gown and a white apron, with a cap on her hair. She bobbed a curtsey.

Wycliff folded his arms over his chest. "What were you doing up here?"

The maid glanced behind her before answering. "My morning rounds, milord. I look for anything left outside doors to return to the kitchen. Miss Stewart always has a tray and I collect that. I saw the door here partway open and thought the guest was going to ask for something. When I got closer, I saw he was stone like the other lord."

"Does Miss Stewart always leave a tray out?" Hannah asked, wondering if the maid had seen anything the night of Stannard's murder.

The maid turned to her with wide eyes. "Oh yes, your ladyship. A cup of tea and three soft-boiled eggs every night. She leaves the tray out because she doesn't like the smell of the eggshells."

*Three boiled eggs before bed? How odd.* "Has she always had such a tray at night?"

"Yes, milady. Ever since she came here as Lady Frances's companion." She bobbed again.

Hannah tucked the information away in her mind, where it wriggled and scratched, as though she wiped her brain with a stinging nettle. What *was* it about Miss Stewart's request for eggs?

"Thank you, you have been most helpful," she said to the maid, who jiggled from foot to foot as though she was prepared to bolt down the stairs.

"Mage Tomlin will be here today. Perhaps he will shed some light on these deaths." Lord Pennicott waved to the statue. "Godrich, why don't you have a horse saddled for Wycliff so he can fetch the boy?"

"Of course, my lord." The butler bowed and disappeared on silent feet.

"I shall leave you to your investigation. Keep me

abreast of what you find." Lord Pennicott also took his leave, waving the staff back to work on his way past. They scattered like flustered chickens.

"We have much to do and should get dressed, Hannah. Robins won't be going anywhere." Wycliff leaned on the wall as Hannah contemplated the situation.

"In a moment." She gauged the available space around the doorway. "Someone slender could squeeze under his arm and through the door, but I'm not sure they would then be strong enough to move him back to admit anyone else."

From what she could see, Robins had undressed for the evening. He wore a robe with a plaid pattern and tassels on the ends of the tie. The neck of the robe showed his linen nightshirt underneath. His hair was tousled. Had he been awakened by a knock at the door, or caught before he went to bed? Until they could get past him, they wouldn't be able to tell.

The small gap between door and frame also made her question whether a potion had been used. It couldn't have been thrown through the gap, or if it had been, only a small portion of his face and shoulder would have been splattered—and surely there would be residue on the door shielding the rest of him? She needed to discuss this with her mother. It might be a charm that froze the victim once they looked upon it.

She cast her gaze downward and paused. "There's something by his foot."

Hannah knelt and inspected the man's bare stone

feet. She had seen a similarly shaped object before, clutched in Stannard's frozen hand. "Small and round, like an egg or billiard ball."

"Such as Stannard is holding?" Wycliff offered his hand to help her rise. Then he took her place and wedged his head in the opening. "I think you are right." He sat back on his heels and rubbed the back of his neck. "It cannot be a coincidence, but is it a clue?"

"Or a message from the murderer? We should see if the billiards room is missing any balls." Ideas whirled in Hannah's mind. First, she needed to contact her mother. Then an unpleasant thought ran through her mind.

Mage Tomlin. *Please don't let him arrive until we have finished here.*

"Clothes, Hannah." Wycliff coughed into his hand.

She had quite forgotten she wore only a robe and had bare feet. It would be more appropriate to be attired before running around the house chasing the ideas in her head. "Yes, clothes."

As Wycliff led her along the hallway, she glanced backward at frozen Mr Robins. What was going on under this roof?

Hannah considered her clothing options while Wycliff hurriedly dressed and dashed off to ride to Doctor Colchester's. Once alone, she put on her most practical dress and laced boots on her feet rather than indoor shoes. If she had to walk outside in the pursuit of clues she didn't want to muddy the pretty silk slippers.

The clock chimed eight o'clock as Hannah exited the bedroom and rubbed the ring on her finger. Time to summon her mother and apprise her of events. She went through the double doors in the parlour and strode out on the grass, where she turned a slow circle looking for her mother's proxy.

"You are early today, Hannah. What has happened?" Her mother's voice came from the chaffinch that alighted on Hannah's outstretched hand.

Hannah lifted the bird closer to her face. "Mr Robins was turned to stone last night."

"Oh, dear," the bird chirped. "In circumstances similar to those of Lord Stannard?"

"Not exactly. Stannard was out in the garden. Mr Robins is peering around his bedroom door. Whatever turned him immobile took effect through the few inches the door is open." Hannah walked with the bird over to a bench set under a nearby tree.

"Not a potion that is thrown, then. Otherwise, the door would have afforded some protection. We are looking at some sort of charm that works when looked upon." The bird scratched its head with a claw and ruffled its feathers.

"I shall leave it in your hands to continue searching for the answer to that riddle. One other thing, Mother. Mage Tomlin is due today to collect the statue of Lord Stannard and return him to the marquess his father." Hannah dropped her voice and glanced around.

The bird fell silent and its beak tilted down. After a prolonged silence it raised its head and hopped closer to Hannah. "Be careful of him, Hannah. The animosity between us is no secret and he is vocal in his condemnation of the Afflicted."

A chill took up residence in Hannah's bones. The mage led the magical council and directly advised the Regent. While not as powerful as her mother, Mage Tomlin had a long reach. "I will watch what I say, Mother. Now I must go—I spy Wycliff and Timmy. I shall report back this evening."

Hannah returned to the house and met Wycliff and Timmy in the foyer. The house began to stir around them and staff glided back and forth to tend to the guests upstairs. Muttered conversations and the occasional cough came from behind closed doors.

They stopped at Mr Robins's partly open door. "Can you squeeze through, lad?" Wycliff asked.

Timmy eyed the gap. "I think so, milord." He slipped through the gap like an eel evading a net and disappeared into the room.

"What do you see, Timmy? Is his bed undisturbed?" Hannah called.

"It's been slept in, milady. The blankets are thrown back," Timmy answered.

That changed their timeline. Mr Robins must have been awakened sometime after he went to bed.

"Can you do as you did with Lord Stannard, please, Timmy? Let us know what your gift can tell us. And take your time," Hannah said through the gap.

Wycliff paced up and down, his steps keeping time with the tick of the grandfather clock.

After several silent minutes, a quiet voice came from the other side. "He's gone, milady."

Wycliff pulled out his pocket watch, glanced at the face, and then shoved it back into his waistcoat. "It is close to nine o'clock. We know Stannard's heart took some six hours to surrender to the spell, so our murderer struck before three this morning. The staff said Robins retired after midnight, leaving us a window of opportunity of less than three hours. More likely two hours, since Robins was disturbed from his slumber." Wycliff rubbed his chin. "We must move him back so we can enter the room."

"Timmy and I might be able to work together to slide him back enough to admit you," Hannah suggested.

"If you wouldn't mind trying. Or we can find a slender footman." Wycliff gestured to the door with an open expression on his face.

"Since I am already here, let me try first."

Hannah sucked in a breath and wedged herself into the gap under Mr Robins's arm. For a horrible moment, she thought she might be trapped by the heavy statue on the other side. Then she brushed aside the panic and wiggled. Inch by inch, her body eased through into the bedroom.

Timmy smiled at her as she made her way past the barricade. Hannah cast a quick glance around the room. The bed still bore the impression where Robins had rested before throwing off the blankets to answer the fatal knock at his door.

Unfortunately, there was no rug under Mr Robins's feet, or they could have pulled that along the polished floors. "Come, Timmy, let's have a go. You take the other side. Don't try to lift him. He will be far too heavy for us. We wish merely to shuffle him back."

They took a side each, clutching Robins around the middle, and they pulled and strained. An adult male was heavy enough. One made of solid stone was significantly heavier again. They were both red in the face and puffing by the time they had dragged the man back a mere inch. With his fingers wrapped in a death grip around the door, he opened the door further as he was scraped backward.

"Another inch, Hannah, and I shall be able to make it through," Wycliff's voice came from the hall.

Timmy rolled his eyes and Hannah heaved a sigh. He might as well have asked for a mile. An inch alone seemed a vast distance.

"We can do it," Hannah said, to convince herself and the lad.

Once more they grabbed Mr Robins's limbs and hauled on him. A scraping noise came as they dragged the statue another inch or so. The oak planks would no doubt have to be replaced after this.

"That's enough!" Wycliff called, and soon he had pushed himself into the bedroom. "Let's move him away from the door to make it easier to come and go."

Timmy emitted a low sigh, but then applied his slight shoulder to the object. With three of them and Wycliff's additional strength, they soon had Robins standing to one side. The bigger difficulty was his hand curled around the door; even in death he refused to let go.

"Good, you managed to move him," Lord Pennicott said as he appeared in the more open doorway.

Hannah looked around and swallowed the words she was about to say. Lord Pennicott was not alone. Beside him stood a tall figure wrapped in a deep purple cloak with gold runes embroidered around the hem. A grey beard formed a sharp, eight-inch-long point, as though the wearer stroked it constantly. A balding head was covered by a velvet cap that matched the cloak, a gold tassel dangling from the tip. Cunning eyes peered out from a lean face.

Mage Tomlin dressed like a storybook magician to ensure that everyone knew who he was.

"Your Grace," Hannah murmured, and bobbed a curtsey. Her heart hammered in her chest. The man created a magical wave around him that stung her skin like nettles. She wanted to protect herself, their investigation, and Timmy from the magic wielder's cruel gaze.

The earl gestured to the man at his side. "Mage Tomlin arrived early and will investigate the means used to kill Stannard and Robins."

"He is welcome to offer his expertise, but this enquiry falls under the authority of the Ministry of Unnaturals." Wycliff moved to Hannah's side and folded his arms.

Hannah edged closer to her husband. His presence

shielded her from the invisible nettles the mage seemed to be launching at her.

Tomlin narrowed his gaze and peered around Wycliff. "As Britain's most powerful mage, I'm sure I can clear this up in no time."

Hannah bristled and bit back a snort. Her mother was Britain's most powerful mage—death had not stripped her of that accolade. But then, Tomlin was one of those men who refused to see the skills and merits of talented women. Or their offspring. She glanced at Timmy. The lad had gone pale and hid behind the statue and the open door. Did he know Lord Tomlin was his grandfather, or did he instinctively want to avoid the notice of a man with a rank the equivalent of a duke?

"My mother is seeking the answer to what brought these deaths about," Hannah said.

Mage Tomlin laughed and waved a dismissive hand. "This is no business for sticky-nosed matrons with nothing better to do."

She didn't realise she had taken a step toward the insufferable man until Wycliff shot out his arm to act as a barrier, keeping her in place.

"My wife is the daughter of Lady Seraphina Miles," Wycliff said.

The mage's nostrils flared and he bared his teeth. "I should have known. She emits the foul stench of her mother's dark arts."

Lord Pennicott stepped forward, perhaps sensing Hannah was about to start an incident by scratching out the mage's eyes. "Any news, Wycliff? Does Robins's heart still beat or are we too late?"

Wycliff turned to their host. "We are too late. I calculate that the killer knocked on his door sometime between one and three this morning."

At that moment, Timmy shuffled from foot to foot. Like some lumbering rhinoceros whose vision is based on movement, Mage Tomlin swung his head and glared at the lad. "What is a stable boy doing here?"

Hannah moved to stand in front of Timmy. "Timmy is a very talented aftermage. He has used his gift to determine how this effect was wrought, and was able to detect a faint heartbeat in Lord Stannard that unfortunately failed. He just now was able to confirm that Mr Robins has passed and cannot be saved."

"Aftermage, is he?" Tomlin sneered as though Hannah had told him the boy was a form of slug.

"He's third generation, and Sir Hugh Miles anticipates a bright future for him." Wycliff glared and engaged Tomlin in a staring competition.

"Third generation?" The mage's eyes widened as he looked anew at Timmy.

Hannah didn't wait to see if he would figure it out. While it was petty of her, a need surged inside her to ensure the mage knew that he was depriving himself of a relationship with a wonderful and talented child. "We found Timmy working as a stable boy. It is most unfortunate that his grandfather chose to cast off his mother, but he has a loving home now with us. My parents will nurture his talents to their full extent."

Lord Tomlin rocked back on his heels and his jaw hardened. Then he stared at Hannah with a look of pure vitriol. "Unwanted pups, regardless of their pedigree, should be drowned at birth rather than disgracing noble families."

"*Noble* should be a verb, not a noun." Wycliff stalked closer to the mage. "Too many peers think themselves better than others when by their actions, they show they are the worst among us."

"Shall we begin with Stannard, Your Grace?" Lord Pennicott interjected.

"Yes. I cannot work where the air is fouled." Tomlin spun on his heel, causing his cloak to swirl out around him as he departed.

"Good riddance," Hannah muttered under her breath.

Wycliff barked in laughter. The wide smile breaking over his face stole her breath.

# 20

When Hannah wrapped an arm around Timmy and hugged him, the youngster glanced up at her with a tremble to his lips. "That was him, wasn't it? My ma's father."

"Yes, but he is of no consequence to you now. You are part of *our* family and we are not giving you up." Then she ruffled his hair.

A glint crept into his eyes. "I prefer my new family. Bet he doesn't have a Barnes to play with."

Hannah laughed. "No, he doesn't look the sort to tolerate a disembodied hand running around his hallowed halls. Now, let's see what we can find here."

They searched Mr Robins's room, but found nothing of interest. The man's clothing was scattered on every surface and even dumped on the floor, as though no one had ever taught him the purpose of a drawer or a peg. On the night table was a small, worn book that Hannah thought was poetry with accompanying pictures, until she looked more closely at the drawings. While the people on the pages were naked, it was most certainly not an anatomical text. She held the book at arm's length and waved it at Wycliff. "Perhaps you should dispose of this, so it doesn't fall into the wrong hands?"

He raised one dark brow and took the volume. He opened it at a random page and both eyebrows shot up. Then he slammed it shut. "I cannot bring myself to throw a book on the fire, even one such as this. Instead I shall find a dark and dusty corner of the earl's library in which to hide it."

*I cannot bring myself to throw a book on the fire.* Hannah held in a sigh. The more she learned of her husband, the more her heart softened toward him.

"From the sounds coming from the rooms around us, the rest of the guests are stirring. Shall we head downstairs to begin our questioning of staff and guests?" Hannah turned to the statue. He would be awkward to move down the stairs. Perhaps Mage Tomlin could make himself useful and use his magical abilities to levitate the stone man down to the foyer.

"There is nothing more we can do here. There are no notes to indicate an assignation last night, nor anything that hints at someone with murderous intent."

When they emerged from the bedroom, they found Lady Frances, flanked by Captain Armstrong and Mr Mowatt.

"Is it true—Robins is dead?" Fanny demanded.

"Yes. Murdered in the same fashion as Stannard,"

Wycliff answered. He stood in the open doorway, obscuring their view of the statue still clinging to the door.

"By Jove, what is going on here?" Captain Armstrong said.

Mr Mowatt paled and shook his head, but remained silent.

"Might I suggest you finish dressing, Lady Frances? Then we can discuss this downstairs." Hannah stood next to her husband, Timmy behind them. It didn't seem appropriate to discuss the most recent murder while they were attired only in their robes.

Lady Frances narrowed her eyes. "Yes, very well. We shall reconvene in the morning room. Come along, gentlemen."

Captain Armstrong walked next to Lady Frances as they headed along the hall. Mr Mowatt paused with the look of a man with something to say.

"Do you know something, Mowatt?" Wycliff asked.

Mr Mowatt glanced up and down the hall and then shook his head. "No." With the one syllable, he returned to his room.

"Shall I go back to the doctor's house?" Timmy asked as they descended the stairs.

Before Hannah could answer, the earl appeared at the bottom of the steps and waited for them.

"We have little to report, Lord Pennicott. There was nothing in Mr Robins's room to suggest he was expecting anyone this morning." Hannah reached the bottom and stepped onto the tiles.

The earl laced his fingers together in front of his stomach. "That is disappointing, but I have a slightly different matter to discuss, Lady Wycliff. I must ask that you remove yourselves from under this roof."

Beside Hannah, Wycliff tensed. "We have an investigation to conduct."

The earl smiled and the tips of his pointy ears vibrated. "I appreciate that, and I will not deny you access to those you need to question. Mage Tomlin will not undertake his return journey for a day or two. In the meantime, he wishes to examine the scene himself and he says Lady Wycliff is a distraction. Something to do with a residue of Lady Miles's magic detectable upon her."

Hannah bit her tongue. Had Mage Tomlin detected her mother's spell to freeze the curse within her? Blast. He was the last person in the world she wanted to know *that* secret.

Wycliff folded his arms and huffed. "Rubbish. More likely he feels threatened by our heading the investigation. He knows he cannot wrest it from the hands of the Ministry of Unnaturals despite all his bluster."

The earl cocked his head as though he listened to the guests above their heads. "That aside, there are also guests who do not wish you under this roof, particularly in the early hours of the morning."

"You think *I* did this?" Wycliff stepped forward and this time it was Hannah who had to restrain her spouse.

"We will have Timmy and Old Jim bring round our carriage. That will give us time both to pack and to ask our questions of the guests. Will that satisfy yourself and Mage Tomlin?" Hannah glanced from Wycliff to the earl.

Lord Pennicott bowed to her. "Yes. Thank you for your understanding, Lady Wycliff."

"I'll help Old Jim harness the horses," Timmy said once the earl had walked away.

"Good lad." Wycliff patted the boy's head in an easy manner, but he still had a tight set to his jaw.

Timmy shot off, leaving Hannah and Wycliff alone.

"I will talk to the staff, if you will approach the women," Wycliff said.

Hannah glanced up. "Of course. Here they come now."

Chatter carried along the halls as the guests made their way downstairs. Wycliff took his leave and strode off toward the servants' stairs. Hannah walked through to the morning room and composed herself. No doubt she would be inundated with questions, but she needed to ask her own. She would need to be more forthright this time. Since they had been pressed to leave, she couldn't wait for an opportunity to find each alone. Instead, she would draw each woman to one side.

Lady Frances entered first, her eyes narrowed and a scowl between her brows as she walked to the large picture window.

Miss Stewart leaned on the arm of Mrs Armstrong while the two women sat on a sofa before the fire. Miss

Stewart looked grey and wan. Her breaths came in shallow gasps. The woman appeared decidedly fragile this morning. Her hair was caught up in a cream turban that only emphasised the sickly cast to her complexion.

"Are you quite all right?" Hannah asked as she approached.

"A spring cold has me in its grips, I'm afraid." She tried to smile, but her lips only twitched before she leaned back on the arm of the sofa clutching a handkerchief to her chest.

"When you placed your tray outside your door last night, did you see anyone in the hall?"

Miss Stewart clutched the locket around her neck. "No, it was as quiet as a church, without so much as a mouse running to its hole."

"What of you, Mrs Armstrong? Did you leave your room last night?" Hannah wondered if she might have confronted Mr Robins about her missing letter. It was possible he might have known where Stannard had concealed it.

Her eyes were wide behind her spectacles. "Oh, no. I didn't budge all night, despite the captain's snoring."

Next Hannah took Mrs Wright-Knowles by the arm and led her to a corner.

"Were you in your own chamber last night?" Hannah whispered.

Pippa shook her head. "But I swear I saw nothing. I made certain that the hall was empty before venturing forth."

Lady St Clair gave the same answer as Mrs

Armstrong, and said she had no cause to leave her room during the night. Then she fell silent and moved to join Miss Stewart by the fire.

When Hannah approached Lady Frances, she found the woman intent on her own interrogation. "Could your mother turn a man to stone, Lady Wycliff?"

"Yes, I believe she could. Were you in your room all night?" Hannah tried to wrest back control of the conversation.

Lady Frances's eyes darkened in intensity and she waved her hands as she spoke. "Of all my guests, only one has the ability to turn a man to stone, yet here you are, questioning us."

"My mother is not a guest here. While she may possess such an ability, I do not." Hannah wondered how Wycliff's questioning of the staff progressed below stairs. She didn't imagine he had to fend off such accusations.

"But she could have given you a spell with which to do it?" Lady Frances was like a dog with a bone and would not drop her theory.

"Are you suggesting that I came here with murderous intent toward two men I had never met?" The mere idea was farcical.

Lady Frances's arms waved in bigger circles and her eyes had the glint of hysteria. "Your husband had dealings with both of them. Robins shot him just yesterday, and Lord Wycliff is known for his temper. It seems more likely that he lashed out in anger and used a spell that, perhaps, he found among your luggage."

The other women murmured agreement, but when Hannah turned, none could meet her gaze.

"The very idea that my husband turned murderous over a verbal taunt and an accident is utterly preposterous." Hannah's temper rose. Why were people so quick to judge based on so little?

Lady Frances walked over to the other women and took Miss Stewart's hand. "Yet we shall all sleep better tonight knowing that Wycliff does not roam the house."

"I see there is nothing more for me to learn here. Good day, Lady Frances. Ladies." Hannah dropped the smallest of curtseys before leaving the parlour. She hurried to their bedroom and while she ranted about small-minded people, gathered together her belongings, and packed them into her trunk.

"I assume that, from the way you are tormenting that dress, your questioning did not go well?" Wycliff asked as he joined her. He moved with efficiency to clear away his things.

"No. Lady Frances is now quite convinced that *we* are responsible for the deaths, using a spell from my mother. Honestly!" Hannah balled up the dress that refused to be folded and threw it into the open trunk.

"We shall prove them wrong, once we unearth the truth." He moved with a calm deliberation around their room that soothed Hannah's fractious nerves. "Ready to leave?" he asked as two footmen arrived to assist with their luggage.

She cast one last look around the room to ensure they hadn't left anything behind. "Yes. I'd rather not stay where we are not welcome."

She took his arm and held her head high as they walked through the house and down the front steps. Wycliff handed her into the carriage and Hannah glanced up at the building as she settled. She had much to be thankful for about their stay with the Pennicotts. Proximity had allowed her and Wycliff to reach some common ground and they worked well together. He had kissed her and the memory still made her lips tingle. The ember of hope flared in her chest that their marriage would yet prove to be a happy one.

If only people would stop getting murdered.

Wycliff tapped on the roof for Old Jim to drive on. Then he drew a book from his jacket pocket and placed it in her hands. "I asked the earl if you could finish reading a particular book you had found in his library and he graciously said you could keep it."

"Oh! How marvellous." Hannah held up the slim volume about the Fae. "Did he not object to losing a valuable book about the fairy folk?"

"I may have omitted that bit. I said it was a history book, but didn't mention the particular subject." He winked and seemed in an oddly good mood, given that most people thought him a murderer and they had been evicted because of a petty mage who didn't like Hannah's mother.

"I shall treasure it as a reminder of our time here." She placed the book on her lap. "I learned nothing from talking to the ladies, I am afraid. Only Mrs Wright-Knowles left her room last night, and she was very careful to ensure no one saw her. Lady Frances decided to interrogate me about you. Her theory is that you colluded with my mother to murder Lord Stannard and Mr Robins."

He snorted, a dismissive noise that accurately reflected Hannah's sentiments about that topic also. "I called Stannard out for what he said. I would face a man with a gun or sword in my hand if he wronged me or someone I cared for. I don't sneak around at night casting spells."

"Exactly what I said, but she would not be diverted. Miss Stewart looked terribly ill this morning. I fear these unpleasant events have taken a terrible toll on her delicate constitution." The woman's health niggled at Hannah. She had seemed perfectly well their first night, then had fallen ill, only to recover and relapse again. A tonic of honey and brandy might fend off the cold that had her in its grip. Or was her malady related to something else?

They journeyed along the quiet country roads in silence, both of them lost in their own thoughts. Soon the carriage rolled to a stop outside the quaint cottage of Doctor Colchester.

The doctor rushed out to meet them with a smile of welcome. "Miss Miles! Or I should say Lady Wycliff—it has been too long since I last saw you."

Hannah climbed down and hugged the doctor. As a dear friend of her father, he had visited their home often and Sir Hugh had even taken her with him on rare visits to Swindon.

Hannah was relieved to find genuine warmth in his welcome—not all of Swindon thought them murderers. "Doctor Colchester, it is wonderful to see you. I do hope you will forgive our imposing upon you, but it would appear we are no longer welcome at the Pennicott estate."

The doctor tucked Hannah's hand into the crook of his arm. "Martha and I would be delighted to extend our hospitality to you, then. Timmy did say there had been another murder. How terrible to be turned to stone—but what a fascinating process to watch."

Hannah was enveloped in Martha's embrace that smelled of freshly baked biscuits. "I'll show you upstairs, Hann—my lady. Then you must come down to the kitchen for a cup of tea and a biscuit like you always used to do."

Their room was cozy, intimate, and much smaller than their previous one. There was no screen to hide behind when changing. Conversely, Hannah wouldn't need as many changes of clothes. With the informality of staying with the doctor, she could wear the same clothes practically all day long.

"I'm going out to the garden to summon Mother, to let her know we have moved," Hannah said to Wycliff, and made her way down the stairs and outside. As she walked, Hannah rubbed the peacock feather wrapped around her pinkie.

She found a bench seat under a gnarled old apple

tree. Before long, a sparrow flitted to a branch at eye level and chirped.

"Mother? We have been asked to leave the Pennicotts' because Mage Tomlin thinks I smell, and the other guests think Wycliff responsible for the murders!" She unburdened herself without waiting for confirmation from the bird that it channelled her mother.

"Tomlin is an arrogant fool. Pay him no heed, Hannah," the bird said in Seraphina's voice. "Why do they suspect Wycliff?"

Hannah let out a sigh. Where to begin? "The gentlemen were shooting yesterday, and Mr Robins accidentally shot him. They think he killed him in retaliation."

The bird let out a squawk and flapped its wings. "Wycliff was shot? Why ever didn't you say?"

Hannah waved a hand. "It is a small flesh wound below his collarbone. I removed the ball and stitched it. He is very nearly perfectly well already."

In truth, she was more perplexed by what had happened afterward, when her husband had sprouted fur made of smoke along his spine and heat shimmered from his skin.

The bird hopped from the branch to the back of the bench. "Well done, Hannah. You have learned so much at your father's side. But why would they leap to the conclusion that Wycliff had turned him to stone?"

Hannah let out a sigh. Wycliff did have a temper, but he was no murderer. "He argued with Lord Stannard and broke his nose our first night at the Pennicotts'. Both men were cursed only hours after their arguments with him. Lady Frances's evidence consists of his known temper and the fact that his mother-in-law is a mage."

"Poppycock and nonsense. My being a mage is irrelevant. Do they think I can give someone else my ability? Besides, if Wycliff were inclined to end someone's life, it would be with a knife in his hand in broad daylight." The bird flapped its wings like someone raising their hands.

"Is there a potion or spell that could bring about the same effect? Only a small portion of Mr Robins showed around the door, yet he was still struck down." They were missing something, but what? None of the aftermages at the Pennicott estate were powerful enough to cast such an enchantment, but could they have obtained one from another mage?

"A spell. Possibly. Did you feel any magical residue or disturbance at the time it was cast?"

Hannah couldn't remember any tingle of magic, only what emanated from the statues. Nor had her sleep been disturbed, even with the long body of her husband next to her. Oddly, his nearness allowed her to sleep more deeply, as though he guarded her slumber. "No, nor did any pull of magic wake me."

"Not a spell that is cast, then, but some other form of enchantment. We are close, Hannah. I will return this afternoon to confer with you." The bird fluttered to her shoulder and rubbed its head against her cheek, then took flight back to the treetops.

"Not a spell that is cast, but another form of enchantment." Hannah turned over her mother's words as she walked back to the cottage.

What if it were an enchanted object that froze the victim once they gazed upon it? Like a pendant or a small painting? Try as she might, she could not imagine what could have been used.

But there was one seed planted in her mind by Wycliff that reached for the light and whispered to her.

A Greek legend that might have its roots in reality.

# 21

Hannah spent an hour in the cozy kitchen with Martha Colchester, nibbling biscuits and catching up on their respective families. Once pleasantly full of tea, she excused herself to find Wycliff. He sat at a writing desk in the parlour, positioned under a window and looking out over the riotous front garden.

"What ought we to do now?" Hannah asked as she dropped into a worn and overstuffed sofa. Peacocks fanned their tails over the fabric and she traced an all-seeing eye with a fingertip.

"We start from the beginning. Let us go through all the guests and evaluate their possible motives." Wycliff pulled folded sheets of paper from his jacket pocket and laid them out on the desk. He flipped open the pot of ink and took up the quill.

Hannah began with the most obvious motive they had unearthed. "Mrs Armstrong sought to retrieve a letter from Lord Stannard that could humiliate her husband and she threatened consequences if it wasn't returned. Yet that doesn't explain the death of Mr Robins."

Wycliff added notes next to her name. "Unless the letter changed hands and was in Robins's possession. Or he might have had it for safekeeping all along."

To what lengths would the devoted woman go to shield her husband? "Then why freeze him as he opened the door? He blocked the way, so she could never have entered his room to retrieve the letter. Nor did we find anything in our search."

More scratches of the quill. "Let us mark her as possible and move on. We know Mowatt and Mrs Wright-Knowles are engaging in an affair, and that he sought to distance himself from the other Devil's Triplets."

An ache speared through Hannah as she thought of Pippa's unhappy situation. "Do you think it could have been Mr Mowatt? Philippa said that when her father refused his request for her hand, he vowed that no longer would he have any part in the games of Stannard and Robins. Is it possible they would not let him go?"

Wycliff rubbed his chin. "I can't imagine that Stannard would release his minion easily. Mowatt came to the estate with them, either voluntarily or by compulsion. The two deaths do put a permanent end to the Devil's Triplets and leave him free to change his ways."

"You suspect he killed his former friends to remove himself once and for all from their influence?" Hannah shuddered despite the warmth of the sun coming in through the glass. Such a desperate way to end a friendship, when all he had to do was move to a different part of the country. "To what end, though? Philippa is still married to Mr Wright-Knowles." Then a gruesome idea struck Hannah. "Unless he is intended to be victim number three, leaving the path clear for the wronged lovers?"

Wycliff turned in the chair and fixed his midnight stare on her. "To what ends would a man in love go to secure the woman who holds his heart?"

"Or what would a woman do for a man, for do we not love as deeply?" But when did devotion cross a line into madness? Then a most horrible thought crossed her mind. "What if *Philippa* is removing the obstacles to their being together? The method does seem to indicate a woman. We should warn Mr Wright-Knowles." Although to do that, they would have to divulge why he might be in the path of danger. Could she betray the other woman—one her best friend, Lizzie, considered a friend—like that?

"Let us discuss the other guests first, before we decide if Wright-Knowles is about to leave a grieving widow seeking solace in Mowatt's arms." Wycliff made more notes.

Hannah rubbed her arms to dispel the chill that descended over her. She couldn't imagine Pippa turning to murder to gain the freedom to marry the man she loved. But then, neither had she ever considered that the charming Lord Dunkeith was killing women who resembled his Afflicted beloved, and piecing their bodies together to create a new home for her mind.

"Moving on," Wycliff said, "we know that Lady St Clair dallied with Stannard who, as she claims, left her room and she didn't see him again. No one has yet admitted to being the woman hiding in the shadows, so we cannot verify her version of events. If the woman was even there."

Hannah considered what she had learned of the lovely widow. She seemed a woman indulging in harmless flirtation after having escaped a constrictive marriage. "But why murder Lord Stannard? Nor does that explain the death of Mr Robins. Even assuming she were conducting an affair with both, she is not a praying mantis who kills her lovers. Not to mention they were turned to stone. We might examine her more closely as a suspect if their heads had been removed."

Wycliff barked a laugh and made more notes. "What have we learned of Miss Stewart?"

"A gentlewoman fallen on hard times. Apparently, when her sister, Celeste, came out, she made some unfortunate choices, which cast the entire family in a poor light and resulted in Edith's fiancé calling off their engagement. Celeste died two years ago, but that is probably a coincidence. I cannot see how the death of a loved one could ruin a family." Hannah recalled the sadness on Miss Stewart's face as she had shown her the portrait of her sister. The closest Hannah had to a sister was Elizabeth Loburn; she would be devastated if anything ever happened to Lizzie. She could not imagine her life without her best friend to share the journey.

"If Stannard were involved, there was no recognition between them. Nor when I asked Mowatt did he have any memory of her." Wycliff studied the paper and ran a hand through his dark hair.

There was one thing about Fanny's charming companion that bothered Hannah. "I do not know if it is relevant, but every night Miss Stewart has three soft-boiled eggs delivered to her room on a tray."

Wycliff shrugged. "I don't think the consumption of eggs means she is our killer."

Hannah couldn't let the subject go while the niggle in her mind remained. "She also appeared grey and faint the morning after each murder."

"Which could be the reaction of any sensitive woman to such news." Wycliff set down the quill and countered Hannah's every idea.

"It is also a common reaction among those who have used a great deal of magic and drained their resources. I have seen it happen with Mother." The woman's fainting episodes were very coincidentally timed with each death.

"But Miss Stewart is an aftermage who talks to spirits. Your mother did not think it was possible for an aftermage to wield such a spell."

He was right, of course, but the niggle did not dissipate. She would have to worry at it later. Hannah ticked off the guests in her mind. "That leaves us with Lady Frances, who appeared to think the Devil's

Triplets *good fun*, which is why they were invited. Apparently, she became acquainted with them when she, Mrs Wright-Knowles, and Miss Stewart were attending Granger's Finishing School."

He turned back to the spread pages. "Has your mother found the method used to turn them to stone?"

It seemed as though they went around and around in circles, like Sheba the puppy chasing her tail. "There are a few spells that could bring on such an effect, but they require a mage to cast them. Mother doesn't think an aftermage would have sufficient magic, not without nearly killing themselves with the effort."

"So, it is possible?" Wycliff leapt on the small area of doubt.

"Without knowing *who* or *how*, we can only speculate. Anything is possible, but we need to find what is *probable*." Hannah picked up the cushion next to her and plucked at the cord edging. They had a few possibilities and no way to narrow them down to the person responsible. "Perhaps Mage Tomlin will be able to identify the spell after he has examined Lord Stannard and Mr Robins."

She didn't like the old mage, but she wouldn't eschew his assistance in solving the murders.

Wycliff folded his notes and tucked them back into his pocket. Then he rose from the desk. "I shall ride back to the house and enquire."

Hannah picked up a cushion. "I shall stay here. I am told I smell of my mother's magic."

Wycliff rode into the Pennicott stableyard and handed the horse off to a groom. Laughter drifted from the lawn that rolled from the house down to the lake. The remaining houseguests played croquet and chased the coloured balls over the short grass.

Ignoring them and their apparent lack of mourning for another death, he strode toward the house and gestured to the first footman he could find. "Where will I find Mage Tomlin?"

"In the library, milord." The footman bowed and then made his retreat on silent feet.

The charged atmosphere in the house made the hair stand up on the back of his neck. He wondered if the mage could have succeeded in turning Stannard back into flesh and bone.

The halls were quiet and the staff noticeable by their absence. Perhaps the mage had turned them all out for disturbing the air he inhaled through his large nostrils. Wycliff ground his jaw as he recalled the way the mage had accused Hannah of reeking of her mother's magic. At least Lady Miles had served her country during the war. Tomlin had hidden in the mage's tower in Woolwich.

He pushed open the double doors to the library and found the mage seated at the large desk. His hands hovered above the leather insert.

His head snapped up at the intrusion and he

narrowed his eyes. "I did not give you permission to enter! You disturb my casting."

Wycliff approached the desk. There was little to see apart from a small cream pebble, or it might have been a lime chip from a pathway. "If you wish privacy during a house party, perhaps you should lock the door, place a footman outside, or set some magical ward."

The mage sat upright and the tassel on his ridiculous velvet cap swung. "I could turn you into a loathsome creature for disturbing my work."

There was another mark against the man—Tomlin was a toothless dog who barked but couldn't bite. Lady Miles would have turned him into a frog the moment he stepped over the threshold. Why did the man bluster when he never delivered on a threat?

Wycliff studied the man who claimed to be the foremost mage in England. His complexion was florid and a single droplet of sweat travelled down the hairline at his temple. Whatever he was trying to do, it taxed him to his limits.

"Some would say I am already a loathsome creature. But that would not aid what needs to be done here. Have you succeeded in turning Stannard and Robins into flesh and bone?"

"No." Tomlin's shoulders slumped and he tucked his hands into the sleeves of his purple robe. "This is a chip taken from Robins's nightshirt. I have been trying different incantations to revert it to its original form. Once I find the spell that works, I can cast it over both of them."

"Have you determined what spell resulted in their deaths?" Wycliff asked, looking down on the mage.

Lady Miles had discounted the possibility of a potion, due to the way it would work through their bodies. A spell was possible, but nobody except a mage would have sufficient magic to cast it. A charm of some sort was another possibility. His wife's mother was doing her best to find the method despite her not being present. Surely it would be easy for England's top mage to solve the mystery right here in the house.

"I believe a potion is most likely. Something they ingested that turned them to stone. No doubt purchased from a mage who has no difficulty in wielding the dark arts." He unfolded his hands and pushed off the desk to stand.

Wycliff tensed every muscle in his body, commanding himself to hold his position and to not to betray his disgust at the man before him. "Lady Miles discounted a potion. That would have seeped outward from the inside, yet they were both turned to stone from the outside in, their hearts being the last to succumb."

Tomlin laughed and waved a dismissive hand at Wycliff. "She is wrong. Never understood why people thought she had any talent. A female mage is an abomination who can only perform shallow entertainments. Her only decent act was to get herself killed and transfer her magic to a fine boy."

Wycliff growled and lunged. He had his hand

wrapped around the mage's throat before the magic wielder could so much as utter a surprised *oomph.*

"Lady Miles is an extraordinary woman who worked tirelessly to help our troops abroad. Unlike many *men* who hid under their beds on English soil. Speak ill of her again and I shall assist you in performing one *decent act.*" He let the anger flow through his veins until it heated his grip and spilled from his eye sockets.

Tomlin sucked in a breath. "You are an abomination just like her! Get your filthy hands off me."

One by one, an invisible force peeled Wycliff's fingers from around the mage's throat. The man might not be anywhere near as powerful as Lady Miles, but he had significantly more magic than Wycliff. The mage threw out both hands. A blast of air hit Wycliff in the chest and slid him back along the polished wooden floor.

When he came to a halt, Wycliff pulled on the ends of his waistcoat and then adjusted his cuffs. The heat still coursed through him and he considered each word he would say carefully, so as not to throw more fuel on his internal fire. "For all your claims, you have determined less than Lady Miles—who isn't even present. I shall continue with my questioning of the guests. If by chance you do discover something of use, please have a footman pass the information along."

He inclined his head in the briefest possible bow. The man was still the equivalent of a duke, even if he wasn't worthy of such a rank. Then he turned on his heel and left.

"I shall solve this without your interference," Tomlin called. The library doors slammed shut behind Wycliff. A metallic rattle sounded as chains materialised and looped themselves through the door handles.

"Arrogant fool," Wycliff muttered under his breath.

Shame that Lady Miles had never challenged him in combat for the position of England's foremost mage. Defeat and humiliation by a woman seemed exactly what Tomlin needed to cut him down to size. Instead, Wycliff would settle for ensuring he and Hannah solved the murders. Once his wife showed the foolish Tomlin what women were capable of, Wycliff was going to have a good gloat.

# 22

"Tomlin is an idiot," Wycliff announced as he strode into the parlour and tossed his hat on the sideboard. He stripped off his gloves with jerky motions. "He asserts that Stannard and Robins ingested a potion that turned them to stone."

"But we have already discounted that method." Hannah slid a bookmark between the pages of her novel and set it aside. "Timmy said that they were transformed from the outside through to the inside. Mother believes it is either a spell or some sort of device, used externally."

"England's foremost mage dismissed your mother's findings out of hand. The only thing he is *foremost* of is a host of idiots." Wycliff stalked to the window, seating himself on the ledge. Bad humour rolled off him as though he were a bear awakened from hibernation too early.

"I will assume, then, that Mage Tomlin has not

discovered anything to aid the investigation?" Hannah asked.

Afternoon drifted into dusk behind Wycliff's head and the setting sun backlit him like a dark angel on a tomb. One in a particularly foul mood. "No. He has chipped a piece off Robins and is trying to turn it back into its original form."

Chipping pieces off the unfortunate men seemed rather horrid. Hannah hoped the mage hadn't broken off a finger. Robins might be dead, but there was no need to desecrate his form. Although she could see the advantage of working on a smaller piece first. It would use less magic than trying to revert a whole man to flesh and blood. "Let us hope he is successful, so that they may be returned to their families in a less distressing state."

"You are too charitable." Wycliff's grim expression softened as he regarded her.

Hannah rose from the sofa and smoothed out the wrinkles in her sage green morning dress. "His lordship makes his own choices about how he treats others and one day, he will have to climb into bed with the consequences. Because he is that way does not mean we have to emulate him and be equally closed-minded or spiteful."

"You are a far better person than I. I spent the ride back thinking of ways to torture him should I ever have the opportunity." A small smile pulled at Wycliff's lips. "I have certainly had my fill of Mage Tomlin for today.

Shall we adjourn to the kitchen and start afresh tomorrow?"

"An excellent idea." Hannah took his offered hand and they walked through to the kitchen.

Meals were informal in the doctor's house, where Hannah, and by extension Wycliff and Timmy, were treated as family. They dined at the large table in the bright and cozy kitchen, rather than in the less used (and rather cold and small) formal dining room. Dinner was a raucous and warm affair, held at the long pine table. Even Timmy laughed at the stories Doctor Colchester told, and the tense set to Wycliff's shoulders eased as the meal progressed.

Despite the excellent company, Hannah excused herself early. Pressure was building behind her eyes and her fingers tingled with numbness. "My apologies, everyone, I find I am quite worn out."

By the time she stripped off her dress, donned her nightgown, and plaited her hair, her eyelids were heavy and she couldn't stop yawning. Sleep claimed her, just as she pulled the blankets up over her shoulders.

THE NEXT MORNING, Hannah awoke to an empty bed. She reached out and touched the depression where Wycliff had slept. The blankets were warm; he couldn't have been gone for long.

She rose and dressed, before heading downstairs. She found Martha at the kitchen table, drinking tea and chatting with the housekeeper. “Good morning, Hannah,” Martha greeted her.

“Good morning. Have you seen my husband this morning?” It was most odd for him to have slunk away without telling her where he was going. Hannah took a seat opposite Martha.

“Yes. The menfolk have gone fishing. They decided last night over coffee, after you had gone to bed. Lord Wycliff said he couldn’t figure out who is killing those guests of the Pennicotts’. My George said a spot of fishing aids a man’s thinking, so they left just before dawn.” Martha fetched a teacup and saucer for Hannah, then poured tea.

“Fishing?” How did fishing aid thinking? Hannah tried to conjure the image of Wycliff sitting under a willow on the banks of the river, a fishing rod held in loose fingers as the line played out in the water, his features relaxed as he laughed and talked. An odd ripple ran through her, not unlike that which disturbs the water when a fish takes the bait.

Martha retook her seat and slid the toast rack toward Hannah. “Yes. Bit of trout would be lovely for supper. Wouldn’t it be good if he had a revelation while dangling his line waiting for a bite?”

Hannah didn’t have to wait long to find out. The men returned mid-morning while Hannah was still seated in the kitchen, keeping her hands busy by shelling a bowl of peas. The doctor carried a half dozen fish strung together, which Martha exclaimed over as though they were expensive jewels.

"A successful venture, I see." Hannah pointed to the fish.

Wycliff wore a smile. "Yes. In more ways than one. I have decided we need to stop concentrating on potential suspects and return to examining our victims. Something bound Stannard and Robins in death, and who do you think would be most likely to know that?"

"Mr Mowatt." Hannah whispered the name of the third, and sole surviving member, of the Devil's Triplets.

Wycliff arched one black brow. "I believe he knows something that he hasn't had the courage to admit. Permit me to wash up and we will discuss it in more detail."

Hannah watched her husband leave the kitchen and wondered if she would return to Westborne Green with an individual quite unlike the one with whom she'd left. He seemed much changed and the uneasy, brittle atmosphere between them had dissolved and turned into something warmer and more companionable.

She was seated on the sofa in the parlour when Wycliff returned—scrubbed and now smelling vaguely of lemon rather than fish. Before he could open his mouth to speak, Martha came in on his heels.

"A Mr Mowatt is here to see you, my lord," she said.

Hannah glanced to Wycliff, who shrugged. "Perhaps one can summon one of the Devil's Triplets by saying his name three times."

"Please tell him we will receive him, thank you, Martha," Hannah said. She clasped her hands in her lap.

Mr Mowatt entered and bowed. "Lord and Lady Wycliff. Thank you for seeing me at such an early hour."

Hannah held in her amusement. Wycliff had been up at dawn to go fishing and even she rose some hours before the fashionable set. She gestured to the sofa. "Please be seated, Mr Mowatt."

"I'd rather stand, if you don't mind, Lady Wycliff." He clutched his hat in his hands and appeared unable to settle. He paced back and forth and while his lips moved as though he spoke to himself, he addressed no remarks to either Hannah or Wycliff.

The Colchesters' rug didn't deserve to be worn out in one visit. Hannah pondered whether there might be a way to prod the man into speaking, and chose his most obvious Achilles heel. "Did you seek us out, Mr Mowatt, in order to unburden yourself?"

He paused and glanced at her. A frown pulled at his brows. "Unburden myself?"

"Yes. Mrs Wright-Knowles confided in me that you sought to distance yourself from both Lord Stannard and Mr Robins. Lord Wycliff and I speculated that you might have sought a more permanent distance."

Wycliff stood in front of the window and wrapped his long fingers around the edge of the sill. "If Wright-Knowles were to suffer the same fate, your path would be clear to reclaim the woman you love."

Mr Mowatt's jaw dropped and his eyes widened as he stared at Wycliff. "Good God, man! You think I did this?"

While Hannah appreciated that Wycliff was all for efficiency and cutting to the heart of the matter, if he wanted to elicit a confession, then a more understanding approach might be better. "It is obvious that you and Mrs Wright-Knowles have great affection for each other," she said. "It could not have been easy to see her married to another man after your suit was refused."

Mr Mowatt let out a long sigh and dropped to the sofa. The nervous energy that had made him pace now fled his form as he rested his elbows on his thighs and placed his head in his hands. He was silent for a long minute. Then he scrubbed his hands over his face as though he had made a decision. "As a young man, I was a damned fool, if you'll forgive my language, Lady Wycliff. I fell in with Stannard and Robins because I thought they were great fun."

*Great fun* was exactly how Lady Frances viewed them. People had very different estimations of what constituted fun. Hannah thought them cruel and lacking in any empathy for their fellow man.

Mowatt spoke to his hands, without looking up. "We larked about, drank too much, and got into trouble. Isn't that what all lads do?"

"I didn't." From his post by the window, Wycliff surveyed their visitor with a black stare.

Mr Mowatt glanced up with a sorrowful expression. "I thought they were entertaining. A diverting way to fill empty days when I couldn't see Pippa. It wasn't until she came of age and I asked for her hand that I realised our activities had cost me the woman I love. Her father, as you are aware, denied me."

"Did you consider eloping?" It seemed the solution to Hannah. If you loved someone with all your being, would you let the single syllable *no* stand in your way?

"Yes. But her father's words struck me to the core and I realised he was right. I had nothing to offer Pippa. I had burned through my allowance and had nothing but debt. My father threatened to cut me off if I didn't shape up. People were already talking about us and many doors were being shut in our faces. If we had run away, we would have had no money, no support, no society. I wouldn't see Pippa suffer because of my foolish behaviour." He ran his hands through his hair and tugged at the roots.

"Is this tale of thwarted love going somewhere?" Wycliff looked bored and was inspecting his nails.

Hannah swallowed sharp words. Had he no romance in his soul?

Mr Mowatt leaned back and rested his head on the sofa. He continued in a softer tone. "I vowed to Pippa that I would change my ways and be worthy of her should circumstances ever allow us to be together. We continued our affair even after her marriage to Wright-Knowles, snatching what time we could. I stopped seeing the others so much. I found excuses to avoid being around them. But I did not end our acquaintance. Then, about three years ago, at a ball, I realised there was no level to which they would not stoop."

"What happened?" Wycliff asked.

"A pretty thing in her first Season had led Stannard a merry dance for weeks. Teasing him each time she saw him. That night, he drank more and more and then announced it was time for her to make good on her coquettish promises." Mowatt closed his eyes and squeezed them shut, as though he sought to keep some image from appearing before him.

Sudden certainty gripped Hannah's heart. Instinct told her she might already know the unhappy ending to this story.

"She fluttered her eyelashes and dashed along the hall that led to the billiards room. Robins and I followed, intending to play a game. When we walked in, she was struggling with Stannard and trying to leave. He grabbed her, threw her on the billiards table, and told Robins to hold her arms." He fell silent and leaned forward again, his gaze fixed on the carpet beneath his boots.

"You didn't assist the girl to break free?" Wycliff spat his accusation.

Mowatt swallowed and licked his lips. "I wanted no part in it! I turned to leave and that was when Stannard threatened me."

"Why did you not leave and seek help for the poor creature?" Hannah couldn't comprehend how a man who claimed he was trying to change his ways could be a party to such a horrific act. What threat could make a man complicit in such a terrible crime?

"Stannard said that if I walked out, he would make sure I never saw Pippa again. He had stolen letters from my room. Private things Pippa had written to me, that proved our devotion to each other. He threatened to give the letters to her father and husband. What fate was worse—losing the woman I loved or doing nothing while he had his way with the girl?"

"You watched while he raped her?" Wycliff bit out the words, disgust heavy in every syllable.

Mowatt shook his head and covered his face with his hands. "No. I might be a coward, but I still have limits. I turned my back. When we left the room, there were some other chaps in the hall. They saw her with her legs dangling over the edge of the table as she pulled her skirts down. Stannard lied and said she had satisfied all three of us. We all laughed, but word circulated like fire. By the end of the evening she was disgraced as spoiled fruit."

Simple words with such a heavy consequences. But the facts niggled at Hannah's mind. "No gentlewoman can make an accusation of rape without admitting she is no longer a maid. Either way, she was ruined. How could you?"

"Because I am a weak fool who cannot spend his life with the woman he loves. I vowed to have nothing to do with them after that, and saw very little of them until this week. Fanny invited all of us along and I met up with them at the inn." When he looked up and met Hannah's gaze, his eyes shone with tears.

Wycliff pushed off the windowsill and paced to the door. "You think the rape is connected to their murders?"

Mr Mowatt curled his hands into fists and pressed them into his thighs. "You asked me if I knew of anyone who would want Stannard and Robins dead. We were cruel to so many over the years, but it is that night which sticks in my throat. Nothing haunts me like her sobs and pleas for him to stop. What if she has a brother, seeking vengeance on us?"

Wycliff spun to face the man. "Then I'd say you all damned well deserve it. You worked hard to earn your reputation for cruelty."

Mr Mowatt fixed Wycliff with a stare. "You also have a reputation, my lord. Did you earn that? And do you not seek a different one now?"

Wycliff grunted.

"Are none of us allowed to change, to become someone different? I learned my lesson and sought to correct it. I wanted to be a better person, and yes, I failed when tested. In that moment, the thought of never seeing Pippa again was far harder to bear than the poor girl's cries." Mr Mowatt raised his fists and slammed them down.

"The billiard balls!" Hannah jumped to her feet and stood between the men. "Lord Stannard was holding one. Mr Robins had one between his feet. It could be a reference to that night. Perhaps the killer wants you to know that they are seeking vengeance for that crime."

"Do you recall the woman's name?" Wycliff asked.

Mowatt shook his head and spread his hands wide. "I cannot remember."

"Would you recognise her, if you saw her again?" The answer leapt into Hannah's mind in blazing colour and she sucked in a breath as she took it in.

"Yes. How could I ever forget her face? But I assure you, she is not among the guests, nor have I seen her prowling the halls." He relaxed his hands to tug on the hair above his right ear.

"I believe, however, that we have a vengeful sister—Miss Edith Stewart," Hannah said.

"Surely not. She looks nothing like the woman Stannard ruined." Mr Mowatt frowned, the lines deep between his brows.

Hannah couldn't stop, now that the idea flowed through her. "Miss Stewart told me she favours her father, while her sister took after their mother. Around her neck she wears a locket containing a portrait of her sister, now deceased. She was a pretty thing, with dark hair and sparkling eyes."

Mr Mowatt let out a low whistle. "That sounds like her. But Stewart? She seems too mousy."

The more Hannah thought about it, the more it made sense to her. "Mrs Wright-Knowles confided to me that Miss Stewart was set aside by her fiancé and the family disgraced because her sister earned the reputation of being *spoiled fruit* in her first Season. The poor girl was brutalised by Lord Stannard and the family ostracised from society for it."

What if, even worse, it had resulted in her death? Miss Stewart had never mentioned how her sister died. What if the unfortunate girl, unable to bear the weight of the shame, had taken her own life? If Lady Frances's companion had known of the atrocity committed against her sister, Hannah could only imagine the anger directed at the Devil's Triplets.

"We do not know that for certain yet, Hannah. But it does all seem to fall into place." Wycliff rapped his nails on the writing desk as he thought.

Hannah did know for certain. "We need to show the locket to Mr Mowatt to confirm whether Miss Stewart's sister is the girl he saw, and then determine how Miss Stewart murdered the other men."

Wycliff grinned. "Let us set a trap. And we'll use Mowatt here as our bait."

# 23

"BAIT?" Mr Mowatt repeated the word, gazing uneasily from Hannah to Wycliff.

"Yes. We don't yet know how Miss Stewart turned Stannard and Robins to stone. We will dangle you before her and make her lunge for whatever charm or spell she has concealed." Wycliff's face remained impassive as he pronounced sentence upon Mr Mowatt. There was no hint of emotion or even a twitch of an eyebrow.

Mr Mowatt's eyes widened and he swallowed, his Adam's apple bobbing against his cravat. "Is there not some other way? What if it goes wrong? I don't fancy spending eternity as a garden ornament."

Wycliff shrugged and inspected his fingernails once more. "Given that you did nothing while a woman was raped, consider yourself lucky I will use you as *live* bait."

"Do you have a plan, Wycliff?" Hannah asked. Or

did he intend to literally dangle Mr Mowatt like a piece of mistletoe at Christmas? Granted, she was repulsed that Mr Mowatt had done nothing to aid the woman brutalised by Lord Stannard, but did that mean his life should be forfeit?

Wycliff continued speaking from his post at the window. "The ball is tonight. If Miss Stewart follows the same pattern as the other deaths, she will look for a moment to find Mowatt alone. We have only to keep watch over him. Perhaps, Hannah, you could find some way to ask to see her locket with Mr Mowatt nearby? That would confirm the identity of her sister as Stannard's victim."

"I shall try." Hannah didn't think that would be too difficult. But there was another loose end that niggled at her mind—how to help Mrs Armstrong? "There is a separate matter that Mr Mowatt might be able to assist us with. Were you at all aware of a letter that Lord Stannard possessed, with which he intended to expose one of Lady Frances's guests?"

Mr Mowatt let out a sigh and his shoulders relaxed. "I know of its existence, but not of its contents. Stannard used to chortle that it would destroy the person's life once he had it published in the newspaper."

Wycliff pushed off the windowsill and moved to stand behind Hannah. "Did he carry it on him? I searched his room and went through his satchel, which contained many letters, but not that one in particular."

Mowatt leaned back on the sofa, more at ease now that the conversation had moved away from an examination of his character faults. "No. He wouldn't keep something like that on him unless he intended to wave it at the poor unfortunate. But it wouldn't have been far away, hidden where it would not be found either by accident or the curious."

Hannah turned to gaze up at her husband and her cheek brushed Wycliff's fingers where they curled into the back of the sofa. "The staff have packed up his belongings to be returned to the marquess. We have surely lost our opportunity."

Mowatt tapped his thumb against his forefinger as he thought. "It won't be among his things. He always said nosy people would poke about in your luggage but ignore the everyday furniture in a room. He was particularly fond of tucking things into the base of a shaving mirror."

"It could still be there," Wycliff said as he glanced down at Hannah, a fire lit in his eyes.

"We may not be welcome at the estate, but at least we still hold our invitations to the ball." A trickle of relief wormed through Hannah. What a weight they could lift from Mrs Armstrong's shoulders if they could return the letter to her!

They advised Mr Mowatt to take care not to be alone with Miss Stewart, and to be on his guard. Then he took his leave of them. Hannah walked out to the garden, to contact her mother before they left for the ball and their covert operation to save the reputation of Captain Armstrong and the life of Mr Mowatt.

She rubbed the peacock ring and settled on the

bench under the apple tree, waiting for her mother's proxy to make itself known. Within a few minutes, a chaffinch fluttered to a nearby branch. The brown chest and blue-grey stripe over the head signalled it was the male of the species.

"I have news, Hannah," the bird said.

"So have I. We believe we have found the inciting event that connects the murders—a woman raped three years ago by Lord Stannard. I suspect she was Celeste, the sister of Miss Edith Stewart, Lady Frances's companion." The words tasted heavy in Hannah's mouth. Stannard had committed a heinous crime and Robins and Mowatt were complicit by not stopping him. Society had compounded the crime by ruining a woman who was no longer a maid—despite the fact that her virginity had been forcibly taken from her.

"Oh." The bird fell silent and groomed under a wing.

"What did you discover, Mother?" Hannah reached out a finger and bumped the bird's feet, causing it to swap branch for digit. Then she brought the creature closer to her face so as not to strain her neck looking up.

The bird's claws clenched and unclenched around her finger. "My findings also relate to Miss Stewart. I found her and her sister both in the genealogies. They are fifth generation aftermages. Both sisters possess a mild ability to commune with the dead. I also discovered that their father is a shapeshifter with a specific affinity for reptiles."

Hannah screwed up her face. She would rather share a home with a lycanthrope than a man who transformed into a lizard, crocodile, or snake.

*Snake!*

Again an idea sparked in Hannah's mind. It came with a certainty so incredible and yet logical, she had to give it voice. "Miss Stewart told me she resembled her father, while her sister favoured their mother. Do you think it ran deeper than appearance? Could she also have meant his gifts?"

The bird flung out its wings and fluttered closer to her face. "By Jove, Hannah, *there* is an incredible possibility."

Hannah wasn't entirely sure what happened when mage blood mingled with that of other Unnatural creatures. Did they produce something entirely different, or stay true to one side or the other? "Would it even be possible for the combination of aftermage and reptile shifter blood to produce...a gorgon?"

"Anything is possible with magic, Hannah. Legend tells us that after Medusa was raped by Poseidon, she was turned into a gorgon by Athena. There are similarities to this situation. Regardless, your father will insist on hearing all about your findings when you return home." The bird shook its feathers and inched along her finger.

Hannah pondered the cruelties of life. Even Medusa had been punished for the crime committed against her. Was it possible that Miss Stewart had been born with gorgon tendencies? Or had rage at her sister's fate triggered something dormant in her blood?

The bird chirped and pulled her from her thoughts. "There is one other thing about Celeste, Hannah. The poor woman died in childbirth."

"Oh!" Hannah's hand flew to her chest. "How did you ascertain *that* detail?"

The bird's head drooped with the weight of its news. "There is a babe notated as her son in the genealogies, his date of birth Celeste's date of death. Sadly, he was never given a name. His entry only reads *baby boy*. He died only hours after birth, and drew breath only long enough for the mage genealogies to record his brief existence."

"How terribly sad for the family." Hannah leaned back against the bark of the fruit tree. A sister cruelly raped, ruined in the eyes of society, who then died delivering her rapist's child. Now Hannah understood the series of events that had caused the downfall of the Stewart family and that had seen Edith become Lady Fanny's companion.

All of it because of one man and his cruel appetites. What fuel for revenge. While two wrongs didn't make a right, as the old saying went, in this instance Hannah could understand the depth of outrage and need to see someone punished for what had happened to a much loved sibling.

"Thank you, Mother. I shall consult with Wycliff and then we will attend the ball to lay our trap for Miss

Stewart." Hannah stroked the bird's head with a fingertip in thanks.

"Stay safe, my child, and remember, if Miss Stewart has gorgon tendencies, you must not look directly at her. As much as it galls me to say so, you may need Mage Tomlin's assistance." The bird shook itself free of the enchantment and took flight.

Thoughts collided in Hannah's head as she ran back into the house. Heedless of decorum, she called, "Wycliff? Wycliff!"

Her husband trotted down the stairs, a frown on his face. "What is it? Is there news from your mother?"

"I believe Miss Stewart is a gorgon!" Hannah blurted.

His lips twitched and humour flashed in his eyes. "And *I* believe I suggested that some days ago."

She rocked back on her heels. So he had. Well, the fullness of time had revealed that he was right after all. "Mother found Miss Stewart in the mage genealogies, which also revealed that her father is a reptile shifter. We believe she may have inherited his ability—perhaps amplified by the misfortune that befell her sister. If so, she may conceal another form."

He took a step closer to her, his hand still resting on the newel post. "That would explain the cover of darkness for the murders—to ensure no one else saw her transformation."

"How does one defeat a gorgon?" Hannah mentally rummaged through the spells she carried and pondered which one to tuck into her bodice.

"In Greek mythology, Medusa was beheaded." Wycliff's nails rapped thoughtfully on the polished timber.

Hannah grimaced. A beheading during the ball would ensure that Lady Frances and her parties would be talked about for months to come. "Mother also revealed the circumstances of Celeste's death. By my reckoning, Miss Stewart's sister died some nine months after she was brutalised by Stannard."

Wycliff's hand ceased its tapping as the arithmetic soaked into his mind. "She was with child?"

Hannah swallowed the lump in her throat. "Died in childbirth. The little boy survived long enough that his birth was noted in the mage genealogies, before he joined his mother in death."

He let out a low whistle. "There is a motive for revenge, with echoes of the old myth."

"Mother also suggested we may need Mage Tomlin's assistance to apprehend her." The mage's name tasted sour on Hannah's tongue. Regardless of her personal feelings about the man and his horrendous treatment of Timmy's mother, he could yet prove of service to them.

"I will seek him and the earl out when we return to the estate. I shall apprise them of our suspicions before we confront Miss Stewart. Better to have Tomlin standing in the wings should we need him." Wycliff's lips tightened as though he, too, had difficulty swallowing the idea of asking the mage for help.

Hannah managed a smile. "We have much to accomplish this evening."

"Yes. Why don't you take the bedroom first to wash and change, and I shall see if the good doctor has any books about Greek mythology on his shelves." Wycliff nodded and then set off for the doctor's study.

Two hours later, Wycliff took her hand as she climbed into the carriage. Hannah wore a cream silk dress with an overdress of deep orange bearing an embroidered pattern like flames around the hem and neckline. Martha had helped her arrange her hair and heated the tongs to make the ringlets grazing her cheeks. A strand of topaz was wound through her hair to match the overdress.

"You look lovely this evening. Bold colours suit you," Wycliff murmured as the carriage jolted and they set off on their journey.

Hannah cast her eyes downward as the compliment slid hot inside her. She swallowed, not sure how to respond apart from a whispered *thank you*. There were aspects of her marriage for which she realised she was wholly unprepared. What Hannah desperately needed was a confidential talk with dear Lizzie. The sort of conversation that they conducted at night, by glow lamp, while draped in a blanket.

The Pennicott house blazed as though afire as they rolled into the sweep of the drive. Carriages lined up, each waiting their turn to disgorge their passengers. Some more robust locals had walked, chatting loudly as they trod the gravel toward the house.

Hannah squinted against the glare coming from the windows, far brighter than any candle could throw. Mage Tomlin, Hannah guessed, had probably added enchanted light to the evening. How like a man to turn the ballroom into daylight so that it lost all its romance. Women and diamonds were made for golden warmth, not harsh white light.

Wycliff took her hand as they mounted the steps into the house. "See if you can find Miss Stewart and determine, carefully, whether she is carrying a cursed item upon her. I doubt she will strike until she finds a way to lure Mowatt out of the house on his own. I'm going to search Stannard's room first and find that letter."

Wycliff kissed her cheek and disappeared into the throng of people.

Hannah touched her cheek. It was the first time he had kissed her since she'd stitched his wound and he'd taken her in his arms. They needed to have a conversation about that night and there was more to discuss than how delicious she found his kisses. There was the matter of scorched paw prints and smoking hackles.

But first, Hannah needed to brave the ballroom alone and find a gorgon.

# 24

Hannah took a breath to steel her spine and then stepped into the ballroom. Local society had converged on the house and the parquet floor had disappeared under a sea of silk, satin, and best muslin. White and cream were interspersed with bold splashes of red, green, and blue as though a careless artist threw paint at their canvas.

She descended the stairs and scanned the revellers. Lady Frances frowned in the receiving line and Hannah returned her dour look with a bright smile. While Lady Frances might not wish to receive them, the earl had promised not to impede their investigation and no one would be telling Hannah or Wycliff to leave before they got to the bottom of this.

Captain Armstrong stood to one side surrounded by other gentlemen and appeared to be telling a story with much gesticulation of his hands.

"Lady Wycliff!" Mrs Armstrong hurried over from

a corner with a welcoming look behind her spectacles and a smile on her lips.

Hannah clasped hands with her, thankful that at least one person was glad to see her. "Mrs Armstrong. I do not wish to get your hopes up, but my husband has gone to search for that which you are missing."

"Oh," she breathed. She pulled her lips into a tight line as though she steadied herself in preparation for disappointment. "I shall be eternally grateful if Lord Wycliff locates the item."

A footman glided past and Hannah plucked a glass of champagne from the silver tray. She watched the dancers, but saw no sign of the one she sought. "Have you seen Miss Stewart this evening, Mrs Armstrong? I am concerned whether she managed to shake off the spring cold that had her in its grip." With the benefit of hindsight, Hannah suspected the companion's fainting fits and grey pallor were more likely caused by magical exertion than any change in the weather.

"No. I understand she is suffering a headache and keeps to her room," Mrs Armstrong said.

*Bother.* Their plan hinged on dangling Mr Mowatt as bait and catching Miss Stewart in the process of transforming into a gorgon before she turned him to stone. Now what would they do? It didn't seem proper to barge into her bedroom and demand a confession instead.

"Perhaps she might join us later." Hannah sipped her wine and silently wished the companion would be compelled to leave her room.

Out on the floor, Mr Mowatt partnered Mrs Wright-Knowles, in a deep pink gown, for a country dance. Her oblivious husband was deep in conversation with the group surrounding Captain Armstrong. There was no sign of Mage Tomlin. Perhaps Wycliff had encountered the mage and the earl, and was apprising them of the plan. There was little Hannah could do until he returned or they located Miss Stewart.

Laughter tinkled over the music and Hannah turned to the source. Wearing a bold imperial purple gown, Lady St Clair stood surrounded by men. She laughed and employed her fan expertly, leaving only her sparkling eyes visible.

"Some women are born with all the gifts and reap all the rewards," Lady Frances said as she appeared at Hannah's side. Mrs Armstrong retreated and took a seat with a cluster of matrons whispering among themselves.

"Do they, though? Beauty is no guarantee of happiness. Indeed, from what I have observed of Lady St Clair, I think she has experienced more than her share of sadness." Hannah watched the young widow. While she appeared an innocent surrounded by predatory men, it was an illusion. Lady St Clair was the wolf luring the sheep close. She waved her fan and batted her eyelids, but they concealed a cunning mind. Having married for duty, she now sought a happier arrangement.

"What of you, Lady Wycliff? Are you happy in

your marriage?" Fanny's sharp black eyes peeled away Hannah's layers.

"Yes." She replied without thinking, and the word rang true through her, like the crisp note of a bell. "I married a man with qualities I admire and find I am most content with my decision."

Lady Frances huffed and worried at her bottom lip. "My father has negotiated a marriage for me with a quiet man possessed of a steady temperament and intelligence. Yet I delay giving my final consent, wondering if there is something better out there. Is it wrong to want both happiness and excitement?"

Was this the real reason Lady Frances had invited Hannah and Wycliff—to inspect an arranged marriage to compare to her own prospects? Wycliff had offered Hannah a marriage of convenience that was to be in name only. Yet she discovered that a whole new world waited to unfurl before her, if she had the courage to reach for it. "You do not know what might come of the match, until you try," she said at last. "I rather think happiness is something we must find within ourselves, instead of expecting it to be delivered by someone else's hand. If your intended is an honest and intelligent man, then isn't that a sufficient foundation on which to grow your own excitement?"

A rare genuine smile broke over Lady Frances's face and she tapped Hannah's arm with her folded fan. "Thank you, Lady Wycliff, for you have given me something to ponder. On another topic, I do request that you keep your husband to the more crowded areas of the house. Nobody wants to encounter him alone in a dim hall."

Hannah followed Lady Frances's gaze as Wycliff cut a path toward them through the guests. They parted before him like the ocean receding from the shore.

He bowed to their hostess as though she had never thrown them from the house. "Lady Frances, please forgive me, but I must steal my wife away."

Lady Frances arched one eyebrow. "I never knew a married man could be so keen for his wife's company. You give a woman hope, Lord Wycliff."

Wycliff stared as Lady Frances winked at Hannah and took her leave. His frown turned upon Hannah and he raised his own questioning eyebrow.

Hannah rested her hand on his forearm as he indicated they should walk to a quiet corner. "Lady Frances is contemplating her own nuptials. I pointed out the advantages to marrying a man with abilities one can admire, such as honesty and intelligence."

Wycliff's frown fell away and he flashed her a smile. Then he patted his pocket. "I found the letter where Mowatt thought it would be—under the base of the shaving mirror."

Hannah leaned in closer to him. "And?"

He spoke to her while he glanced from one dancer to another. "As you suspected, Captain Armstrong's account is not entirely accurate. It seems the French mage was killed by a falling timber while the captain was some distance from him. In the confusion and swirl of smoke, no one saw what happened, and so he was able to cast himself as the hero of the hour."

"At least we may return the letter to Mrs Armstrong. It will be a weight lifted from her shoulders." The woman in question was engaged in a lively conversation and if she could not dance, Hannah was relieved that she had found good company.

"What of Miss Stewart?" Wycliff asked.

"Apparently she has a headache and has not yet come down." Hannah scanned the dancers, looking for the elegant blonde.

"It is early yet, and she does favour the small hours of the evening to exact her revenge. Shall we occupy ourselves while we wait for her to appear?" Wycliff gestured to the dancers.

Hannah stared at her husband, convinced he had gone quite mad. "You wish to dance?"

"Yes. Quite apart from enjoying my wife's company, it allows us to keep an eye on Mowatt." The musicians finished one song and the next dance was announced. Wycliff led Hannah out on the floor.

In the quiet moment before the music started, Hannah considered the possibility that her mother had thrown some enchantment over Wycliff to turn him into a polite gentleman. If so, she hoped it was a transformation that lasted.

They danced three together, by which time Hannah needed a glass of punch to relieve her dry throat. Never before had she enjoyed a ball this much. Odd how Wycliff's company now set her heart aflutter

—though it was probably the unexpected exertion of dancing that made her breathless.

The earl approached them and nodded to Hannah. "Lord and Lady Wycliff, I must have a private word." They followed as he wound his way through the guests and then the double doors to the quieter hall beyond. "I sent a maid up to Miss Stewart's room, but she is not there," the earl said once they were alone.

Wycliff clenched one hand into a fist. "Blast. I have not seen her in the ballroom. Could she have gone somewhere else in the house?"

The earl raised both hands in the French manner to indicate he did not know. "I have the staff looking for her."

At that moment Mrs Wright-Knowles burst into the hall and called to Hannah, "Oh! Lady Wycliff, you must find Mowatt. I fear he has done something foolish."

"Whatever has happened?" Hannah stepped toward the other woman.

Philippa reached for Hannah's hand. "He said he had done something terrible and the only way he could ever seek my forgiveness was first to stare into the face of justice."

Wycliff swore under his breath. "Damn fool. Last I saw him, he was still in the ballroom. We instructed him not to go anywhere alone."

Hannah's blood ran cold. "He has gone to find her." If Mr Mowatt found Miss Stewart first, then the Devil's

Triplets would be as permanent a trio of statuary as the Three Graces were a painting.

"They could be anywhere. This is a large estate," the earl said.

Something cold brushed Hannah's skin and she glanced down. "What do you have there?"

Philippa lifted the hand that touched Hannah's arm. When she opened her palm, she cupped a cream-coloured ball. "Mowatt handed it to me before he stormed off. Is it a clue?"

Wycliff peered over Hannah's shoulder. "A billiard ball. They are in the billiards room."

"He means to finish it where it began," Hannah whispered.

Wycliff turned to Lord Pennicott. "Find Tomlin at once. We will need the mage's help in the billiards room."

"I'll help look." Philippa picked up her skirts and took off at a run down the hallway. Hannah didn't have time to watch her disappear around the corner—Wycliff grabbed her hand and pulled her in the opposite direction.

They raced along the corridor to the double doors of the male sanctuary. Wycliff threw them apart to find Miss Stewart facing down Mr Mowatt. As Hannah and Wycliff burst into the room, the companion pulled on the end of her turban and the silk tumbled to the ground. Among her blonde locks, something slithered and hissed. Three snakes peered out from her curls and rose higher to stare at their victim.

*Of course,* Hannah though. *Snakes like eggs. She required the three soft-boiled eggs every night to feed them.*

"Don't look directly at her," Hannah yelled. She cast around for anything that would shield Wycliff's eyes.

Wycliff threw himself at Mowatt, knocked the man to thc ground, and rolled him under the billiards table and out of the way.

"He must pay for what they did to my sister!" Miss Stewart shrieked.

Hannah snatched up a silver platter from the sideboard and held it before her face like a shield. Unfortunately, that meant she could only see the bottom half of Miss Stewart, who rushed around the large table.

"Taking their lives will not bring Celeste back," Hannah said. Why could she not find something that would protect Wycliff? The immobilisation spell was no good—if she were that close there was a high chance she would lock gazes with one of the snakes.

"They destroyed her innocence, ruined her reputation, and then stole her life," Miss Stewart sobbed. "I held her in my arms as she took her last breath."

Hannah's heart squeezed and shuddered at the woman's raw emotion. Tragedy had been heaped upon tragedy. There would never be a happy ending to this tale. "Mr Mowatt should have come to Celeste's aid, but we cannot change what is done. He must face the consequences of his cowardice. But that does not mean his life is forfeit."

Hannah assessed the items on the sideboard. Wycliff would need a way to see the gorgon while he sought to restrain her. A shallow bowl held an assortment of apples and pears. A faint bluish hue kissed its rounded side, indicating it was made of crystal.

Hannah upended the bowl and the apples rolled off and bounced to the floor.

Wycliff crawled out from under the table on the side opposite Miss Stewart, but with an arm covering his face to avoid looking at the woman. "Stay beneath!" he yelled to Mowatt.

"Wycliff! Take this—the crystal will refract her gaze and keep you from turning to stone." Well, theoretically she hoped it would. Hannah threw the bowl across the table.

Wycliff caught it in one hand and held it before his face like a strange helm. With his other hand, he grabbed one of the two crossed swords hanging over the fireplace and advanced on the gorgon.

Hannah bit her lip. In theory, the crystal would stop her husband from turning to stone, but she didn't have any practical proof it would work. Hannah had conceived the hypothesis but her husband had to test it.

Hannah turned her back on them and held up the platter, watching events unfold in the polished silver. One of the snakes hissed and lashed out at Wycliff, the other two intent on the man sheltering under the billiards table.

Wycliff swung the blade and severed the head of a snake. It fell to the floor.

Miss Stewart screamed and her hands went to her hair. "No! I must have justice for Celeste!"

"I am terribly sorry for failing your sister, Miss Stewart," Mr Mowatt's voice issued from under the table.

Wycliff thrust with the sword, his movements short and stiff as he tried to strike the snakes and not Miss Stewart.

A draft raised goosebumps along Hannah's flesh as Mage Tomlin swept into the room, his purple velvet cloak billowing around him like an angry storm cloud. He raised his arms and began a series of hand movements while he muttered under his breath.

Prickles scratched at Hannah's skin as his abrasive magic flowed through the room. A ball of what appeared to be lengths of white string pulsed between his outstretched hands.

Hannah angled the silver platter. Wycliff battled the snakes with his back to both Tomlin and Hannah. The mage was either oblivious to Wycliff's presence or did not care that he stood in the way.

Anger surged through Hannah. "Wycliff!" she shouted as the mage threw the object he had conjured.

Wycliff turned and dropped to the carpet as the ball whizzed past his head. The magic ball hit Miss Stewart in the neck and light burst forth. Hannah squinted and lowered the platter.

"As I suspected all along, Miss Stewart is a gorgon," Mage Tomlin said.

Hannah opened one eye and peered cautiously over the top of the tray she clutched in both hands.

Miss Stewart was covered in a fine white net. Two snakes pushed against the holes and hissed, but couldn't squeeze past the ensorcelled constraints. The body of the third snake was pressed limp against the curve of Miss Stewart's head. As she squirmed and tried to pull the net off, it shrank more tightly to her body. Her arms were pinned to her sides and she began to lose her balance.

Mage Tomlin crossed his arms and threw Hannah a smug look, although he kept his distance from the woman.

"Well cast, Lord Tomlin. Will the net stop the snakes from turning anyone else to stone?" Hannah asked.

He snorted. "Of course."

Wycliff rolled his eyes and Hannah bit the inside of her cheek to stop the laughter that tickled through her. She didn't like the man, but his intervention had proven timely.

"He must be punished! They killed my sister!" Miss Stewart cried as she struggled.

"That your sister died in childbirth added to the tragedy, but it is one that strikes down many women. You cannot hold Mr Mowatt responsible for that." Hannah let out a sigh. Men only had to worry about being called to war and dying on the battlefield. Women faced death in their own beds while trying to bring life into the world.

Putting aside the woeful state of medical care that failed so many women, all of society should be held accountable for what had happened to Celeste. What sort of world did they live in, that a woman could be brutalised and then punished for being a victim? A tragedy could have been averted if Celeste had been able to come forward and name Stannard a rapist with the full support of her friends and society. Judge and jury should have meted out his punishment. Now, Hannah could only hope a higher authority would weigh his soul in the balance and hold him accountable.

Mr Mowatt crawled out from under the table. "I truly was attempting to face justice," he said as he caught Hannah's eye.

"Allowing her to kill you would only have added another crime to this sad tally. You must find some other way to atone for your cowardice. I suggest you start by being completely honest with Mrs Wright-Knowles." Hannah moved to Wycliff's side and relieved him of the crystal bowl.

Mage Tomlin muttered another incantation and threw it over the struggling woman. Miss Stewart let out a quiet gasp, her eyelids fluttered shut, and then she crumpled at the knees and collapsed to the carpet.

"What was that?" Wycliff asked, still holding the sword as though he didn't quite trust the other man's magic.

"Sleeping spell. It will keep her under for an hour

or two while we decide what to do with her," the mage replied.

"I shall leave you men to tidy up here while I tell Lady Frances that the murderer is apprehended." Hannah took her leave. No doubt the scandal to follow would delight Lady Frances and ensure her house party would be the talk of London for months to come.

# 25

When Hannah told Lady Frances, their hostess let out a startled snort and clapped a hand over her mouth. Her small eyes widened nearly to regular size. "*Stewart?*"

"Yes. A most terrible crime was committed against her sister by Lord Stannard, and Mr Robins and Mr Mowatt were involved. She sought vengeance in her sister's name." Hannah pitched her voice low. There was no doubt word would spread, but she wouldn't be the one to heap fuel on the fire of gossip.

"*Stewart?*" Lady Frances repeated. "Well, it certainly goes to show you never know what people have simmering beneath the surface."

"In Miss Stewart's case it was three snakes tucked under her turban. Now, if you will excuse me, Lady Frances, I still have much to do." Hannah had barely turned away before Lady Frances was relaying the news to all those within earshot.

Hannah searched the shadowy corners for the next person she needed to find. Mrs Armstrong sipped punch while she tapped her foot to the music. Hannah seated herself in the empty chair next to her and took Mrs Armstrong's free hand. Into it she pressed the letter. "I hope this eases your conscience."

Mrs Armstrong stared at the crumpled letter for a silent moment, then she wiped away a tear. "Thank you, Lady Wycliff. I am forever in your debt. I shall ensure it never sees the light of day again."

Hannah had toyed with throwing it in the fire, but thought the other woman would want to see her own hastily written words destroyed. "I do suggest you counsel your husband to be honest about the mage's death. Miss Stewart is not the only aftermage who can converse with the dead. It is only a matter of time before the deceased tells the truth of the situation to another. Better your husband should correct the narrative now."

Mrs Armstrong nodded. "I will talk to my husband on the journey home. It is time we were frank with each other...about a number of topics."

There was something with which Hannah could wholeheartedly agree—marriage required honesty. How could a healthy relationship grow and flourish if one party or the other was concealing something?

A headache pressed against Hannah's temples. The events of the evening and the loud ballroom were taking their toll. She walked through the open doors to the terrace beyond. A cool breeze lifted a little of the ache and she breathed in the earthy aroma of the grass at night. At the balustrade, she found she was not alone. Mrs Wright-Knowles stared across the lawn at the ha-ha and the hedges beyond. Pippa pulled her shawl tighter around her shoulders as Hannah joined her.

"I made Mowatt tell me what he did—or rather, what he failed to do. He was a horrid coward and he knows that. He should have stood up to Lord Stannard and come to the aid of poor Miss Stewart's sister." Pippa addressed the hedges as though they were an audience of shapeless jurors. "I also share in his shame. If we had been honest from the beginning, then Lord Stannard could never have held our affair over Mowatt's head."

"What will you do now?" Hannah asked.

The other woman let out a long sigh. "Secrets fester when they are left too long in the dark."

"Yes." Hannah thought of the secret between her and Wycliff. She should expose it to the fresh air before it had a chance to ruin their fledgling relationship.

"We are going to tell my husband. He will demand a divorce, and I will grant it without complaint, though I am left with nothing."

A divorced woman was a pitiful creature, treated more cruelly than a homeless dog. Hannah did not envy the other woman the limited choices available to her. She rested a hand on Philippa's arm. "Whatever happens, you will always have a friend in me."

Philippa laid her hand over Hannah's. "Why do we

make ourselves miserable, all to seek the favour of society? So many people are ruined or unhappy because of appearances. I have decided I no longer care what society thinks. Let them gossip that I am a fallen woman and an adulteress. I will be happy with Mowatt and together, we shall make amends. Besides, Wright-Knowles deserves to find a woman who loves him and his toy boats."

"I hope for a resolution for you all." Hannah said her goodbyes before Philippa returned to the ballroom. The revellers were draining out into the night. No doubt by tomorrow all of society would be talking of how a gorgon had been captured during Lady Frances's ball.

What fate awaited the loyal companion? Would Lady Frances stand by her? It seemed cruel that Miss Stewart should suffer for seeking justice for the crime committed against her sister. If only they lived in a society where women could speak out, without fear of recriminations that could destroy their lives more thoroughly than the original crime.

Wycliff emerged from the ballroom and spotted her. "Mage Tomlin has bound Stewart with more layers of magic so that she may be transported to London. We also discovered that Stannard has turned from stone back into flesh, but not Robins as yet. Stannard is still dead, but at least now his family can bury him. We believe that if we were to sever another snake's head, Robins will be released from his stone prison."

"I cannot help but feel sorry for Miss Stewart. If

found guilty of murder, she will either face execution or interment in the Repository of Forgotten Things."

Hannah turned back to the silent night. The temperature dropped and she rubbed her gloved hands up her arms.

"You're cold." Wycliff's voice came from directly behind her. His arms encircled her and he pulled her against his chest.

Hannah was too exhausted by the day to resist, and leaned into him. He radiated warmth and it chased the chill from her skin. "You're so warm, like a brick left before the fire. This must be one advantage to being married to a hellhound."

His embrace stiffened. "How did you know?"

She turned her head and glanced up at him. "I pieced together the clues. Do not blame Mother. She has kept your secret. She only reveals mine."

He let out a sigh. "It was the afternoon you dug out the shot."

Hannah rested her head against his shoulder, careful to avoid the still healing wound. "That provided the final clues, yes. The scar on your neck that is so similar to the lycanthrope bite, yet burned. The heat that radiates from your skin. The smoky fur that sprouts from your hackles under duress."

"Really. You saw fur?" Wonder lay in his voice.

She recalled the ghostlike fur she stroked along his spine. "Like tiny black flames, tipped in red. But when I touched it with my fingertip, it dissolved like smoke or mist. Then there were the scorched paw prints under our bedroom window."

A silent laugh heaved through his torso. "I thought I scuffed those out."

"Not before I saw them. There have been other clues. When you ran after Lord Dunkeith last month, I was certain you dropped to all fours and jumped like a wolf. Then there are the rumours swirling at home of Black Shuck roaming the fields. I was left with the question: What creature is like a lycanthrope but is not a lycanthrope? The only answer is a hellhound."

"Are you not afraid?" His voice whispered next to her ear.

During their week together, Hannah had learned much about her husband and about herself. She had found a new confidence in her married life that she had not possessed before. "No. You said that when we married, I would have the protection of both your name and your person. I do not believe that has changed, nor do I believe you would ever hurt me."

He rested his chin on top of her head. "I would never hurt you, Hannah."

"Hellhounds are the guardians of the dead," she mused aloud. "I wonder if that is why Mother told you that the Affliction is frozen within me."

"Possibly. But I think she pushed us together to help me." His arms moved lower, to tighten around her waist.

Hannah turned in his embrace and frowned up at him. "Why do you need help?"

The lines of his face were relaxed in the lamplight as he met her gaze. "I don't understand what I am or what it means. I only know I can see through this world to the next and it is...chilling. I am beginning to suspect that being close to your dear humanity stops me from losing myself to the underworld."

A hellhound who could move between their world and the afterlife. "Oh, how fascinating. We will have much to talk about on the way back to Westbourne Green."

He tipped up her chin and placed an all too brief kiss on her lips. "Let us go back to Doctor Colchester's house. I don't know about you, but I am too tired to continue with conversation tonight, and we have an early start in the morning."

Hannah slipped her hand into the crook of his elbow and stayed close as they walked inside. Much had changed since they had left home a little over a week ago. Once she had dreaded being alone with Wycliff. Now the idea made excitement flutter inside her.

What would the future hold for them? Hellhounds were the servants of Hades, but Wycliff might yet provide the help they needed to break the Afflicted women free of death's grip. More importantly, would her husband kiss her again?

She thought he might. For she had not missed that he had referred to her as *dear*.

~

The next adventure for Hannah and Wycliff is VANITY and VAMPYRES

# ABOUT THE AUTHOR

Tilly drinks entirely too much coffee, likes to watch Buffy the Vampire Slayer and wishes she could talk to Jane Austen. Sometimes she imagines a world where the Bennet sisters lived near the Hellmouth. Or that might be a fanciful imagining brought on by too much caffeine.

To be the first to hear about new releases and special offers sign up at:
www.tillywallace.com/newsletter

*Tilly would love to hear from you:*
www.tillywallace.com
tilly@tillywallace.com

facebook.com/tillywallaceauthor

bookbub.com/authors/tilly-wallace

Printed in Great Britain
by Amazon

62248672R00184